Patrick's eyes slid over her as if she were a meal he were about to devour. The tip of his tongue traced his upper lip, and dampness formed on his forehead. "Was anyone ever so fair? So womanly?"

Karalee strained against him, twisting her head from side to side to avoid his lips. But he held her fast, lowering his face toward the soft whiteness of her breasts, lower, still lower, until she thought she would faint in his arms. Then his lips found one nipple—and the other. She gasped as her own body began to respond to his wickedness.

"There's my little beauty," he whispered against her ear, sensing the rise of her own passion.

"I despise you."

"Despise me then, if it makes you throb and burn against me so."

"No."

He wrested her to the ground, then lowered himself over her, pressing his mouth against hers. He worked his tongue easily between her clenched teeth, and one hand fumbled with her skirt, inching it upward around her waist. His legs forced hers apart, and she began to sob.

"Nah, girl, don't you cry. It will spoil it for you and for me too. I'm not like some who relish the hurting. There will be many, many times for us. Each better than the last. There now, give in to it."

. . . And then there were roses— bouquets of wild roses . . .

So Wild a Rose

Virginia L. Hart

PINNACLE BOOKS   LOS ANGELES

SO WILD A ROSE

An original Pinnacle Books edition, published for the first time anywhere.

First printing, May 1980

ISBN: 0-523-40543-X

Cover illustration by Norm Eastman

Printed in the United States of America

PINNACLE BOOKS, INC.
2029 Century Park East
Los Angeles, California 90067

One

As one still sleeping, Karalee Nolan moved across the crippled bridge. She turned off the main-trodden road, onto a narrow bohereen that lay hidden from nearby farm cottages by a rain-blackened beech grove. Ahead, a heron stretched its wings on a mossy rock, fluffed its feathers, and with a hop sailed into the mist.

There had been few quiet moments of late. But there would be soon. The men all said it and the women nodded. At first it had been whispered. Then it had been shouted. 1798 would bring freedom to Ireland. But already it was June and nothing had changed—unless they meant the kind of freedom Rory had now.

Karalee thought of Rory again. Not as he had been at his wake, lying in his mother's kitchen with his hands crossed over his chest. His face had been beautiful and as white as the linen he wore, except for the patches of red on his cheeks that the women had dyed with berry juice. No. In life, Rory had not been beautiful. His face had been dark from the wind and the sun and it had been comical almost, with his imp grin and his shaggy peaked brows and the foolish way he had of speaking with barely a moving of his lips.

She had never walked this way before. Never walked. She had run, lifting her skirts high above her ankles so she would not stumble over the rocks that poked their way out of the spongy earth. She had never been here alone before, either.

Always there had been Rory racing with her, teasing,

1

laughing—and Theresa. But now Rory Fitzgerald lay beneath the earth, gone to her forever. Theresa would be gone too in only six more days. She and her family were fleeing to the colonies. To that cold, savage land where the grass was brown and sparse and where girls lost their teeth and the color in their cheeks by the time they were eighteen. They were old women at forty and never bathed any more of their bodies than what poked out of their dresses.

A great wall of stone loomed ahead of her and she stopped, as if seeing it for the first time, flinging one arm over her eyes to shield them from the sun. It was as if this castle had been dropped by mistake out of the barbarous past into the middle of the lush meadow. Its north wall was coated with a thick layer of green slime and its ruined gate barely hung in place, tugged low by choking briars.

Its forbidding look had never intimidated Rory or Karalee. Theresa had followed more reluctantly as they scampered across the remains of a moat, through the gate, past the chancel arch, up the crumbling stone steps, past the broken saints on their sunken pediments, golden sunlight sifting through the remains of the collapsed roof above them.

From the west tower, where they found the only safe footing, they could see the little road, twisting its way toward the distant spires of Limerick, the stone wall moving with it, as if to keep it company. Behind them were the misty-topped blue and purple hills of Clare.

What was it they had found to laugh at in those days? Karalee wondered.

She shivered and started off again. She did not want to be late and give Brian a reason to leave without her. She picked her way through the weed-choked cemetery with its crooked crosses and poor flat slabs of stone, then threw her legs over the wall, turning her head away from the bramble-covered mound, where stood a gate, and beyond it four steps leading down into the damp blackness, to a coffin.

The land rose before her and subsided, then rose again and she was there. She found the flattest of the stones on the bank and glanced around before sitting. She lifted her skirts and let her dusty bare feet paddle in the icy stream. There was only the lapping of the water and the soft bird talk and she closed her eyes, trying to imagine that all the world was at peace. That no one was bleeding or dying.

2

A bird shrieked and she cried out, leaping onto the grassy bank again, where she stood, staring at the clear gray-green water rippling its way to meet the Shannon. With her eyes shut, the bird's shriek had been a scream and the water had been red as it had been only weeks before. Red with the blood of a dozen fine Irish lads. Red with Rory's blood.

A chquid! Beloved Rory. Beloved—yet not truly loved by her, and there was the tragedy of it. The tragedy she could share with no one, but must carry to her grave.

It began in April when everything was so busy bursting into bloom, it seemed the world was having a second try at being born all over again. It was the second day of turf-cutting, and the bog was splendid with tiny white cean-a-bhans. The neighbors had gathered to do the job, moving their wagons across the bumpy marsh-earth, making a picnic of it.

Each bog bank was to be peeled down to the brown and the sod molded into rough bricks and carried clear to dry. The harvesting of enough turf to last throughout the year was an enormous job and every able-bodied person was expected to do his share, from the youngest to the oldest. The turf-fire was important for more than warmth. It was the symbol of the family and it was believed that if it were allowed to go out, night or day, the souls of the people who lived there went out with it.

There were songs and fiddlers were playing, and Rory, never taking a prize for being the swiftest turf-cutter, had pulled Karalee away from the others. Laughing, they skipped across to the other side of the hill where the grass grew thick and waist-high and was mixed with honeysuckle, foxglove, and wild daisy. Karalee collapsed, rolling, out of breath, and Rory stood over her, still crooning softly the song the others had been singing when they left camp. Suddenly, he stopped singing and she looked up at him.

"Married, we must be, soon, girl."

"I am far too young to think of that, Rory Fitzgerald. And yourself too," she answered, not adding what they both knew. That she loved him, truly, but not in the same way he loved her. Oh, no man could ever have been loved so dearly. But never could she have taken him to her bed.

"Your own sister was married at sixteen and had two wee ones by the time she was your age. You had best decide on it, or I might begin to look at greener stock."

3

To marry—only to be married—was a temptation. The unmarried, no matter their age, had no say in village matters. They were subject to the rule of their parents as if they were still children.

"The times are wrong."

"The times are as we have always known them to be."

"We are poor."

"We will always be poor. We can live as others do on a few roods of potatoes, if we have devotion for each other. We can own a houseful of children, can we not, if we are allowed to own nothing else?"

Karalee laughed and raised on one elbow, but Rory held her down, dropping to his knees beside her. There was none of the comic in his face.

"Such a brilliant blue your eyes are, girl."

"Ach, they are not blue at all, Rory Fitzgerald. They are green and a muddy green at that. Let me up now. We had best be returning."

"They are blue with the sky in them."

"Rory . . ."

He touched calloused fingertips to her lips to silence her. "I have a need for you that cannot be put off, Karalee."

His shoulders were twice the width of hers and his big hands were clumsy and strong. Yet she could have stopped his kisses had she wanted to. He tussled with her, but would have held off at her slightest outcry, so afraid he was of hurting her.

"A lhaie, Karalee," he whispered. "We always knew how it would be someday. My head is dizzy with wanting you."

It had been wicked of her, but she had wanted to taste his lips then too. She had never known the feel of a lover's kiss and ached to try it. Rory moved over her and a hotness swept through her as his body pressed down on hers, close—but somehow, not yet close enough. Then she felt his swollen hardness against her and tried to roll from under him. But it was too late. There were voices and Timothy Roe's freckled face was grinning down at them.

"It's no marvel you did not win the turf-cutting contest, Fitz lad."

"Never found your way down to the bog, eh?" someone else added, laughing.

"He has no more vigor left in him for the cutting," another sang.

Karalee's giving in, lying in the meadow, mouth-to-

4

mouth with Rory Fitzgerald, was mistaken for agreement to the marriage. There was no stopping it. His family visited with hers, discussing the merits of the alliance and then her family walked the land with the Fitzgeralds. The nanty-maker set to stitching up Karalee's bridal dress and cloak and the tailor began sewing a fine suit of clothes for Karalee's intended.

Rory—her husband. No. Karalee dreaded the day and in private prayed that somehow it would not happen.

Rory set off in high spirits for Wexford, the place of his birth, to inform relations there of the wedding-to-be and to bring as many of them back as he could to attend it. While there, he was drawn into the middle of an uprising and joined into battle with fiery Father John Murphy and a few hundred farmers who, armed mostly with pitchforks, drove back a party of over ten thousand soldiers and succeeded in holding the town.

He was on his way home with a group of his kinsmen, eager to share the news of their glorious victory and the victories they were sure would come now under Father Murphy's leadership, when a group of marauding Yeomanry fell on them from ambush at the Shannon and left them all dead or dying.

Had Karalee's own prayer caused it?

There was a rustling and she brushed her skirt down about her ankles as the bushes parted in the center of the lumpy hillside and a red-cheeked man in black homespun emerged.

"Good afternoon, Father O'Glanny."

"Acting sentinel for our little classes this day are you, girl?"

"It seems so, Father."

Father O'Glanny nodded and squinted off, first in one direction, then the other. When he was sure the way was clear, he turned back to the cave and beckoned.

"All right, lads. Off with you, now."

One small boy-face appeared in the opening, then another, and suddenly lads, all sizes, poured into the clearing, their eyes nearly closed against the burst of sunshine, gray knapsacks of schoolbooks bouncing on their shoulders and rude pens tied with cord swinging about their necks.

Father O'Glanny studied Karalee's face for a moment, then reached out to clasp her white hands between his red,

5

freckled ones. "It has been too many days since I saw a smile in your eyes, Karalee Nolan."

"I know that, Father."

"And you know you should be proud of your Rory Fitzgerald and the valiant way he died."

"I know, Father."

"The boy himself would grieve to see you so mournful on his account."

"Please, Father."

"We must talk it out, girl. Pray about it. It does no good to turn your face from truth. Come and see me—soon."

"Soon, Father," Karalee promised, avoiding his eyes, knowing she would not—could not—tell him or anyone of her feelings.

Scowling through coarse strands of black hair that fell into his face, Brian dragged his feet toward her, pulling his schoolsack behind him. "None of the others have sisters here to guide them home."

"Nor is it to my liking to be here, gorsoon," Karalee snapped, matching his tone, though it was a lie. It was her own concern for the safety of her youngest brother, more than the concern of her mother, that brought her here to watch out for him. "It eases Mother to know you are safe. So we must both accept it while times are unsettled."

"What kind of protection would you be against a British soldier?" Brian sneered. "It would be me having to protect you at that."

It was a fair question, Karalee realized, and one she had asked herself. But there was no answer to it, so she offered none. "At least I can see you travel a straight path. Hurry along now."

How brave Father O'Glanny was, she thought as she watched him disappear through the trees. When the law was passed banishing Catholic priests, many of them had fled. And who could blame them? Had not Father Lucas, who openly defied the law, been flogged near to death and then hanged in full view of his students? The same had happened to many another good man of the cloth, who dared to stay on. And that was not to count even more who rotted away in English prisons.

There were men—if you could call them men—who made their living as priest-hunters, discovering in what ditch, or behind what hedge, a priest was conducting his forbidden classes. Sometimes the students themselves, yet

6

boys, were caught and punished inhumanly. A favorite atrocity was the pitch-cap. Boiling pitch was poured into a bowl and then clamped over a prisoner's head. When it had cooled, it was ripped off, more often than not tearing the unfortunate's scalp off with it, and ears, as well as his hair.

"Ah, here you are, you two."

Patrick Roe sat on the low stone wall just ahead, chewing on a crabapple and making a sour face to go with it. "I've been so long in waiting, I can feel my beard grow."

Karalee managed a smile for Patrick only because he was husband to dear Theresa. His was surely the most handsome face in the village and he had enough charm for a dozen like him. But there was something of an animal in the way he watched her move, and she had no liking for him. Even his most innocent remarks or movements seemed to have some hidden, shameful meaning. Had she been alone, she would have darted. But with Brian trudging beside her, she would be safe enough from his wandering hands.

"And why is it you are waiting for us?"

He swung himself over the wicket gate, then paused and hurled the half-eaten crabapple out of sight with a whiz. "Your mother asked me to fetch you. You are not to go home."

"Not go home?" Karalee stiffened and clenched her fists to her face as if expecting a blow. "Oh Patrick, tell me now, quick. What's wrong? Is everyone safe?"

"Calm yourself, little beauty. It's Theo again. Your brother has been named as one of those who burned some Protestant homes in Athelone. They're searching for him and he has gone into hiding."

"Again." Karalee sighed. "Why does he put us into danger this way?"

"Flinging a stone at the giant."

"Where has he gone this time?"

"Some say he slipped off to the outer islands near Galway Bay. Others claim he's taken to the mountains. Either way, I'd wager he'll be safe enough and you are welcome at our hearthside until the incident is forgotten. Your mother and sister are there now and we expect your father by suppertime."

Karalee nodded, not able to voice her thanks. At least there would be some good from this new trouble. She could visit with Theresa before the girl sailed to America. They

7

had had little time together since Theresa's marriage and none at all since the birth of the twins.

Karalee had never seen childbirth rob all color from a girl's cheeks before, or put such circles under her eyes. It had to be something more. There was a quiet resignation in Theresa's manner that was entirely unlike the manner of the Theresa she had always known.

"You don't curl your hair, girl," Patrick said, catching a silky strand of black hair between his fingers. "I like that. The way it falls straight and free down your back. And the smell of it. Like spring rain."

Karalee quickened her pace, measuring her stride against Brian's.

"Theresa crimps her hair with rags every night, until it curls into stiff little frizzles all over her head."

He wrinkled his nose in distaste and Brian giggled. If Karalee had not detested Patrick before, she would have begun at that moment. Still there was no need for open antagonism. In a few more days she would be free of him forever.

"We are all comic in some way, I think," she managed. "If our secrets were revealed."

"Ah, and that sounds mysterious." He caught up to her and pulled his face close to hers. "What of your secrets?"

There was a child's squeal behind them and a pattering of feet. Two orange-haired boys, one a few inches taller than the other, raced by them, yanking at Brian's sleeve as they passed.

"Come along with us, Brian. Mother has made oaten bread and we're going to play Horse Fair. My cousins are here from Cork with fine presents for us."

"He cannot," Karalee said quickly.

"I can. Mother lets me."

"But not today."

"Ach," Patrick broke in, "you forget what it was to be a child, Karalee Nolan. The days of nonsense and games are too soon gone. Let him go. Mind you, lad, be home in an hour or I'll come after you with a boolhawn."

"You have no right, Patrick Roe. Brian, you stay here."

"Take my book-sack with you," Brian pleaded. "I mustn't be caught with it."

"Take it yourself, gorsoon." Karalee turned her head from him.

8

"I'll take it." Patrick caught the grey linen knapsack and gave Brian a resounding smack on the rump to send him on his way. "Leave belly-room for the potatoes and blood-pudding."

"You will answer for this, Brian Nolan," Karalee screeched as the boy raced out of sight.

Patrick edged close and their legs brushed together as they walked. "Now you can tell me your secret, little one."

"Were I to tell you, 'twould no longer be a secret, now would it?"

The flirtatious banter between them was unseemly, as was the way her pulses raced at his nearness. Karalee longed for a glimpse of Theresa and the safety of the Roe cottage. They moved into the deep glen and she silently counted the footsteps it would take to bring them into the clear. The path was shadowed with close-growing trees. So thick was the feeling of loneliness and gloom in this spot, in spite of the pinkish heather that bloomed there, the villagers declared it was haunted.

"Ready are you then for your departure?" Karalee asked abruptly. It mattered little to her how Patrick felt about leaving Ireland. Indeed, she resented his hasty decision to go. It would rob her of her dearest friend, Theresa, forever. But the question would serve, hopefully, to guide his thoughts in a safer direction.

He sighed. "Not ready. No. But go, we must. I've had my fill of the fighting."

"Better the fighting here, to my way of thinking, than the loneliness of another land. I would not leave if our own front yard were a battlefield. I couldn't. I'd die of missing the gentle rains, the green hills, the warmth of the turf fires . . ."

"Ay." Patrick nodded, serious now. "And the sound of lilting voices, of dogs barking in the still night."

They passed a ruined house whose owners had no doubt been turned out many generations before. Its poor roof was battered, its gates were hanging and it was so overgrown with weeds it might easily have gone unnoticed, but still the wild roses flowered over its broken walls and trellises. Patrick plunged his hand through the thick-growing nettles and plucked a single flower. He handed it to Karalee, then touched a finger to his lips to soothe his flesh where a

9

thorn had bitten into it. "I'll miss the sweet, wild roses most of all, I think."

"There are roses in the new land. I have heard there are elegant parks entirely planted with them."

"I do not doubt it. Roses planted in carefully spaded beds. Perfect roses. Twisted and tweaked and coaxed according to the whim of a practiced gardener. But they will not be like this one, Karalee. There is more sweetness in a single wild rose sighted among the nettles then in all the gardens of the new world." His eyes touched hers and held them. "The one you hold is yet a bud. The loveliest of all. Like love unawakened, they say."

He moved closer to her, but Karalee dropped the flower into his hand and doubled her steps to take herself out of his reach.

"I would guess your secret has something to do with the way none of the village lads ever gets a look from you."

Karalee's face felt warm and she knew she was blushing. "It is not right of you to speak to me of such things, Patrick Roe, with Rory only late in his grave."

"Rory, is it, then?" Patrick's laugh was a taunt. "I think not. There's a fire blazing in you, girl, and it was never quenched by poor Fitz."

"Believe what you wish."

"I believe what I see. And I should know, shouldn't I? Bound in wedlock to a pasty lump who lies under me like bread dough, squeezing her little raisin eyes shut until her duty is done. She disrobes herself under cover of darkness and holds her bony fingers over her eyes so she will not have to look at my manhood."

"I will not hear this!"

"She turns the holy pictures to the wall as if t'were some black sin we were committing."

"Shame on you."

"And shame on you, colleen, for wasting a body such as yours with a lie. Wrong am I, for thinking you want the same thing I want?"

When she did not answer, he circled in front of her and caught her wrists easily with one hand. "Wrong am I?"

His lips were full and finely moulded and his skin was more fair than Rory's had been. He looked very much like a painting she had seen once of a long-ago poet.

"Don't you dare to touch me."

"Tell me I am wrong."

"You are wrong. I'm a decent girl, Patrick Roe. I have never in my life been intimate with any man."

"Now you sound like Theresa."

"There were never more than kisses between Rory and me—and few of those. A gentleman—with respect—he was, content to wait for marriage."

"A fool, he was, then. But I do not believe it." He laughed, his white teeth flashing, and pulled her against him, catching her blouse sleeves and yanking until her shoulders were bared.

His eyes slid over her as if she were a meal he were about to devour. The tip of his tongue traced his upper lip and dampness formed on his forehead. "Was anyone ever so fair? So womanly?"

She strained against him, twisting her head from side to side to avoid his lips. But he held her fast, lowering his face toward the soft whiteness of her breasts, lower, still lower, until she thought she would faint in his arms. Then his lips found one nipple—and the other. She gasped as her own body began to respond to his wickedness.

Oh merciful God, I must be entirely wicked too, if I feel this way, she thought.

"There's my little beauty," Patrick whispered against her ear, sensing the rise of her passion. "How did you expect me to believe your act of innocence? Did you forget my brother and me were among those who found you and Fitz lovemaking in the meadow? You, rolling and groaning under him? I have not been able to get the sight out of my mind. I can hardly sleep for thinking of it at night, reliving it over and over. Then I reach for my woman and imagine it is you I am pleasuring."

"I despise you."

"Despise me then, if it makes you throb and burn against me so."

"No."

He wrested her to the ground, then lowered himself over her, pressing his mouth against hers. He worked his tongue easily between her clenched teeth and one hand fumbled with her skirt, inching it upwards around her waist. His legs forced hers apart and she began to sob.

"Nah, girl, don't you cry. It will spoil it for you and for me too. I'm not like some who relish the hurting. There will be many, many times for us. Each better than the last. There now, give in to it."

11

"Please . . ."

"Next time you will be saying your 'please' for wanting me inside you, beauty. There now."

Too weak to fight him anymore, she relaxed under him, trying to regain her strength. Her only chance, if there would be any, would be to catch him off his guard. She accepted his kisses as they nearly smothered her, as his lips pressed against her neck, then slid to the base of her throat. Breathing hard, he raised himself to his knees in a half-crouch, and began pulling at his trousers.

With a shriek, she sat up, butting her head against the bridge of his nose. He yelped in pain and tumbled off-balance. Free of his weight, she rolled to her feet and ran, afraid to look behind her. Afraid she would see him gaining on her and this time, full of rage, he would not be gentle.

At last she was safe at the top of the hill. Below her was the cottage, its side stones left natural, its round thatched roof whitewashed so that it looked snow-capped from where she stood. And beautiful—so beautiful. Theresa stood in the doorway, watching for them, a red kerchief tied around her brown hair.

Karalee waved at her frantically, until Theresa waved back. Then she began to move forward, her legs weak as flower stems beneath her. She smoothed her hair and her blouse as she ran. There was a rip at her shoulder, but hopefully it would not be commented on. Theresa was running now too, and calling to her, across the turnip field that separated the cottage from the road. Only then did Karalee dare to glance around. Patrick was nowhere in sight.

Two

"Sha, Napoleon will save us from the English, you say? Is that it? Then I ask you, who will save us from Napoleon?"

Feargul Roe's swollen, purple-veined nose held a fascination for young Brian who, despite elbow-digs in the ribs by Karalee, sat staring at it as the older man talked—too loud—as they do who are full of poteen. He seldom spoke of anything but the cause, and of keeping Ireland for the Irish. He did not share the popular opinion that Wolfe Tone and his United Irishmen—Presbyterians and Catholics who had joined together for common good—would be the salvation of the country.

"Sure and didn't Tone take first his own loved ones to the colonies where they would be safe, before taking up the battle? There's a mark of confidence in the outcome, I'm saying."

"A wise move by a wise leader," another man said, a stranger who had knocked on the door just before they gathered together for supper. He had brought with him a sullen, black-eyed lad of about thirteen who chewed his fingernails and a narrow-faced woman with no lips to speak of, who sat huddled in a corner eating one boiled potato after another, as fast as she could peel it and dunk it into warm milk.

Visitors were seldom turned away from any door in this land, where it was believed a bit of Christ dwelled in each stranger. To close the door to a man could mean having Christ do the same to you some day.

13

"We've an extra potato hot on the fire," was the common welcome such travelers found, even during barren times.

"A man can put his whole heart into his duty when he knows his women and babes are safe from harm."

"There is truth in that," Grandfather Roe said through teeth still clenched over his pipe.

"Aye?" Feargul broke in, leaning closer to the old man. "And how about Bantry Bay? Forty-three French ships, he had, and the men and arms to go with them. No help at all is what they were that sad day." He pressed a fist to the hollow just above his great stomach and belched. "They did not even set foot to shore."

"The winds were fierce," the stranger said, his voice rising. "No mortal man could have brought those ships in."

"Well now, so your Wolfe Tone is mortal, is he? I'm surprised to hear you admit that, from the talk I have heard this night."

It was too warm for such a fire and the peat smoke tasted bitter at the back of Karalee's throat. A dish of boiled potatoes still steamed on a three-legged pot, kept warm for her father and the others who had not yet arrived.

The man-talk was the same every night and Karalee only half listened, staring into the fire to avoid meeting Patrick's eyes. She could feel them searing through her relentlessly, promising her what would happen when they next met. He had not voiced his opinion once that evening. Did he share his father's sentiments, she wondered? Did he care at all about the cause?

The top of her own head still ached where she had struck him in escaping. Had she truly injured him? The bridge of the nose was a sensitive spot. She had stolen a side-glance at him as he was washing his hands for supper and had seen a crimson drop on one edge of his shirt collar and another on his cuff. She had certainly made his nose bleed. Well, it served him fairly and she would do better not to consider it.

Timothy and Margaret Roe sat across from her. Copies of each other, they were and, in turn, copies of their auburn-haired mother, tilt-nosed, open-faced and frank, their eyes wide with interest in what was being discussed. But Patrick looked not a whit like her, with his raven hair and fine carved cheekbones and nose. Was it possible that

14

Feargul Roe had once been as dashing as his eldest son? Were it so, there remained not a trace of it. Was it possible that he had excited passion once in someone—anyone? Could the years, even twenty-five or thirty of them, make such cruel changes in a man?

At least Karalee would never see dear Rory grow old and bloated. He would not shout down opinions of those who disagreed with him, nor drink too much and belch and spit on the hearth to make it sizzle.

This was a fine room—one such as she would like to have when she wedded. The wall lamp flickered warmly on the great polished chest with its fragile set of blue willow dishes, on the copper pots gleaming from their hooks over the fire, and on the picture of the Holy Family, which had been the Nolans' own wedding gift to the couple. In the far corner sat two full bins—one of yellah meal, the other of flour. Patrick had done well in providing for Theresa and for their wee twins, Daniel and Deirdre, who now lay sleeping in their cribs. Theresa must surely have been heartsick at having to leave all this behind. So little of it could she pack and carry with her on the ship.

Karalee reached over to squeeze her mother's hand. But the woman did not seem to notice. She had not taken a bite of supper and sat twisting a frayed thread of her shawl, her eyes moist with yet-unshed tears. At every sound, she stiffened and stared at the door as if she expected the devil to burst in.

Theo was her firstborn. The son every mother hopes will become a priest. She had borne him in great pain and now he was somewhere in the black night, hiding in the ruin of some monastery, or perhaps in the hands of the enemy. This was the tragedy of motherhood.

Theresa rose from her bench and stretched herself, more to attract Karalee's attention than from the need of unfolding. She widened her eyes and nodded toward the door. Karalee returned her nod and murmured her excuses to the circle. She was glad to leave it. Talk of uprisings unsettled her.

"I don't want to go," Theresa wailed when they had walked outside. "It is not only leaving this house and you and my mother and father that sorrows me so. It's that this is where I was born and all my people before me. I want Daniel and Deirdre to hear the songs and the fiddles and to run the green hills as we did. I shall hate this Philadelphia and everyone there will hate me. Mercifully, I will not live to see its wretched shores."

"Ochone! Let me hear no more of that!"

"Why? It is true. Coffin ships they call them, because so many die while aboard. My health is poorly enough right here."

"If you were to die, I would want to die too."

"How would you know of it? My body would be dumped into the sea along with the bodies of all the others who died along the way."

"What is this talk of dying? Think of your journey for what it is, a great adventure. Like the adventures we used to plan when we were girls."

"Adventure, is it?" Theresa drew her shawl more tightly about her thin shoulders. "You say that only because you are staying here."

There was no argument Karalee could think of that would hold up against such a truth, so they stood in silence. The night was thick with threatened rain, the sky inky with patches of blackish-gray clouds. Beyond the gate there was nothing. The call of a night bird, the bleat of the sheep.

"Then tell Patrick you will not go. Stand up to him. He might even rejoice at your courage."

"Patrick rejoices at nothing I do. You do not know him or you would not ask me to stand up to him. I dare not quarrel about it."

Dare not? Dare not? Karalee marveled at what had become of the girl's independent spirit. The Theresa she used to know would have stood chin to chin, fist to fist, for her right to make such a decision about her future and the future of her babes. Hadn't the two of them at twelve—or had they been younger?—been cornered by the wicked Lynch boys who were jeering at them and pelting them with stones? Hadn't she and Theresa flown at the boys with teeth and nails and kicking feet and driven them over the hill with shirttails flying?

But that was long ago.

"Perhaps your Patrick is right. There is no chance for the young here."

"And are the colonies better? There are hordes of red savages ready to scalp us and carry off our children to enslave them."

"Can they be worse than the British in our own land?"

"My mother's eldest brother spent two years in America to earn bread for his family and was only too anxious to return here, strife or no. He said that women twist their hair up tight onto their heads so they never have to wash it and that they fairly crawl with lice. He told mother that during their time of the month, women put on a colored skirt they keep aside for that purpose. A skirt they never change or launder until it falls apart from use."

"At least you need not follow the ways of the unwashed there. You can bathe as you like. Here, Catholics are not allowed to be educated or to own property. Not even a horse worth more than five pounds. Our churches are not allowed to have bells or even to be called churches. It may well be that soon Catholics will be denied the water for bathing and the air for breathing."

"Hark." Theresa's icy fingers clutched at Karalee's wrist and she moved closer. "Someone is coming."

There were footsteps, but it was too black a night to make out whose they were. Whoever approached traveled fast and carried no lantern.

"Most likely, my father," Karalee whispered. "And none too soon. I have never seen Mother so wretched with worrying."

"Perhaps he has word of Theo."

"No, see there. It's Father O'Glanny. And Thomas Doolin with him."

"Wisha, quickly, both of you," the priest told them, waving them inside. "Let us close the door against the night."

Sheila Nolan rose fearfully as Father O'Glanny entered. Margaret Roe, sensing tragic news, slid an arm around the woman's shoulders to steady her.

"Have you seen Theo, Father? And where is my husband?"

The priest sighed and lowered himself into the chair Timothy vacated for him. "I will not lie to any of you and say things are good." He took with both hands the mug of hot tea Patrick's mother handed him. "Thank you, Nora. Informers, I fear. May the Lord punish them. Now hold. As yet, Theo has not been captured. Nor Micheal. And God be praised, they are together. Waiting."

"Waiting?" Sheila repeated dully. "For what?"

"Micheal has been working like ten men. Making preparations. Now he has sent word what you must do."

"Do? Ochone!" Karalee's mother wailed, clutching her

stomach as if she were in agony. "What is it I can do? What can any of us do? The trouble is too terrible this time. I had a dream about Theo last night. The same dream as always. About the cursed mole."

"What are you saying, woman?"

"When Theo was born, Father, there was a crooked-backed old pishogue who lived in a cave she had dug out of the hillside with only a sharp stone. Wise, she was, in spells and charms. When she saw the mole under my Theo's left ear, she screamed and began to tremble and pale. She declared that those born with such a mole—"

She stopped, her voice too wracked with emotion to continue. Karalee knew she should have run to her mother's side to comfort her, but she could not. She had always found the woman's spells of crying embarrassing, even if they were justified. Fortunately, Margaret Roe was beside her, and with mumbled words of comfort led her to the window seat.

"Those born with a mole under their left ear are slated for hanging," Grandfather Roe announced in a loud voice, tapping his walking stick on the floor for emphasis. "I have heard it often."

"You want to know what you can do?" the priest thundered, rising to his feet. "First, you can calm yourself and listen to me. Or it won't be Theo Nolan's mole that slates him for hanging. It will be your waiting and your useless lamenting. There is little time. For any of you. You must leave at once."

"We have already made plans to sail six days from this, Father," Patrick told him. "I have decided I want a better life for my son and for my daughter."

"You must leave in the morning," the priest said.

"But we cannot. We cannot." Theresa sailed forward and dropped to her knees in front of the priest. "There is too much to do first."

"Theresa girl, there are treacherous men who earn money by supplying names. Men who even make up lies to ingratiate themselves and to earn favors."

"I will not budge from my hearthside," Feargul said, tamping his pipe against the hearthstone. "Let them do what they will."

Father O'Glanny raised his hand. "The two of you, Feargul and Nora—yes, and you, Margaret, should be right enough, if you leave for your own homes at once and

18

if you stay clear of the Ennis Road. But the Nolans have been named because of Theo and his tie with the Defenders. Patrick and Timothy are wanted for harboring the Nolans. A crime likely to be punished by hanging. Or if not that, certainly by imprisonment."

Father O'Glanny talked on and Karalee watched his mouth, without really listening to the words. She only knew that all day she had been pitying Theresa for the journey she would have to make. Now Karalee herself would be making that journey. There would be no time to go home for any of her treasures or even to get her good dress.

Brian had fallen asleep on his straw mat in the corner and his little sister, Shauna, lay next to him, her pile of dark curls tickling his nose, so that every few breaths, he reached up to brush it away.

The priest handed Patrick a piece of paper signed by the captain of one of the "coffin ships," as Theresa called them. It stated that their passages had been paid. Then he sat sketching a map that told them what roads they should take, where the ships would be waiting, where they would hide and sleep while they awaited the black hour, and where they would be reunited with Theo and her father.

Theo was the cause of it all. It was hard not to bear him malice even if he was her brother. For this—and because he had more of her mother's love than she, Brian, and Shauna all joined together. More even than what love she had for their father.

Timothy would ride in one wagon with Karalee, her mother, and the two children. Patrick would follow in an hour or two with Theresa and the twin babes. They could take only what they would be able to cram into a single bag.

Karalee could offer no arguments. Her father had risked his life to arrange the journey, and had by some miracle managed to scrape together enough to pay this privateer who would carry them to the colonies. Loving his homeland the way he did, he would suffer more than she from the exile.

Everyone was silent as Feargul raked over the fire, damping down its glowing center with ashes so it would still live through the night. People all over the country were doing the same thing—in thousands of other tiny cottages. They had always done it. When these ashes were poked aside at dawn, when someone knelt low to blow upon the faintly glowing turf, flames would rise and fresh peat would be added.

" 'Twill not be long before you will be returning," Feargul said at last, pulling first Timothy, then Patrick, into a rough embrace. He sniffed and wiped his nose across his shirtsleeve. "Father John Murphy and his brother are gaining great strength in Wexford. It will all be as I have said. Together at this same hearth come St. Stephen's day."

There would be no hearth come St. Stephen's day, or even come tomorrow, Karalee thought. If their family and the Roes were truly sought, men would come to batter the cottage down and burn it. They would do the same to the Nolan cottage.

"Feargul." Thomas Doolin stepped forward, scratching at his bristly gray side-whiskers. "It is sad I am to be telling you this, knowing how you feel. But you would no doubt discover it and perhaps not so gently. Father Micheal Murphy was killed on the battlefield. I only today got the news of it. The good man is gone to us and to our cause."

"May the Lord give glory to his soul," Nora Roe cried, slipping an arm around her husband's shoulder.

"And there is more. Worse. Father John Murphy has been captured. There is talk of breaking him away. But it is only talk. The forces are too great around him. He will surely be hanged."

Karalee closed her eyes, trying to close out their talk. They were speaking of this man—or that man—who would come forward, take up the battle, and win. They all clasped hands and smiled and assured each other again and again that the exile would be only for a short time. But their voices were hollow as if they did not believe it at all.

Karalee did not join in their talk, or utter a cheery word. But she knew, no matter what any of them thought, that she would come back some day. That she would finish out her life here—in this green land which had given her birth.

Three

Karalee lay on her stomach at the cliff's edge, gazing out at the miles of green sea ahead and the jagged gray crags stretching on either side as far as she could see. Below was a sheer drop, hundreds of feet, to the swirling water.

Gulls, squalling, chased each other in and out of the black hollows in the cliff face. Black sea crows swooped by, unmindful of her, and dived headlong into the water, sinking from sight, only to reappear, soar upwards, and dive again. One scrawny grayish kittiwake, a leg dangling pitifully, dropped to rest with a flock of others of his kind. They hopped apart from him, shrieking. When he did not take this warning, they flew at him, pecking his injury until he fluttered away, crookedly—exiled.

The sky was beginning to darken and bits of salty sand bit Karalee's cheeks. The breeze that had gently rippled her hair when she first lay down here, now was a wind that blew savagely. The waves that had been foamy and green were now boiling and brilliant blue, hurling blackened strings of sea plants against the rocks, then pulling them back again.

She knew they would be wondering about her. That they would send someone to look for her. Perhaps Patrick. The thought of being at his mercy, here, brought her to her feet.

She walked down the narrow road, but stopped a moment where it leveled and the sea wall began. A cluster of women had gathered on the beach and several men ran toward them, waving their arms and shouting. A girl with green sea slime coating her bare feet scrambled over the

21

wall and joined them, yanking at one of the women's skirts.

Karalee followed their gaze to a black dot on the horizon. It was the boat with the three men she had seen earlier. They had run into the water, their shiny, tar-bottomed curragh swung over their heads, so that only their legs emerged. They had looked like a giant insect.

Now a wind was up and their tiny boat was being battered against the rocks. It disappeared behind a jutting cliff and one of the women below screamed and dropped to her knees. The curragh reappeared, larger now—closer. The crashing waves were hurling it toward the shore, then away.

One of the men cupped his hands over his mouth and shouted a warning, but Karalee could not even hear any of his words from where she stood. They were lost in the howl of the wind and the sea. The boat still rocked toward the jagged shoreline.

She had seen this happen before. Sometimes the curragh would be smashed to pieces and the men with it. Other times a gash would be torn into the boat's sides and it would sink. The men would never be seen again. Then sometimes they made it to shore safely, and would be pulled onto the high beach by those who had watched their struggle.

She had never seen anyone go in for a rescue, though. Her father had told her that such attempts were futile. But she knew it was more. There was an awe of the sea—a fear. The sea was a living spirit that did not like to have her victims snatched from her grasp. She would remember those who had cheated her and would lie in wait for her sweet revenge. She would surely drown the rescuer himself when she got her chance, making him take the place of the man he had saved.

Karalee moved along, not wishing to see the outcome. She would rather imagine that the three men fell safely into the arms of their loved ones. Imagination usually gave happier endings to such stories than did reality.

Night had closed in by the time she reached the village where her family had been given refuge. There were lights in the high, plate-sized windows of all the cottages and they looked alarmingly alike, peat smoke rising from the chimneys and through the open doors. Then she remembered that a fishnet had been nailed to one side of their cottage and two felled trees had been placed before the door for sitting, and she found it easily enough.

Her father had arrived and was sitting on an overturned bucket before the fire. A pale-haired man, with a jutting, broken-looking jaw and arms that seemed to hang to his knees, was holding forth about Oliver Cromwell and how he had crushed the Galway of the tribes.

It was surely Robert Kerrigan, Karalee decided, the man whose hospitality they were accepting. He was a Presbyterian, Father O'Glanny had told them, but his sympathies lay with their cause. His eldest son had turned Catholic when he married a girl of the faith and he hoped that by helping people like the Nolans, someone would, in turn, offer the same kind of help to his dear boy who was somewhere—he knew not where.

Micheal Nolan rose and opened his arms for Karalee to run into.

"A gilla," he murmured with a weak smile.

She had seen him last only three days before, yet he had changed. He seemed taller and more gaunt. Had not his hair been bushier—less gray? She had always adored him with his ready jug of poteen for guests and his wheezing laugh that made everyone join in, his store of tall tales that set her to giggling and made her mother cluck in vexation. Now there was a dignity and strength about him that had not been there before.

Something was amiss. Her mother sat shrivelled in her corner, the exact place she had been sitting when Karalee left, still clutching her shawl about her as if it were not the hottest day of the year. The faces in the flickering shadows were grim. No one spoke.

"Where is Theo?" Karalee asked, afraid to hear the answer.

Micheal Nolan turned from her, clasping his hands behind his back. "Theo is not coming with us."

"Not . . . coming . . ." she stammered. "Has he been hurt? Is he . . ."

"No. The boy is in fine health. He does not wish to leave. There is great need for him here and his conscience will not allow him to run away."

"His conscience, is it?" Karalee stormed. "So he does not wish to leave? I do not wish to leave. Mother does not wish to leave—and neither do you. But we must. All because of

23

him. The choice is no longer his. He must leave and the devil take his conscience!"

"I cannot force him to do what he feels will be a betrayal of his comrades."

"And do we—his family—mean so little to him?"

"It is for us he stays and fights."

"Sha, for us! Only tell me where he hides. Let me go to him. I will change his mind, I promise you that."

Karalee knew it was true. She had her way with Theo when no one else had. Perhaps it was because they thought so much alike. Born on the same month, they were, a year apart almost to the day. She could often turn back his protests before he voiced them.

"I will not have you go. It would be dangerous."

"No one would suspect a girl, Father. Only tell me where he hides."

"And have you lead the soldiers to him?"

"I will not."

"I forbid it."

"Then forbid Theo to stay."

"I did," he told her after a long moment. "He will not listen."

Suddenly Patrick was beside her, holding her elbow, steering her away from the circle, to where an iron pot steamed over the fire. "You have not tasted of food this day, Karalee. Hunger makes us speak without thinking at times."

"I am not hungry," she protested, trying to pull away.

"And I say you are." Patrick dug his fingers deeper into her flesh.

"'Tis the times," Robert Kerrigan said, nodding. "We are none of us the way we wish to be. You should be proud of your Theo, Micheal Nolan. 'Tis a fine thing he does. Too many of our young men are seeking refuge in faraway lands. Letting their women dictate to them. The fight cannot be won that way."

Patrick jabbed a potato and plopped it onto a plate. Then he sliced off a thick wedge of raisin cake and slapped it next to the potato. He spooned steaming broth and chunks of fish into a thick mug. "Eat now. There is no one can tell what kind of food we will be getting aboard that rat-filled vessel."

"What is it to you if I eat, amadhaun?" Karalee whispered.

24

"Nothing at all, bonnaveen. It might be well for you to miss a supper or two, so as to weaken your black temper."

"Then eat of that plateful yourself."

"You will eat it. You cannot talk with your mouth full of bread and disgrace your father the way you were doing—yammering at him so in front of strangers. If you were my woman, I would wallop you so you would not be sitting throughout the journey. I might well do that anyway if you do not hold your sharp tongue . . ." He shoved the food at her. "Silence!"

Karalee ate without another word. It was not from fear of Patrick Roe. Him, she would stand up to with good showing if she had to. Rather, he had struck a grain of truth. She had never spoken so harshly to her father before. Now she felt shamed for the shame she had brought to him and in front of strangers.

She glanced across the room to see her mother watching her, her eyes wide with a strange kind of glow. The woman lifted a finger and beckoned to her.

"My daughter," Sheila Nolan cooed when Karalee sat beside her. She reached out to smooth back a strand of hair from her daughter's forehead. "You are my only hope for life."

"Everything will be fine, Mother," Karalee whispered, touched by her mother's unusual show of affection.

"You must go to Theo."

"I cannot. Father forbids . . ."

"Hush!" She clutched both of Karalee's hands between her own. "You must go. Heed my words."

"Mother . . ."

"I heard them speak of it. In the morning, while everyone sleeps, you must slip away. Follow the main road that winds through the city. Lombard Street should be easy to find. It is bustling with people, so you will not be noticed. There will be a death's head and crossbones over the door where Mayor Lynch hanged his own son three hundred years ago."

"Please . . ."

"A few doors farther on the same way will be an apple stall, where squats a red-haired woman, selling her wares. You will tell her you have come from Connemara to buy a gift for your sister who is ailing. Ask her how much she will take for her beautiful shawl."

"Her shawl? I don't . . ."

25

"It is only a sign. It will let her know you are one of us. She will take you to Theo. The woman's name is Hannah Bray."

"I cannot go unless I tell Father."

Sheila Nolan stiffened and thrust Karalee's hands from her. "You must know that Theo means more to me than anyone in this world."

"I know, Mother."

"When I was in labor with you and with Brian and Shauna, I wore your father's coat. The pishogue said that in such a way, your father would be able to bear some of my pain with me. But with Theo, I refused the coat. I wanted to share my agony with no one. He was my first. And my son. Can you understand?"

Karalee nodded.

"Have you marked my words well?" Sheila Nolan persisted, in a voice that was like the voice of a stranger. "Will you promise to go tomorrow morning? Promise to see Theo and to tell him that his mother's life is on his head? Convince him that his first duty is to me? To us?"

Karalee could not look into her mother's eyes. She felt a chill in spite of the turf fire.

"I promise," she said.

Four

"I have a sister in Connemara," Karalee stammered, certain that everyone in the square knew she lied.

"Buy a juicy apple?" The red-haired woman did not seem to hear Karalee over the marketplace din.

Blue-cloaked fruit women, tinsmen, and ragmen hawked their wares, each attempting to outcry the next. Scrawny beggars wailed their tragic stories, yanking at each prosperous-looking sleeve which passed. Pigs, shrieking for their right to pass, trotted through the narrow cobbled street as if people were the intruders. Geese, squawking, waddled after them.

"Bite into a sweet pear, then? Only tuppence apiece."

"No, thank you. I'm not hungry." Karalee tried not to wrinkle her nose at the baskets of green fruit, the trays of fly-inspected oaten cakes and the chunks of reeking fish and scrap meat spread out before her. "I have a sister in Connemara," she tried again.

"Aye, we all have sisters. Six, I have, meself." The red-haired woman squinted at her through pale, straggly brows that met at the bridge of her nose. "Gooseberries, just picked?" She slapped at the hand of a grubby child who snatched up a dirty oaten cake and ran with it.

"God bless your color, ma'am," someone whispered so close to Karalee's ear that the surprise of it nearly toppled her forward into the fruit woman's lap.

She turned toward the voice, but the man who had spoken was well away now, the tails of his gray frieze coat flapping behind him.

"Cool buttermilk to quench a parched throat?" The woman dipped into a foaming bucket and came out with an overflowing mug. The stumpy hand that extended it was covered with warts.

"My sister is ailing," Karalee went on. "I thought I might . . ."

"Will it be herring you want then?"

"Here's a comely Papist wench for you, eh, Phillip?"

Karalee swallowed hard and dug her clenched fists into her sides. She had never seen so many military men and orange-ribboned yeomen in one place before. Now a group of dragoons had stopped before the apple-stall, and one of them, a slim, golden-haired officer, was smiling at her. Had she not known him for the wicked creature he must be, she would have thought him handsome in his scarlet coat, white, fitted waistcoat, blue pantaloons, cocked hat, and feather.

"She's comely, all right, lad," one of the older soldiers said, "but look how brazen she is with her color. She needs to be taught a thing or two her croppy lover' doesn't know."

Color. Karalee's hands flew to the ties of her cloak. She had forgotten she was wearing green.

"I might take the job," the young officer said, still smiling at her.

"No time now, lad," the first man said with a chuckle. "We must report."

"Later, then." The golden-haired one touched a gloved hand to his forehead in mock salute. "You might stop by the ale house at the end of Lombard Street this evening, my pretty. We're barracked there temporarily. I'll buy you a new cloak and maybe a new bonnet. One with orange ribbons." He leaned so close that his lips brushed her ear. "Major Phillip Shepard is who you'll ask for. You won't be sorry."

"I noticed your shawl," Karalee began quickly when the men had moved away. She was anxious to get her business finished before they came back. "It's . . ."

She stared at the patched, mud-colored shawl. How could she offer to buy such a rag? Too many idlers stood about, listening. They would suspect something.

"My shawl, is it?" the woman growled. "If it's nothing you intend to buy, step away for them who does."

"Please . . ."

The woman lunged forward with a shriek and shoved Karalee aside with the strength of a man twice her size. "Bless you for a fine gentleman," she cooed at a stout well-dressed man with white chin whiskers and shiny boots. "Buy an apple and help a poor widow?"

The man barred her way with a thrust of his silver-knobbed walking cane and strode toward an elegant coach which stood waiting in front of the Royal Oak Inn.

Karalee rubbed her fingers across her forehead. Had she forgotten something? Had she gotten the words wrong? The woman had not responded to the supposed signal that she was a friend. Perhaps among the throngs of fruit women, there was another with red hair. Of course. That was it. But how would she be able to tell? Most of the women wore hoods, or shawls pulled so low that only a narrow strip of face showed.

"Are you Hannah Bray?" she asked in desperation.

The woman's face flamed and she bared her teeth as if she were about to bite. "I asked you kindly to move along. Ye—without a shilling in your pocket to spend. Ye—with rolling eyes for the shiny soldier boys. Shall I be calling the magistrate to see you on your way?"

"No—please. I am sorry."

Karalee whisked around the corner into the alley, where a dozen ragged urchins paddled through a stinking stream, yelling, playing pitch-and-toss. Hastily-built hovels rested against the walls, with openings big enough only for a person to crawl into and thatched roofs not high enough to stand straight once inside. A bare-breasted girl, younger, it seemed, than Karalee, sat in a wretched doorway, nursing a babe who looked large enough to jump up and join the games when he had sucked his fill.

The next street was wider and the people who traveled it better dressed and more hurried. The shops were cleaner, fresher-smelling, and more finely built, like small fortresses. Karalee stopped to marvel at the Doll Emporium, where little china people wore fancier dresses than she had ever seen on a breathing being. Next to that was a wig shop and beyond that a shiny window of silk dresses in rainbow colors —except that none of them was green. After that came a fine display of china goods and plated ware.

She moved toward the bridge where she could see Lough Corrib shining in the morning sun, and hear it roaring and swirling beneath her feet.

"Bless your colors, girl," someone said, and then again. But Karalee did not turn to see who spoke.

A row of tall red-painted warehouses stood along the bank and at the end of them a huge gray mill, square-notched like an ancient castle. Dozens of ships lay at anchor along the quay and even more small craft floated in and out among them. Could it be that one of them would carry her and her family off tomorrow morning, long before the sun rose?

She had no call to be here dreaming. She could not face her mother without still one good try at finding her brother—dragging him back with her, if she had to take a cat-o'-nine-tails to him.

The mixed feelings of dread and fear Karalee experienced as she retraced her steps from Lough Corrib to the Lombard Street marketplace—at the thought of facing Hannah Bray's wrath again, if indeed the woman were Hannah Bray—were replaced by feelings of frustration. The fruit woman was gone. A toothless grandmother sat in her place.

"Herring? Shoals?" the woman offered.

Karalee shook her head. She was certain she was in the right place. The same weather-beaten sign dangled above the shop door next to the archway where the red-haired woman had displayed her wares. Someone had begun to paint "Hugh Rafferty, Cobbler—Leather—Nails" in fine, swirling letters; but midway through the "Rafferty" had realized he was running out of space, and the printing became more and more cramped until the "Leather—Nails" was finished by painting it sideways on the edge.

Karalee felt the tugging at her skirt, but ignored it, deciding it was another beggar, holding out his cup for a coin she could not give.

"You. Come with me, girl." The ragged boy who held fast to her skirt was perhaps ten, with sunken yellowish eyes and a pointed chin.

"And why should I, little maneen?"

"You want to see Hannah Bray? Stop your puithernawling and come. Hurry."

Karalee trailed the boy, running to keep up with him, as he slid through half a dozen alleyways, down broken steps to what seemed to have been a linen shop once, before the rats and spiders had discovered it, through a twisting corridor and into a dim, windowless room. Empty boxes and heaps of straw covered the floor and the air was so tight with dust she could hardly get her breath.

"Hannah Bray?" She moved forward cautiously toward an even more dim room beyond, like a closet, where she thought she caught some movement and the outline of a seated form.

"What do you want with Hannah Bray?" A man's voice boomed from the darkness of the inner room, and Karalee cursed herself for the little glugeen she was to have come here by herself.

"Someone asked me to inquire of her health. I . . ." She took one step backward—then another, and another, reaching for the door. She would run as she had never run before, the way she had come, out of the town and across the bridge, never stopping until she reached the cottage where her dear family waited.

Behind her was a muffled voice and the clink of coins. The door slammed and a skittering of feet on the other side of it echoed away to nothing. The boy was gone.

"Someone asked you to inquire about Hannah Bray's health?" the man asked. "Your sister in Connemara?"

"Yes."

"Perhaps I know her. Would her name be—Thomas Farrell?"

"Thomas Farrell?"

"Ian Cassidy then?"

"I don't understand."

Someone laughed close behind her and she gasped, moving away from the sound. "Come, come, girl. Is Thomas Farrell your sweetheart? Or is it Ian Cassidy? Robert Murphy?"

"I don't know any of those names," she answered truthfully. "Please, now. I would like to leave. Let me pass."

"When you leave—I should say, if you leave—it will be after you've told us what you know."

"I know nothing." Karalee was surprised at the strength that remained in her voice, trembling as she was inside.

Her eyes were growing accustomed now to the lack of light. The man who sat before her was dressed in coarse farmer's clothes, such as her own father and brother wore. His head was bare and his long brown hair pulled back at the nape of his neck and tied. As he stood and came to-

31

ward her, she noticed that he was no older than Theo. His square chin was smooth-shaven and his gray eyes close-set and piercing.

The other man looked like a drawing she had seen once of a snake St. Patrick had driven from Ireland. His eyes were slits, his skin was ashen, and his tongue darted out repeatedly to moisten his thin lips.

"By rights we could drag you to the triangle, rip off your dress and cut the flesh from your back. I'll wager you would beg to speak after the first lash. You skin is so soft, 'twould cut like butter." The snake-like man reached out to touch her cheek, and Karalee bit her lower lip so that she would not cringe from him. Men of his sort were only more enflamed by a show of fear.

"I've done nothing."

"Haughty, ain't you, Kate?" the snake-man snarled, yanking her by the hair—pulling harder and harder until she cried out. "Tell me your name."

"Does my name matter to you?" she sobbed.

He laughed and released his hold, showing a row of brownish teeth. "Not a whit. You're all Kate to me, you bare-feet wenches."

The younger man stepped forward, his voice quiet now. "I'll have her first."

"Who gives you that right?"

"I take it. Do you want to challenge me?"

For a moment, it seemed the snake-man would reach for the knife that was stuck in a leather flap fastened to his belt. He hurled Karalee to the floor behind him and crouched, his narrow eyes glittering.

"Well?" There was a faint smile on the younger man's lips, as if he hoped the snake-man would try for his blade.

Hardly daring to breathe, Karalee pulled herself across the floor, inch by inch, praying their quarrel would provide enough distraction to cover her escape.

"Just a wench she is, eh, Hugh lad? Just like many another, when you've dallied as many as we have. Not worth good friends spilling blood." The snake-man's voice was syrupy, but his right hand still curled, quivering above his weapon.

"I'll have her first," the other man repeated.

The floor creaked under her weight and Karalee froze, expecting rough hands to drag her back. But neither of the men seemed to have heard.

"I only thought to have her first, to show you how it's done." The snake-man sniffled, then wiped his forearm across his nose. "But—hey ho. What's this?" He did a jigging step, hopping in front of Karalee, and crushed her wrist with the heel of his boot. "Stay awhile, won't you, sweet Kate? The fun is only now beginning."

"Stand watch," the younger man said, his eyes fastened to Karalee's face.

"Go ahead, Hugh lad." The snake-man folded his arms across his chest and leaned against the wall. "But don't tarry at it too long. I'm already burning for a feel of that wiggling body. Would you like me to hold her for you?"

"Stand watch outside the door."

"Awr, lad. I'll stand watch here well enough. Don't take all the fun out of it."

"Outside the door. I don't want one of those damned croppies jumping me with my breeches down."

The snake-man growled, then snatched up his bottle and upended it with a long gurgle, before he left with it.

"It's been a while since I had such a woman," the one called Hugh said, sliding toward Karalee. "You're so fair. So fair."

"Please, sir," Karalee said, ashamed at the sound of her own begging. "Please don't use me."

There was a softness in the man's look, and for a moment as a narrow beam of sunlight struck him, she was certain she had touched his heart. He might even be a sympathizer, as was the good Protestant man who had given them shelter while they awaited their ship. Perhaps he had been drawn into this evil against his will. He might overpower his terrible partner and help her escape.

"Such a face." There was a lilt to his voice as he touched a finger to her chin. "Do you know how lovely it is, girl?"

Before she could answer, his fist struck her cheek with such force that her head jerked backwards, hitting the floor. She lay nearly unconscious, staring up at him.

"A lovely face, indeed." His voice was still a croon—his face bland. "After I have done with you, it may not be so lovely." He pulled her to a sitting position and knelt, straddling her. "Your name. Quickly."

"Karalee," she whispered.

He struck her with his open palm this time, making her ears ring. She could taste blood. "Your whole name, girl."

"Karalee Nolan," she managed.

"Nolan. Nolan. Ah—of course. Theobald Nolan." He nodded and let her slump to the floor again. "Husband, is he?"

"Brother."

"Good. Theobald Nolan's sister. A real prize." His fingers worked at his belt buckle. Then the fastenings of his breeches. "I see the likeness. Yes, through the eyes. Theobald Nolan, is it? 'Twas him who ran with those who torched my father's mill. 'Tis a pity he cannot be here now to see this."

Karalee scarcely heard him as he talked on, taking his time, relishing her helplessness. She was thinking of Patrick Roe that day in the glen and how she had raised herself suddenly and thrown him off-balance. And Patrick was easily as big a man as this one. Could she do it now? Was there a use in it? Even if she got clear of him, she would have to deal with the other in the corridor. No matter. She had to try.

She started, but her first movement seemed to bring her stomach to her throat. Her head still throbbed and spun from her attacker's blows. It was too late. He fell on her, ripping her dress, biting her, wedging himself between her legs, then tearing them wide apart. Suddenly he tensed, raised himself with an animal-like cry and lunged down, forcing himself inside of her, thrusting and twisting until she thought she would split in two from the pain.

At last, when she thought she could bear no more, he went limp, his body crushing hers with its weight. Karalee fought for breath, afraid to move from under him, for fear that to do so would be to bring on a fresh assault. She closed her eyes and wept silently, waiting.

The door creaked open and there were footsteps.

"Get back, Sneed," her attacker snarled, cursing. He raised himself groggily onto his elbows. "I haven't done with her yet."

There was a gargled cry and a cracking sound and he fell again—heavy and lifeless this time. Dear Mother of God, she thought. It will be the other one and I will die. I want to die. Let me die.

"Karalee," someone whispered. "Little glugeen. What a plague you are to those who love you. Hie up from there."

She opened her eyes fearfully, certain her ears deceived her. "Patrick." She moved her lips, but there was no sound.

34

"A chree! What in the name of Heaven have they done to you?"

He stared down at her a moment, his face twisted in horror. Then he pulled her clothes together and scooped her into his arms. Her attacker lay sprawling on the floor, the back of his head wet with blood.

"Is he . . . ?"

"Yerra, he is that. I hit him hard enough to split him through to his heels." Patrick waved a rusty chunk of iron. "And may the devil be waiting for him down below."

Karalee slid an arm around his neck and clutched him. "There's another one—even worse—outside the door. He has a knife. We can't . . ."

Patrick shook the piece of iron again. "I got him first, girl. How in the devil do you think I got in here? But there may be others coming. Are you able to walk? You feel to weigh as much as I."

"Yes, I can walk," she managed. But before he could set her down, she lost consciousness.

Five

The red-haired woman sat on her haunches in the shadows, like a great brown rat, gnawing at a turnip she clutched with both hands, as if she feared someone would snatch it away. She studied it, dipped it into a bowl of whey and gnawed it again.

" 'Tis too soft, you gaffers be, these times. Running off by the thousands to die in a strange land. Your bones will rest with those who did not know to speak your name."

"Nor will my bones care, when my soul has left them," Patrick said. "I do what I must do."

Karalee peered through half-closed lids, trying to remember where she was and how she had come to be here. Her only memory was of the sweating yeoman and his animal cries as he tore her. She did not wish to speak with these people, whoever they might be, and feel their eyes upon her. Especially, she did not want to speak with Patrick.

She lay on a bed of sweet straw, her cloak wrapped tightly about her nakedness and one hand squashed beneath Patrick's rump. She was afraid to inch it out, for fear someone would notice she had awakened.

From the closeness of the walls and the way they curved inward as they rose, she decided she was in a clochan, a long-abandoned dwelling of an ancient people. She had played in such settlements near Dunmore, the summer her mother's oldest sister had died, and Karalee had traveled there with her family to attend the wake. The clochans were fashioned entirely of stone and moved toward the top to form a kind of beehive. The only light and air came through a single chin-high door cut into the opposite wall.

"At least in these times we have bread to put into our mouths. And fish, don't we? As long as there is a sea."

The red-haired woman chewed the last of her turnip, spat out a bit of stem and snatched another from her basket. "Now 1688. There was a black year. The siege of William of Orange. May his soul burn in hell throughout eternity."

"And you were there, were you, old hag?" A skin-headed man with an empty sleeve lay on a straw pallet next to her. His face was a death's head in the dim light. "It isn't a May frolic we're havin' in these hills now, remember? I left a part of meself there."

"1688," the woman went on, as if she had not heard. "Maura Gilhooley told we gaffers tales of Derry Town 'twould chill your blood. Tales her mother told her. Babes wasting away at their own mothers' breasts for want o' milk. A rat sold for a shilling and a bucket of horse blood the same. Glad they was to get it too. When they could. Five-and-sixpence bought a quarter of a dog. Fattened on the bodies of slain Irishmen."

Karalee shuddered and pressed her face against Patrick's side.

"Ah, my lad, your beauty is stirring."

"I would take it kindly," Patrick said, "if you would leave off such stories for now."

"Stories, sha! The truth they be."

"They may be. But I would take it kindly," Patrick repeated, his voice rising.

"Wisha. Your girl is not made of spun sugar only because she is fair. I was fair once too."

The man on the pallet cackled. "1688. The year of the siege."

"I was fair as she," the woman went on. "My hair sparkled like fire, they said, in the sun. What be it, if some son of the devil ravished this girl and cuffed her about? She breathes, doesn't she? When I was but fifteen, I went into a barracks of four men and let them have their way with me on the promise they would release my father and two brothers from gaol. The next morning, they let my brothers go right enough. But they hanged my father. Before he was cold, they chopped off his head and held it up for all to see. 'The head of a traitor,' they cried."

The woman's turnip dropped onto the dirt floor, but she did not seem to notice. "A month after, when our men rose and burned the barracks to the ground, I ran with them and threw the first torch. I watched while those who had used me were roasted alive. I laughed at their death screams. But—we were stronger in those days."

Patrick's hand moved against her arm, and for the first time, Karalee realized how close together they were wedged. She nudged him away with her shoulder. "Stop."

"Stop, is it?" He laughed softly against her ear. "You, who have been caressing me for hours? Pushing yourself against me? 'Tis I who should say 'stop.' "

"If that is so, I did not know what I was doing and I am truly sorry for it."

"I don't mind."

"But I know now. So move away."

There was a scurrying at the doorway and the yellow-eyed boy Karalee had seen in Galway tumbled in. He scooted over to the red-haired woman and squatted before her.

"You saw them?" she asked.

The boy nodded. His pinched face was more like that of a little old man than it was of a child. Blue veins showed through the skin of his forehead and there was no rosiness in his cheeks or lips. His arms rattled about in his ragged sleeves as if there were no flesh and blood to cushion his bones. But his belly was high and rounded. "Only the girl may go. The man is to wait here."

"Patrick," Karalee cried, tugging at him. "The boy is one of them. He betrayed me—led me into the yeomen's den."

"He had no choice," the man on the pallet growled. "You strutting about in your colors, drawing the dragoons to us, yammering about Hannah Bray. The boy does their bidding, but he is on our side."

"They gave him coins . . ."

" 'Twas the lad who showed me where to find you," Patrick said. "He handed me the chunk of iron and distracted the watch so I could bash him with it."

The fruit woman stood, drew in her cheeks, and with her arms outstretched, minced across the room, her wide hips swaying. "I have a sister in Connemara," she mimicked in a squeaky, comic voice. "Where is Hannah Bray? Tell me, pretty soldier boy, have you seen Hannah Bray?"

39

The man on his pallet cackled until he choked and the boy's shoulders shook with noiseless laughter. Karalee's cheeks began to burn.

"Are you not Hannah Bray?"

Her answer was fresh laughter.

"There is no Hannah Bray, a gilla," Patrick told her. " 'Tis but a pass-name they give to their plot."

"And a name we must change now, thanks be to you." The fruit-woman tossed Karalee's dress to her. "I mended it the best I could, seeing it has been torn to rags."

"I thank you." Karalee glanced around the room for a private nook she could use to clothe herself.

The red-haired woman caught her confusion and smiled, almost warmly, as she stepped forward to hold Karalee's cloak outstretched. "Fix yourself behind this, little one. You are right to cling to your modesty as long as you can. In this wretched world we learn too soon to walk in filth and nakedness." She bumped Patrick aside with a lift of one hip. "Move yourself clear, gorsoon. Out of view of her."

The yellow-eyed boy stretched himself and slapped a flat cap onto his head. "It is time for us to go now, girl. Hurry. I have tired of this jawing. It grows late."

"Go with you? Where?"

"I will lead you to Theo Nolan."

"As you led me before?"

Patrick stepped forward. "She goes nowhere without me."

"Then she goes nowhere." The boy shook his head. "Only one of you is to follow me. That was their order."

"Only one, is it?" Patrick laughed shortly. "Then I go and she stays here. I'll bring Theo back with me."

"And how will you do that, maneen?" Karalee smoothed her skirt down and fastened it. "You could sooner bring the mountain. Theo could knock you flat on your back with one hand. Besides, he despises you. How could you hope to convince him to go with us, when my own father could not? No. It is up to me. You wait here."

"Despise me, does he?" Patrick lunged toward her and grabbed her wrist, his eyes bulging with rage. "I said you do not go alone. That order stands. You'll regret it fiercely if you give me another word of your bad-jawing. No more! Do you heed me, girl?"

She tried to match his glare and to wrest her arm away, but he only squeezed harder until she nodded. "Yes."

"Fair enough then."

"May the Lord in Heaven keep us from this," the fruit woman cried, throwing up her hands. "Save your battling for the British. Jacksy, take both of them out of my sight. Let the others deal with this."

"But they told me . . ."

"Say I gave you leave to take them. Go!"

"Best crop that hair before you go, lad," the man on the pallet called.

"Crop my hair? And why should I?"

The man snickered. "If you don't do it now, I'll wager you'll be cropped before you leave their midst."

"We'll see about that, won't we?" Patrick glared at Karalee and gave her a sharp swat on the backside. "Move along. We have much to do before darkness finds us."

Karalee followed after the boy, relishing the thought of Patrick being held down by half a dozen burly Irish lads while Theo sheared off his wavy locks to the scalp. Better still it would be, if they were to let her do it.

The path led between two hillsides and into a valley. The brown and green mounds of earth that rose around them as they moved out of the valley were beginning to turn blue in the hollows. A white mist was lowering so that it grew difficult to see the way without stumbling. There was no sound but their feet, the cry of the wind in the tall grass, and the faint drizzle of soft rain that had begun to fall.

"Close to me," the boy cautioned. "We twist and turn sharply from here. Get lost and you could wander for weeks and see no one but the pookies."

He grinned at Karalee, then made a wide circle around a fairy rath that rose in front of them. It was a raised patch, flat on top and covered with brambles. To disturb such a mound was said to bring on the wrath of the little people and to invite a siege of bad luck. Few there were who were willing to chance it. Even Karalee's father, who poofed at all talk of fairy people, pretended not to notice the flat-topped hill in the middle of his turnip field, which he left untilled.

They passed through what had once been an abbey, but all its ornaments and carvings had long been removed and only two leaning walls were remaining of it. In the church-yard, battered gravestones with worn-away inscriptions stood among the nettles. Bones lay scattered everywhere, only partly covered with earth. Pieces of broken coffins were mixed with them. Grave-robbing was common, not only by those who thought something of worth might be buried with the dear departed, but more often by surgeons, wanting something on which they could practice.

The boy's foot struck a skull and it rolled against Karalee's ankle, where it came to rest, grinning up at her. She wailed and stopped so short that Patrick, trailing close behind, rammed into her.

"I cannot walk this way," she cried. "The dead are watching us. I cannot."

"You can and you will," Patrick snapped, pushing her forward. "I have carried you far enough for one day. And no thanks is what I got for it. 'Tis the living, not the dead, you need have fear of."

Suddenly the boy paused, studied the land, and cupped his hands to his mouth.

"Boolyah, boolyah, boolyah," he called.

There was silence.

The entrance to the souterrain was little larger than an animal hole and was hidden by a tangled hedge. Patrick wriggled through after the boy and dropped, then helped Karalee inside. They crawled on hands and knees to the first turn, then crawled a few yards further, where they found their way blocked by a standing slab of stone rising waist-high from the cave floor. Behind it hung another slab from the ceiling. A third rose from the floor behind that.

Traps such as this one were common in these underground passages, sometimes a mile long, dug out so that men of the cloth could seek refuge from invaders for themselves and for their holy relics. It had to be entered singly and anyone who climbed over the first barrier without being invited, could be battered over the head or captured before he could manage to duck and crawl under the second.

At last the three stood, panting for breath, in a cave room, lit only by two clay lamps suspended from a ridgepole. They could make out only dim outlines of those who sat watching them.

"Theo?" Karalee called timidly.

"Look about you, lad," a male voice boomed. "Don't you see that all here have their hair cropped? What reason could there be for yours to hang upon your neck?"

"My hair is it?" Patrick shook his head and laughed. "To begin, I cannot see any of you yet to know the length of your hair. My eyes have not grown used to the lack of light. But I can tell you this, I do not crop my hair, because I feel to do so is foolish."

Angry murmurs filled the room. "Scissors. Get the scissors," someone shouted and other voices echoed the call.

A barefoot girl of about eighteen, her pale hair skinned back and tied with a red ribbon, danced out of the shadows. Her face was round and smooth and her lips very red. "And are all our men foolish?"

"I think to crop your hair is the same as to walk up to a magistrate with a label that says, 'I am a United Man.' "

"Then 'tis cowardice that makes you wish to pass yourself for a loyalist?" the girl taunted, holding her face close to Patrick, her chin high.

"No, pretty one. 'Tis common sense and a love of living out my life with my sight and with all my members attached. A man's worth to himself or to others cannot be judged by the length of his locks."

"The scissors," the call began again, louder this time. There was a clinking and a flashing of metal.

Patrick shoved Karalee aside and bent to snatch up a length of firewood that lay near his feet.

"Come then," he invited them, beckoning, his teeth set into a grim smile. "There is little doubt you can shear me against my will. Wee babes can overcome a giant of a man if there be enough to rush him at once. Or is there one among you brave enough to try it alone?"

Karalee sucked in her breath and stared at Patrick as if she had never seen him before. There was a glint to his eye and a flush to his cheek that made him look as dashing as she had always imagined young Brian Boru had looked in the romantic tales she had heard of his battles with the Norsemen. She had never before considered Patrick bold.

As the faces around them became clearer, she could see the enmity in their eyes—the muscled shoulders and huge fists on some of the men who started toward him. She forgot her grudge and could only wonder frantically how she could best help.

"Stop," she cried. "He is one of you. I give my word on it."

"And of what use is your word?"

The woman who asked the question was handsome, and

as tall as any man Karalee had ever seen. She threw her cloak back over her shoulders and stood with fists planted on her prominent hipbones as if she would relish a battle of her own.

"Keep yourself out of this, Karalee Nolan," Patrick snarled, crouching, his eyes fixed on the men who had begun to close in.

"I'll gladly take your offer, lad. The rest of you, give us room." A man of about thirty stepped out of the circle, a pair of long shears snapping open and closed in one hand. He was twice Patrick's size, but none of him fat. His weight was in his bulging chest, his bull-neck and in his long arms. "Hold these for me, Peg, darlin'," he told the woman, slapping the shears against her flat belly. "But stay by. I'll be needin' 'em in a wink of your eye."

In spite of Patrick's warning, Karalee moved between the two men, trying to match the stance and the confidence of the big rebel woman. "I was told you had united to fight those who try to force their will on others. I was told that when you win there will be freedom. A freedom that will allow a man to worship God in any way he chooses. Will it not allow a man to wear his hair any length he chooses—whether it be over his ears or long enough for him to trip over? I came here to see my brother who has been fighting for the cause since he was old enough to carry a pike. He told me it was only the British and their sympathizers who use force to bend men to their way. Did he tell me wrong?"

"Well, now—I—" the big man sputtered, gaping at her, his cheeks reddening. " 'Tis surely the truth this bit of a girl speaks. Or am I so battle-weary that any babbling sounds like good sense?"

The woman handed him back his shears. "The girl is right."

A hunched-over man on crutches came forward, offering Patrick his hand. "Dermot Bigger," he said, "and I, for one, welcome you. We are in dire need of brave lads such as yourself. Have a crust of bread with us."

The big man, who a moment before had been ready to shear him, now slipped an arm around Patrick's shoulder, smiling as if the two of them were fast friends. "I have a grave warning for you, lad. If this woman of yours has such a quick tongue while she's but a wisp, she'll be after wearing down your ears by the time she has as many years on

44

her as my woman. Take a stout stick to her now and then. See to it quickly."

"I will not argue with that," Patrick told him.

"Come now, as Dermot said. Young Jacksy has stolen enough to make us a sumptuous banquet this day." He reached down to ruffle the hair of the boy who sat cross-legged in front of the fire-pit, then with a deep sigh, sank beside him. "Our bellies are as vital to the battle as our arms or our legs."

"Will you never stop shaming me, girl?" Patrick whispered.

"Shaming you? Did you say 'shaming you'? I only saved your worthless neck to even us for what you did for me in Galway."

"And how could that make us even? I would not be here a'tall had not your father sent me to fetch you home and if he does not skin you for sneaking off, I will do it myself." He turned his back, took a few steps, then returned. "So certain are you, that I could not have won the battle?"

"Won? You?" Karalee threw back her head and laughed. "He would have made pudding of you."

Patrick's lips turned white and he clenched his fists. For a moment Karalee was sure he would strike her.

"I did not say to do your taming now, lad," the big man called from his place by the fire-pit, where he sat with a bowl of stirabout. "Such had best be done in privacy, where you can kiss away the hurt. Come, eat before the others swarm over it all and leave not a crumb for you. My name is Darby Finnawn. What might yours be?"

"Patrick Roe."

"Not kin, are you, to Feargul Roe of Killaloe?"

"Feargul Roe is my father."

"Hah, that explains your stand. A fighter in his day. A good man. But his thinking is wrong. All wrong. And the colleen's name?"

"Where did you leave your eyes, Darby?" The woman, Peg, slapped at his arm and hooted. "She said she came to see her brother. Look at the green of those eyes, the tilt of that nose, the blackness of the hair."

"Ay, and her way of throwing the words into the air before a man has time to catch them and sort them away." Darby pointed his spoon at Karalee and giggled like a child. "You are Theo Nolan's sister. What is it—ah— Karalee? A fool I was to ask. The boy speaks of you often."

45

Karalee smiled, nodding. "Where is Theo? I was told I would find him among you."

"And here he will be. He is off with a dozen others on a raid. Collecting arms from the enemy's own stock."

"It's back he should have been two hours ago." The girl with the red ribbon in her hair stood at the cave entrance, clutching her shawl about her as if she were chilled.

"You will bring them back no sooner nor any safer by standing as a statue on that spot, Loretta Fallon. If you do not put some food into your mouth, there will be nothing left upon your bones for your Theo to pinch."

Karalee looked at the girl sharply. She was pretty enough with her child's mouth, her even teeth and her dainty hands and feet. But there was none of the flashing beauty of other girls who had won Theo's favor—girls who dyed their fingernails and their eyebrows and stained their lips scarlet—girls who would have been Theo's at the crook of his little finger. Was she the reason they had seen little of him at their hearthside of late? Was she the reason Theo had refused to leave Ireland? If it were true, then Karalee's mission would be more difficult than she had imagined it would be.

She took the barley cake and bowl of stirabout the woman, Peg, offered her, and went to sit against the wall where she could rest her back. The room was quiet with the sleeping and the eating—and the waiting. Most of the men, obviously exhausted, some still smeared with dirt from recent battles, slept sitting up, their eyes closed, but their mouths gaping as they snored. The boy, Jacksy, lay curled at Darby's feet—his face, in sleep, as innocent as that of any child.

There was not an inch of her that did not feel torn and scraped and in the silence, she had her first chance to dwell on what had happened to her in Galway and how it would affect her entire life to come. She thought of the filthy, box-strewn room and the sweating yeoman who had shattered all her girlish dreams with his animal lust. She would have had little to bring with her into any marriage except her virginity and now she did not have that. When Patrick took his place beside her, she scarcely noticed.

"Do not cry, a lhaie," he whispered, reaching to brush a tear from her cheek. "Everything will be fine."

"Everything will not be fine. I am not the same as I was

yesterday. I will not ever be the same. No decent man will ever want me."

"So that is it, is it? What happened to you will be forgotten. It did nothing to change you. Any man with eyes and with a heart that beats inside him would want you. I, myself, can hardly keep from reaching for you each time you pass. I burn with wanting you."

"You?" she threw at him. "I am speaking of a decent man."

"And you say I am not a decent man?"

"Are you?" She searched his eyes for understanding of him, and of what she had begun to feel for him in spite of herself. "You have a wife who waits for you at home. A wife who adores and trusts you. 'Tis a pity, she does not know you as I do."

Patrick brought a spoonful of porridge to his lips, but let it slosh back into his bowl. "I am not a bad man, Karalee Nolan. And you are wrong when you say I have a wife who loves me. Theresa despises me."

"You lie. Theresa weakens more each day and I ache inside for her. She grows thin and pale, crying her eyes out with your indifference."

"My indifference, is it?" There was no mirth in Patrick's laugh. "You see all, but you see nothing. Do you truly not know that Theresa grieves for the death of her childhood sweetheart—the sweetheart she has never ceased to love? That she wastes away because Rory Fitzgerald lies beneath the earth?"

"How dare you tell such a lie, Patrick Roe? May God forgive you."

"Only think back yourself," he told her, "to when her failing began. Did you not see the look of her at Fitz's wake? Have you never known that she visits his grave each day and weeps upon it until Father O'Glanny must ask me to cart her away? That she leaves her own babes to be rocked by someone else, never heeding when they reach out to her, because they are my seed and not his? Rory, the courageous, who fought by the side of Father Murphy in Wexford, while I, the vain coward, cringed at home in the field? That she does not wish to leave Ireland only because it would put three thousand miles of ocean between her and the buried bones of her dear Rory?"

A boy with sandy fuzz on his upper lip and on his

cheeks sat across from them, his bulging eyes fixed in such a stare that Karalee could not decide if he were intrigued by their quarrel, or if he were caught in a sort of hellish daydream of his own that had carried away his mind and left only the shell of his body behind. The woman, Peg, seemed to be listening too, or Karalee would have taken a seat somewhere else, away from Patrick. As it was, she had no desire to call attention to their private differences, and so remained where she was.

"If it were so," she asked, in spite of her determination to pursue the matter no further, "why would Theresa have wed herself to you?"

"It was arranged by our fathers. You know that."

"Hah! I know Theresa would never have agreed to any but a love match. Nor would her mother or father have forced her to it."

"Fitz loved only you since you were children. Theresa knew that as well as all of us did. She knew there could never be a chance for her in his heart. That is why she hates you even more than she hates me."

"Hates me? Now I am certain of your wickedness. Theresa is my dearest friend. Let me be, Patrick Roe. I will listen to no more."

Across the room, Darby Finnawn leapt to his feet. "Someone is coming. Hush now."

There was a muffled call, such as the boy, Jacksy, had made earlier, before the three had entered the souterrain. No one moved or spoke, until at last, a man, so smeared with blood it was hard to tell he was a man, tumbled through the opening. Another pushed past him, then another, and another. Nine there were in all. Some slid into a sitting position against the wall. Others merely dropped, fighting for breath, to the cave floor. One rolled himself into a ball and groaned, clutching his bleeding middle. Peg and two other women hurried to them to see to their wounds.

"Daniel Lovett?" Darby asked one of the men who did not seem to be seriously injured.

"Dead."

"Paddy Lynch?"

"Taken."

"Ian Murphy?"

"Dead."

Darby cursed and pounded a fist against his own forehead. "And his wife with child, she is," he said.

The girl, Loretta, moved fearfully to Darby's side. "Theo Nolan?"

"Taken."

Karalee wailed and leapt to her feet. "They have captured Theo?"

The man nodded. "Ay, terrible it was. Three times the men we were told would be there. Waiting, they were, like they knew we were coming. Ian reached the door first and when the firing began he lifted his arms, shouting for us to bare our chests to the grape shot. Hardly had the words left his mouth when there was a boom and his head was carried clear off his shoulders to my feet. God help us."

Loretta melted into a heap and began to sob. Too stunned by the news to weep, Karalee knelt beside the girl and slid an arm around her shoulders to comfort her.

"Hush there," she whispered. "He lives. Find hope in that at least."

"Hope?" Loretta lifted her anguished face. "I hope he dies."

"What are you saying?"

"Far better it would be if he were dead." She clasped her hands as if in prayer. "Holy Mother and dear Jesus, please let my Theo die before they put their wicked hands upon him. Please do not make him endure their torture."

Six

"Twelve ships there will be. Five thousand troops. Thirty thousand muskets and all the artillery that could be needed," one of the men said.

"All that is fine," Patrick said, carving off chunks of parsnip and plopping them into his mouth. "But I seem to remember the same being said for May the twentieth—this very year. Then Bonaparte decided his invasion of England could better be made through India. We were told his treasury was too barren for him to come to our assistance."

"This time is different. Wolfe Tone is in Paris at this moment, seeing to it. France will make Irish independence a condition of its peace with Britain."

Patrick decided not to argue and instead knelt beside Karalee and gently brushed back a few strands of hair from her forehead. "You should sleep while you can, a gilla. We leave before long."

"Leave? You must know I cannot leave with my brother in peril."

"The ship!"

"I care not for the ship."

"A child's answer."

"My answer all the same. I must stay. But you, Patrick—you must fly. Tell my father the terrible thing that has happened to Theo. Then take your Theresa and your little ones away where they will be safe, as you planned."

"The plans were changed." Patrick settled beside her and took her hands between his. "There has been no chance to tell you what happened after you left. Captain Redding, the

51

seaman your father paid for our passage, was no captain at all. He had no ship. He took the money and disappeared."

"Then there is no ship. We cannot leave."

"We can. Robert Kerrigan, may God keep him safe, made arrangements for us to sail on two cattle ships bound for Liverpool."

"Liverpool? That city of wickedness? I should . . ."

"Hush, you, and listen. There was room in the first ship for only three. Your mother and father have already sailed, with the two children, Brian and Shauna, being small enough together to count as one person."

"Sailed? Without me?"

"The first ship was leaving immediately and you were not to be found. There was no other way. I gave your father my oath that I would see to your safety on the second ship. We meet them in four days in Liverpool. From there, we all sail together on another ship bound for Philadelphia." He patted his coat pocket. "I have the papers here and by all that is holy, we will use them."

"And I am to abandon my brother? Is that what you think my father would have me do?"

"There is nothing else you can do. Now rest. We leave when the sky begins to darken."

There would be no purpose in further argument, Karalee decided. She waited until Patrick's eyes had closed and his breathing became deep and even. Then she crept to Darby Finnawn's side.

"What can be done to save Theo?" she whispered.

Darby studied her a moment, then shook his head. "Nothing. I stand thinking of it until my head aches. We would all be cut down if we tried to take him and Paddy from the gaol. It would be no use."

"I did not mean you and the other men. I meant—me, alone. By the law. Who could I go to? Who would listen to me?"

"There is nothing to be done without danger."

"I expect there to be danger in it. I am not a child."

Darby grunted. "There is nothing. Unless . . ."

"Yes?"

"Do you know anyone of influence? Anyone who would give you a letter praising Theo's character and the character of your family?"

"No."

52

"Think, girl. Much depends upon it."

Karalee shook her head. "There must be something else. We know only simple folks, such as ourselves. My father is a farmer. We . . ." A face from the far-off past flashed through her mind and she waited until she had caught hold to the name that went with it. "Eileen Rodgers."

"Who might she be?"

"A friend from my mother's girlhood days. She married a man of wealth and property. A Protestant, he was, and a Freemason. They settled not far from here."

Eileen Rodgers had married an Orangeman, and so Karalee's mother had not been allowed to attend her wedding. The woman had come to visit two or three times, holding her skirts about her as if she feared they would be dirtied if they brushed against anything and sniffing as if the air were foul. She had spoken of her new enlightened religious beliefs and of how fortunate she was to have found a man such as her James, who had rescued her from squalor. The last time Karalee saw her, she had brought with her two little girls in crisp yellow dresses and perfumed curls, who stood apart from Karalee and giggled at her bare feet and her patched skirts. She pushed them both into a fresh dungheap, reeking and squishy from recent rains. Eileen Rodgers screamed as if they had been murdered, and wept over them until her eyes were swollen. She raved about "black Irish and about how blood will tell" until Karalee might have pushed her into the dungheap too. But she rode off primly in her chaise, never to return.

"Go to her," Darby said, holding onto Karalee's shoulders and pinning her with his pale, gray eyes. "Entreat her to influence her husband in Theo's behalf. See that he writes such a letter as I said. The major put in charge of trials and court-martials has been authorized to pardon a certain number of men. Do as I say, and Theo could be among them.'"

"Oh thank you, sir. I will."

"Wait. That is not the whole of it. When they allow you to see your brother, tell him he must give them names. To show he is to be trusted."

"Names? Oh sir, Theo would never agree to that."

"He must, or he is lost! Tell him to give my name. Darby Finnawn." He laughed. "No harm could be done. It is a name already written a dozen times in their book. How many times can I be hanged, eh? The same for Thomas Farrell and Ian Cassidy. Tell Theo he is to name us—on my word."

"I shall."

Darby grunted and tossed his head toward Patrick. "You forget your hot-headed young man. He will not stand for you placing yourself in danger."

"I will go while he sleeps, and I had hoped I could count on your help to detain him here."

"My help is it?" Darby's face broke into a wide grin and he held up a tight fist. "Ay. I will detain him. But I am not sure for how long. The lad is so full of you that chains could not keep him from you."

Karalee stood on tiptoes to kiss his cheek, then turned to leave. She stopped at the mouth of the tunnel and looked back at Patrick, a faint reddish glow from the firepit flickering upon his face. "Please. Do not hurt him."

Seven

A single red rose stood in a slender blue vase on the tea table and on the polished wood sideboard was a whole silver bowl of them. Still there was no fragrance of roses in the room. Only the heavy, sweet aroma of James Rodgers' cigar and the oil he used to comb his gray hair and up-curled moustache. He stood in front of the wide bow window, listening, as Karalee sobbed out her tale, rocking onto the toes of his boots, then back onto his heels. He made no comment other than an occasional "hmmm" and every few moments inspected his fingernails, polishing them on the lapels of his wine-hued dressing gown.

"It is a nasty business," he said, when she had finished. "People being cut to pieces at the triangle for no crime but ignorance. It is worse, of course, in the North. I was in Dublin only two weeks ago. A nasty business indeed."

"How is your darling mother, Karalee?" Eileen Rodgers held up a fragile blue cup to the girl and followed it with her own hands, as if she feared it would be dropped and shattered before it could be set down.

"Mother is well enough."

"And your father? Does he still keep himself merry with his jug?"

"Father is well too."

"And your brothers and sisters? I am sorry I cannot remember all their names. Five or six of them, as I remember. There would have been another three had Sheila not borne them dead." She smiled thinly at James.

"As I have told you, Mrs. Rodgers," Karalee said, twist-

55

ing her fingers to keep from shouting. "It is my brother, Theo, I fear for."

"Theo, yes. Her favorite. The son Sheila doted on—saved all the clippings from his hair. And now he has brought her grief. Isn't that always the way of it?"

"A letter," Karalee persisted. "If your husband, James, could only furnish me with a letter."

James coughed against his handkerchief. "I cannot see how such a letter could help the young man. I have never met him. Besides, influence and rank matter little in these times. The Duke of Leinster's own son, Lord Edward Fitzgerald, has died in Dublin of wounds inflicted by the magistrate when they attempted to take him prisoner. Innocence will triumph, my sweet girl. Remember that. If your brother is innocent, they will discover it and free him."

Eileen Rodgers nodded, pursing her thin lips as she poured steaming tea into Karalee's cup. With silver tongs she set two sugar wafers into a saucer beside it.

Karalee tucked her feet under her as far as she could, when she noticed James staring at them. She had bathed them in a stream as the entrance gates to the Rodgers' home came into sight. But they were dusty again from the walk up the road to the house.

Eileen Rodgers' feet were slender and dainty, housed in white slippers without a smidge of dust upon them. The years had been kind to her. Though she had never been blessed with great beauty, there was a serenity about her that had left her face unlined. There was not a single gray hair among the titian ones, though the fine sheen had dulled.

Karalee tried to tell herself that her own mother would have been as handsome as Eileen, if her own hair were dressed with blue velvet ribbons and if she owned a blue silken dress and if she had such a cameo brooch to wear at the throat of it. But in her heart, she knew it was not true. Hard work and worry had turned down the corners of Sheila Nolan's mouth and had robbed her eyes of their sparkle.

"If you would only write the letter, sir," Karalee insisted.

"I still weep for Lady Emily, the Duchess, that her own son should have met such an end," Eileen went on, clutching white hands to her bosom. "He had an inheritance of gentle blood."

"There was wildness in the Fitzgerald strain," her husband corrected her. "Such a wildness cannot long be subdued. Did not Garrett Fitzgerald, the Great Earl himself, burn the church of Cashel? And when he was accused of it, he could only answer, 'I burned it because I thought the Archbishop was inside.' How is that for audacity?"

"Please, Mr. Rodgers. Could you write the letter? There is so little time."

Eileen reached across the table and squeezed Karalee's hand. "Patience, my dear. Patience. James and I must discuss the wisdom of such a letter. We cannot afford to have our names drawn into an affair that is none of our doing. It could be unfortunate for my husband's business. Trade could drop off from it."

"Trade? Mrs. Rodgers, Theo could be hanged."

"Nonsense. Not without a trial." James Rodgers twisted one end of his moustache, then stooped slightly to study his reflection in the window glass. "They took him only today? Justice does not work so quickly."

"It grieves me to think that Sheila's eldest son is a prisoner," Eileen said. "But you must realize that being innocent of any knowledge of what has happened, we should not be expected to suffer for it."

She went on about her husband's fine reputation and about the welfare of her beautiful daughters, who were, unfortunately, visiting with an aunt and so could not see Karalee, though they would be disappointed. They were both gifted, Elizabeth with a paintbrush and Anne at the piano.

Karalee made a show of polite interest, but the woman's words were empty. Time was speeding by. When she had arrived she could see the pond, brilliant blue and as still as glass, through the open window. She had seen lines of green hedges, bright with red and white roses. Now she could see only a black sky and a sprinkling of stars.

The room was decorated in blue and white, with watered silk on the walls and paintings of landscapes and portraits of men and women who, from their style of dress, must have been long dead. The piano was white-painted too, with gold designs, and the tables and chairs rested on trembly spindle legs that seemed likely to tip over with the slightest movement of any who leaned upon them. Far more comfortable to Karalee's way of thinking was their own modest cottage, with its sturdy benches for sitting, its straw mattresses for sleeping, and its glowing turf fire for light and warmth. She did in no way envy Eileen Rodgers.

"If you could but write that you know my family to be honest and . . ."

"Karalee!" Eileen cleared her throat. "I have said we will discuss the letter. Now, we are weary. James traveled by coach all the way from Ennis today and the road was dusty and hot. Had it not been for your visit, we would have retired an hour ago." She nodded toward James, who covered a gaping yawn with the palm of his hand as if to witness to the veracity of his wife's statement. "Constance, my housegirl, will prepare the guest-bed for you. In the morning, we will take breakfast together and inform you of our decision. Perhaps James can show you the grounds. We have four hundred acres. Vegetable and flower gardens. Sheep, cows, chickens . . ."

"The cottages you saw as you passed over the bridge?" A light came into James's eyes and he thumped his chest with enthusiasm. His sleepiness of the moment before was forgotten. "All mine. Thirty of them. And not a shilling do I take from the cotters who live in them and work for me. I ask only that they keep their floors swept and their pigs out of their beds. I could get several pounds a year for the use of any of them. But I decided workers would be grateful enough for their roofs to give me an honest day's labor for my generosity."

"James is much too kind." Eileen wrinkled her nose in the manner Karalee had most remembered her doing in the days of long ago. "There are always so many of that class who take advantage. I insist, therefore, they keep their curtains pulled open at all times, so that in passing, I may glance inside and see that all is as it should be. Otherwise, it would not be long before our cottages would resemble those other dreadful ones we pass on our way to Oranmore."

"I had planned to start back tonight."

"Tonight?" Eileen's laugh was brittle and false. "My dear, I could never forgive myself if Sheila's daughter met with harm because I allowed her to venture out into the middle of the night."

"And what of the harm that could befall Sheila's son?"

There was silence and Karalee regretted her hasty words the moment she had uttered them. Eileen looked at her husband and lifted an eyebrow.

"From the look of you, you could not travel a dozen steps," James said.

58

"Perhaps you are right." Karalee hoped her agreement would soften the impact of her accusation. If James Rodgers refused her request, Theo was lost. "If I rest, I can get an early start in the morning."

"Of course we are right." Eileen clapped her hands and a well-rounded woman in white apron and cap came into the room so quickly that she seemed to move on wheels.

"Yes, Mum?"

"Show Miss Nolan to the guest bedroom and supply anything she might need."

The bed was too soft and the feather pillow had an unpleasant odor. Karalee was tempted to roll onto the floor and sleep on the carpet, which seemed soft enough. But it would not have mattered where she lay. Sleep would not find her this night. She lay staring at the ceiling, trying not to see Theo's face staring back at her.

At first she thought she imagined it when the knob turned and the door opened an inch. She had thrown her window open wide before she got into bed, hoping to allow the unbearable stuffiness to escape. A sudden breeze had merely blown through and carried the door. She waited, watching, and when it opened another inch, she sat up and pulled her sheets about her, peering into the darkness.

The door creaked again, like the soft mew of a kitten, swung open wide and closed. A man stood against it, his breathing so labored that Karalee could hear it across the room. She rolled from her bed and groped on the dresser top for something she could use to protect herself. A hairbrush clattered to the floor.

She was about to cry for help, when the smell of cigars and hair oil reached her nostrils and she realized her intruder was James Rodgers.

"What is it you want of me, sir?" she managed, her voice a whisper.

"I? I want nothing. It is you who want something from me. Is that not so?"

"Yes sir." Had he been drinking? she wondered. She could detect no smell of ale upon him, but perhaps the wealthy drank something finer that had no odor to it.

He moved closer and she could see his puffy pink face in the moonglow. His lips were wet and parted and he blinked repeatedly. "I have never seen such a beautiful young girl. And I have been many, many places. Was your mother beautiful?"

59

"Everyone tells me she was, sir."

"You wish me to help your brother, don't you?"

"Yes sir. The letter for the magistrate."

"Ah, the letter stating that your family is of good character? Is it?"

"Oh, yes sir."

"Then why was your brother storming the barracks?"

"I . . ."

"No matter," James Rodgers lifted a fat hand and shook it. His forehead was damp and his hair stuck to it. "I have decided to write the letter."

"That is kind of you, sir," Karalee said, praying that the letter for Theo was his only reason for being in her bedroom, but knowing it was not. "Do you plan to write it now?"

"As you wish." He slid past her to the bedside table, where he lit a candle and held it close to her face. "Very beautiful."

"Thank you, sir."

He brought pen and ink and note paper from the writing case and set them on the table, pointing with the tip of his pen at his initials in gold swirled onto the top of the sheet. "You see? This will make it seem more official. A man may easily write my name, but he could not so easily have the proper paper to write it on."

"Yes, sir."

"I have done even more for you than you asked. In Dublin, I saw men given protection because they surrendered their arms. Some brought in nothing more than a pitchfork or two. I have a rusty musket and an old blade that belonged to my grandfather, useless, but they will serve. I slipped outside a moment ago and placed them in the chaise. When the sun rises, and Eileen still sleeps, I myself shall drive you to the magistrate. Eh? You will present your letter and surrender the arms, saying your brother asked you to do so."

As he bent over the note paper, mouthing the words he scribbled, his face was that of a small boy who proposed some mischievous prank. His pen made a scratching sound as it flew. He signed his name with a flourish, touched it with his blotter and held it out to her.

"It is more than I had hoped for, Mr. Rodgers."

"I dare say."

"Thank you." She reached for the letter, but he drew it back.

"Are words the only way you know to show your gratitude?"

"Sir."

He licked his lips and swallowed. "I desire to see a young girl's body."

"Sir!"

"To touch plump, firm breasts. To fondle and to kiss them."

Karalee was filled with horror. She stared at the letter as he moved it back and forth, taunting her. She thought of telling him to keep his letter. But no, she needed it. There was no other help for Theo. She thought of snatching it from his hand and running, but she was in her nightdress and would not get far. He might even call the magistrate himself and make up lies about her, if he were angered.

"Unclothe yourself. Slowly so that I may enjoy it fully."

"Your wife . . ."

"She takes a sleeping draught. We have separate bedrooms and she will not know I am not there. Disrobe. Please. I shall not ask you again."

He stood between her and the door and his eyes held a look of madness. Karalee was certain now that if she refused to obey, he would take her anyway. Perhaps he even hoped she would resist.

She lifted her dress slowly, over her hips and her breasts, trying to imagine she was alone, preparing for a bath. When she could stall no longer, she pulled the dress over her head, let it drop to the floor and stood naked before him.

"Oh, yes, yes." Sweat drops ran down his cheeks and he could not have looked more drenched if he had been caught in a rainstorm. He devoured her with his eyes, moaning as if he were in pain and moved around her—once, twice—circling as a wild animal might a chunk of meat he wanted to relish as long as he could, before leaping upon it. He cupped her breasts, one at a time, then both together, gently at first, and then harder, crying out himself when she winced in pain. She squeezed her eyes closed as his mouth found her nipples and he began to suck one of them loudly, kneading her flesh as if he were a babe. She had to press her lips together to keep from vomiting. But a sudden noise made her forget her nausea.

61

The bedroom door crashed open and Eileen Rodgers stood gaping, a lighted candle in her hand. She looked as if she were screaming, but there was no sound. James froze where he stood, his eyes bulging. Karalee gathered up her clothes and dressed hurriedly, too frightened to defend herself.

"Blood will tell," the woman said at last, emphasizing each word as if it contained a curse. "You are your father's own daughter. A Nolan through and through. My heart goes out to your mother. Her son is a common criminal who will deservedly hang as one. Her husband is a drunkard and her daughter is a harlot."

Karalee could stand no more. She was about to explain what had happened, when she felt something pressed into her hand. It was the note James Rodgers had written for her.

He moved to his wife's side, having found his voice. "The girl knocked on my door and said she heard a noise outside her window. That she was frightened. But when I followed her here, she . . ."

"I do not wish to hear." Eileen's eyes never left Karalee's face. "Beauty is a curse when it is paired with such wickedness."

"Leave our house at once." James pointed a trembling finger at Karalee. "I will not allow you to sleep under the same roof with my good wife. If either of us ever set eyes upon you again, we will see that you are prosecuted and thrown into prison alongside your worthless brother. Get out!"

Karalee brushed past them, down the stairs, and into the night. She ran until she got as far as the gate, then knelt beside the hedges, panting. Her eyes searched the darkness until they lit upon a bit of metal glimmering in the moonlight. The chaise was where James had told her it would be.

She would wait until the house was dark. Rest until she was certain everyone had retired. Then she would slip back and get the musket and the blade Mr. Rodgers had promised to her. She would wrap them in her shawl and hope that no soldier would stop her and ask to see what they were.

Eight

The officer seated at the center of the long table wore a scarlet coat and his hair was black, but his bloated face looked much like the face of James Rodgers. There were eight or nine other men seated about the room too—some young and some graying—but Karalee could see little difference in any of them.

"This letter you bring has no significance, young woman." The officer handed the folded sheet back to Karalee and clasped his hands together on top of the stack of papers in front of him. "It does not even plead Theo Nolan's innocence. Why should you expect it to free him?"

"Theo is young and he is foolish. But he is not a criminal. His death would serve no purpose."

The officer cleared his throat and shuffled through his papers until he found the one he wanted. He drew it out and studied it, frowning. "There are many who would disagree with you, Miss Nolan. What I read here tells me your brother is, indeed, a criminal. He has already been named by—seven others of his kind, as being their leader. Hot in the center of the damned revolt. As to his death serving a purpose? It would deter others who might be considering the same treacherous acts."

"I have heard, sir," Karalee began in the strongest voice she could muster, "that it is within your power to send a certain number of those arrested out of the country. That their punishment would be exile."

"Exile? Bah! I questioned Theobald Nolan this morning, and though I have questioned hundreds of others in the last few months, I remember him well. He was arrogant—even bold. He refused to give names. He cursed me when I offered to let him take the oath of allegiance. He struck one of my men and it took three others to subdue him. Were we to put him onto a ship, he would sail straight back here on the first that would allow him passage."

"If I could but see him, sir. Speak with him. I could convince . . ."

"It would serve no purpose. My advice to you, young woman, is to go to this mother of yours whose anguish is your concern, and offer her what comfort you can. Theobald Nolan is doomed." He signalled for the young soldier who stood guard at the door. "Show Miss Nolan the way out. I have no more time to waste."

Through the long row of windows facing the barrack-yard, Karalee could see people gathering outside, their backs to her. She could hear them jeering and the soldiers ordering them to disperse. She could hear the terrible sound of the cat lashing against bare flesh and the piteous cries of its victim. She brushed away the young soldier's hands, wanting no help from him, or from any of them. Again and again the lash fell. Karalee groped for the sides of her chair, but there was no strength in her arms. The floor moved beneath her and the faces of the yeomanry and the officers of the army merged into one.

"Catch her, dammit."

"Hold on, Miss."

"I'll teach you scoundrels to plague me with hysterical women."

"Get a cloth for her head, quickly."

There was a thunderous beating of drums outside and the officer who had been in charge of questioning her rose. "I must attend this execution. Let the woman rest a moment where she sits. But see that she is removed before I return."

Karalee put her hands to her face and wept into them with great choking sobs. The door slammed, opened, and slammed again. There were more footsteps, brisk and clicking.

"Outside, all of you. See to your stations. Give her a chance to recover herself."

Karalee could not stop weeping and she did not look up at the sound of the newcomer's voice. But she heard the creaking of a chair as he sat across the table from her. She could sense that he was watching her, though he did not speak. It seemed to be at least a half an hour before the shots were fired. She stiffened as if they had been fired into her.

"Those men are out of their suffering at least," she murmured.

She would have to find the strength to leave. To face the cruel questioning-officer again would serve no purpose and could be dangerous. She lifted her face, expecting to see disdain or amusement in the officer who sat before her. There was none. She was startled not only by the sympathy in his eyes, but by a sense of recognition.

He was the golden-haired soldier she had seen in the marketplace—the one who had teased her about the color of her shawl and had offered to buy her a new one.

"The girl in the square," he said. "Did you find your Hannah Bray?"

"I must go," she said, without answering his question. His knowledge of her being in the marketplace before the charge on the barracks, could well point to her guilt in the deaths of the two yeomen, if their bodies had been discovered.

When she stood, her legs trembled beneath her and she had to reach out to steady herself. The officer caught her and eased her back into her chair.

"I must not be here when that man returns," she protested.

"Where can you go? You would collapse in the streets."

She had walked more miles than she could count and had run until she thought her lungs would burst, hoping to arrive in time to save Theo. All of it had been for nothing. They would not even allow her to see him. Her feet were swollen and blistered. She had not slept any part of last night, nor had she taken any nourishment since the afternoon before, when Eileen Rodgers had given her the sugar cakes.

She touched her fingers to her forehead. "I—I do not know."

"Come with me then." When she hesitated, he added, "I only wish to help you—and your brother."

Karalee cared nothing for the wide expression of concern in his gray eyes, or for his handsome face, or for the friendly smile he wore to deceive her. She knew he lied. Did not they all lie? But she was beyond caring. She allowed herself to be led through the rear door of the building, past some guards who laughed and called out, "You have the girl under your protection, eh, Phillip?"

"Protect her once for me, won't you, lad?"

They walked down a cobbled alleyway, across a crowded street, up a short flight of stairs and down a corridor. The officer stepped in front of her, at last, and opened a door that led into a small, but neat room, whitewashed and furnished with a well-made bed, a table, and a chair. A single, high window let in plenty of light and air but allowed no view of the street below. Karalee turned to face him, deciding she would not fight. Let him do what he would.

"Sleep," he said. "I will see that you have something to eat."

"You think I can sleep while they murder my brother?"

"I will do what I can for your brother, Miss Nolan. Only sleep. No one will bother you here."

She could not even remember lying down. But when she woke to the clatter of dishes, she realized that she must have slept for many hours. The afternoon sun had come and gone and it would soon be dark.

The young officer, dressed only in a white shirt now and tight-fitting dark breeches, poured water from a pitcher into a large basin and set a cake of soap beside it and a cloth for washing. His coat lay over the foot of the bed.

He smiled when he saw she was awake and swept his hand toward the tray he had set upon the table. There was a steaming bowl of broth, a thick slice of pork-meat, a mound of peas and a mug of sweet milk. She could not remember when she had been served such a feast.

"As I promised."

Karalee was too famished to refuse what he had brought her, but she could not bring herself to thank him as she found her way to the table and began to eat.

He sat on the bed, watching her. "Karalee Nolan. A very pretty name. You are . . ."

Karalee dropped her fork and held her hands over her ears. "Please do not tell me I am pretty. You do not have to say it and I do not wish to hear it."

"Beauty is a curse," Eileen Rodgers had thrown at her the night before, and Karalee was beginning to believe it was true. Each time a man had praised her beauty these last days, he had put his hands upon her and made her feel sinful.

"If you only could see yourself, my lady," the officer said, laughing, "you would not think I was about to say how pretty you are. Only how dirty. Though I do seem to remember admiring your face that day in the square. Now you are ragged and uncombed. Your eyes are so swollen with weeping I cannot tell what color they are."

He knelt beside the bed and dragged from under it a long, flat box secured with a string. Inside was a dress of deep blue, ribboned with velvet in a paler shade. There was lace at the throat and at the cuffs.

"I refuse to wear any dress that you have bought for me."

"I believe you will. Your own is nothing but rags. You could not possibly visit your brother as you are."

"Visit . . ."

"The water in the basin was meant only for you to wash your hands and face before you ate. The rest of you will require more soaking. I'm having a bath prepared. You will wish to look your best in the morning."

"But the Major said . . ."

"Major Mahon left for Gort three hours ago. There will be no more interrogations this evening. I took the liberty of removing your brother's papers from the desk and replacing them with new ones which reduced the charges against him."

"Why would you do this for me, sir?" Karalee was unable to believe it was actually happening. "Why do you take this chance for a complete stranger?"

"You remind me very much of a girl I once knew. Once loved. I was struck by the resemblance when I first set eyes upon you. I even went back to the square later to search for you, but . . ." He hesitated, as if he suddenly realized that he was revealing too much of himself to her. "But we must talk of important things now, Karalee. When they allow you to see your brother in the morning, it will be only for a few moments and there may be little privacy. You must not waste time wailing over him. You must be strong. Convince him to take the oath of allegiance when it is offered him. Tell him that to do so is no disgrace. Many good men have done it before him to save themselves."

"I will, sir." Karalee wished she felt as confident of her ability to do so as her words and her tone implied.

"If he does this, I think I can arrange for him to enlist as a foot-soldier with Captain Harris and he will be sent to the

West Indies. There is danger in the regiment too, but at least it is a chance for life."

"Oh, thank you, sir." Karalee hurried to him so quickly that her chair toppled behind her, clattering to the floor. She stooped to right it, but he pulled her back.

"Leave it."

"Bless you for your kindness, sir," Karalee told him, her face warming from his closeness and from the way he stared into her eyes as if trying to see her thoughts through them.

"You make me feel very old when you call me sir. My name is Phillip."

"I know."

There was a brisk knock at the door and a male voice sang out, "Your bath, sir."

"All right, Howard. Go and leave me to it." Phillip lifted Karalee's chin with one finger and touched her lips lightly with his before she could protest. "Your bath, my lady."

From the manner in which he crept ahead of her down the corridor, looking both ways, then slid through the open door at the end of it, she decided he was not permitted to have a woman in his quarters, though he did not say so. Once inside the tiny, gray-painted room, he closed the window, took bath linen from a cupboard and laid it across a shelf next to the steaming bathing-vessel, swung his leg over the only chair, and sat waiting.

"I will not be watched as I bathe."

"A pity." He pulled a sorrowful face, and turned his chair to the door. "Does this suit you, my lady?"

" 'Twould suit me better if you were to wait outside the door."

"That I cannot do. You have my word that I will not peek at you."

Karalee could have told him that the word of a British soldier was not to be valued highly. But he had been kind to her, whatever his motives might be. Without him, she would be without hope.

She did not soak as long as she would have wished to. It was not easy to relax when a man, and the enemy at that, sat only three feet away. Besides, there was the ever-lurking danger of discovery. She stepped from the water regretfully, rubbed herself with a towel, and wrapped around her the coarse-woven dressing-robe that had been provided.

"I am sorry there is no pier-glass, so that you can see

yourself," Phillip said, later, in the room, as she stood brushing her hair.

"I do not need it."

"Had I known you would be here, I would have found the cave of one of your pishogues and had her sell me a bundle of her fairy herbs for your bath."

Karalee looked at him in surprise.

"A cook of ours came from County Cork," he explained. "When my father was not about, she filled me with tales of your Irish heroes and of your little people and their enchantments. Had you soaked in a bath steeped with fairy herbs, you would have flung yourself into my arms by now."

"And that is what you want?"

"That is what I want. More than I can tell you."

"And all your help has only been so that I would bed with you?"

"Does it surprise you?"

Karalee shook her head. "No."

"I have a heart, Karalee, which makes me feel compassion for the trodden-upon and for the tortured. I have known great pain myself, though perhaps of a different sort. But my heart is the heart of a man as well. There was a time when I swore off women. When the girl I trusted proved herself unworthy of my trust." He smiled sadly. "I thought of your St. Kevin—was it?—who fled from his beloved Kathleen? Climbed a mountain to escape her? Beat her away with brambles and finally pushed her into a lake?"

He placed his hands upon her shoulders, tugging gently at her robe until it fell open and dropped to the floor. His eyes swept over her every curve, glistening as if he were pleased with what he saw. "I am not a saint, Karalee. I mean to make love to you. I do not claim to be noble."

"I will not try to stop you," she answered, trying not to shrink from his gaze. "But it is not my will."

"I wish that it were. Perhaps if there were more time for us . . ." He swept her into his arms easily and carried her to the bed. "Will it be the first time for you?"

"No."

Karalee was surprised at her own answer. Had she lied and told him she was still virginal, there was a chance he might have allowed her to dress herself again and he would not have touched her.

Phillip Shepard was taking a great risk on her behalf and so she would pay him for it with the use of her body. But she did not owe him passion. She would lie like a stone until he was through with her.

The light had nearly faded. He undressed quickly, but she caught a glimpse of his firm, lean body and his swollen manhood, before he stretched out beside her. Though she had been certain she would be, she did not feel repulsed by the sight of it.

He threw off the sheet she had pulled up to cover herself and a narrow beam of moonlight fell upon her naked body, making it appear almost silver-white. He tightened his arms around her, gathering her to him, so that her head lay against the damp, faintly golden hairs of his chest and she could hear the wild thumping of his heart. Or was it her own?

"I did not buy the dress for you, Karalee," he whispered. "I bought it a long time ago. But I am certain it will fit as if it were made for you."

Bewildered by his confession, she waited for him to say more, but he was silent. So he had bought the beautiful gown for another girl—the one who resembled her—the one he had loved. Perhaps—still loved? What strange sense of honor had compelled him to reveal it now with his flesh warm against hers? Was it somehow necessary to let her know that it was not really she, he was about to make love to? That he would be pretending all the while she was someone else?

Except for his fingers which tangled themselves absently through her still bath-damp curls, he lay motionless. Was he falling asleep? Karalee waited, tense, more and more aware of his thighs naked against hers, and she discovered, to her shame, that she had an undeniable need of her own.

His hips shifted slightly and without thinking about it, she found her hips following. He caught her response, and fired by it, rolled onto his back, pulling her so that she lay on top of him. With his fingers still twined in her hair, he brought her mouth down to his. Her trembling lips parted for his exploring tongue and the warm tingling she had a moment before felt between her legs, became a feverish throbbing. It was no longer enough to feel his hardness against her. She wanted it inside her. Now—oh, please, now—rose a silent cry within her and all argument about right and wrong flew away. Still he did not take her.

70

He rolled again, straddling her this time, hardly giving her time to breathe between his searing kisses. She squeezed her arms around him with a savage fury, wanting to let him know how desperately she wanted him. Yet he drew back, studying her face in the darkness, savoring her frantic need.

He cupped her breasts with his hands then, and moved down to circle her nipples with his tongue until they grew rigid and she could no longer keep herself from squirming. She didn't even try. His lips moved still lower—to her belly. And lower, until he found the soft moistness between her legs. Not until she cried out for him, did he enter her, first easing her legs farther apart, then lowering himself slowly—in and out—again and again—holding back until she strained to engulf him.

At last there was sweet release. Her whole body quivered with it when she felt Phillip stiffen and shudder atop her. She was so limp she hardly felt his movement when he turned onto his back. For a long time they lay side by side, without speaking. One of his hands moved lightly along her thighs—then between them, coming to rest on her silken triangle of hair. Her response was not as demanding this time, but it was just as undeniable. He raised up to kiss her, then moved over her again. He whispered words against her ear that she could not understand and she answered with moans of fulfillment. With his flesh still within her flesh, they slept.

Nine

The guardhouse, which had once been a stable, stood only a few paces from the barracks gate, and when Karalee looked up, she could see vacant faces peering down from the long row of windows in the upper story. The naked body of a man lay next to the wall, and other corpses, bloody and twisted, lay in an open cart beside it.

She had heard that it was the practice to toss executed men into a common grave they called a "croppy hole," covering them hurriedly, so that loved ones could not locate the remains for proper burial. But the horror of it had never touched her before. She shuddered and turned away.

"Curious business, this," the guard grunted, studying the pass Karalee had presented to him. For a moment she feared he would not honor it. That he would tear it up and send her on her way. But he cursed, scribbling something on it, opened the creaking gate, and beckoned for one of the soldiers to escort her to Theo's cell.

They passed through a room reeking of urine, vomit, and death. Twenty or more men lay on scattered heaps of filthy, flea-infested straw. Some were sleeping, some praying, and some moaning, their naked backs hideously marked by the lash.

They climbed rickety stairs and stopped at a heavy, splintered door, with a half-circle cut into it at chin level.

"You have five minutes," the soldier said.

There were four men in the cell that measured only about eight feet in either direction. Three of them were going ravenously at a basket of bread and a jug of tea. The

73

fourth, Theo, lay on the straw, his back striped and swollen from a flogging.

Karalee pressed her hand to her mouth to suppress a scream. "Theo," she managed. "Theo, it's Karalee."

When at first he did not respond, she thought perhaps it was not Theo after all. But when he raised himself and squinted at her, it was more than she could bear. His fine black hair was matted and snarled, falling across his face as if he were some wild thing. His eyes—green as the sea and so full of the devil before, were dull and red-rimmed. His face, so like her own they might have been twins, had lost its youthful roundness. His proud, wide shoulders were stooped and his chest sunken. She cried out and stretched her arm through the peekhole at him.

"Sister of my heart," he murmured, staggering to the door, where he clutched her hand as if he would break it and pressed feverish lips against it. "The sight of you is what I've needed. I thought by now you would have sailed."

"And you think we would sail without you?"

"I think you must."

"I have come to beg you, darling." She held his hands so that he would not be able to pull away. "To beg you to take the oath of allegiance."

"I did not hear you ask that."

"You must. For us. It is the only way. I have been promised that if you do, they will allow you to enlist as a foot-soldier."

"Oh, allow me will they?" He wrenched his hand free and turned from the door. "If I am to die, by Heaven, let it be for a righteous cause. Not on some foreign beach where my blood will run defending a people I despise."

"You need not die at all."

"You are wrong, my sweet one, that son-of-a-snake Major Mahon is determined against me. Against all of us."

"Major Mahon has gone."

"And another exactly like him has taken his place. Go now, my heart's darling. I fear for your safety. You have grown so beautiful that the sight of you makes me weep. Tell our dear mother and father that you saw me and that I looked well."

" 'Twould be a black lie."

"But not the first you have told, eh?"

"Theo." She clutched at him, sure that once she left, there would never be another chance for words between

74

them. She had to force him to listen. "How will it help the cause if you are hanged? Darby Finnawn himself wants you to name him when you are questioned. Thomas Farrell and Ian Cassidy too. Darby said it would do him no hurt as they already have his name. And it would win you favor."

Theo pressed himself against the door, bringing his face as close to hers as he could. "Karalee, you saw Darby?"

"I did. And it is his will that you give testimony against him. He . . ."

"Silence, girl. Enough of that. Can you find your way to Darby again?"

"Why should I? It is you I must concern myself with."

"You must take a message to him."

"Theo, dear, there is no time."

"Tell Darby—and be sure he is alone when you tell him—that Harvey Banon is the informer. 'Twas Banon who told the yeomanry of our raid. Now he has promised to lead them into the tunnel. It must be abandoned at once and there is no more trust to be placed in that black-hearted devil, Banon."

"If I do as you ask, Theo, then you must do something for me. Take the oath. Give testimony."

"I make no bargains with you, my dearest sister. Your blood and my blood run the same course. You will do what you must do. I know your ways as if you were part of me. Only, heed. Take no risks. See you are not followed."

"Do you know how you grieve our mother?"

"I know how our mother can grieve—and grieve." Theo smiled crookedly. There was a bruised swelling on his left cheek and a gash, like the cruel cut of a blade, below that. "I have seen her expression of sorrow so often that I remember it more than I can remember an expression of joy. It is a part she plays well. But she is stronger than any of us. I owe her my love—and she has it. But I do not owe her—or even you—my life."

With regret she thought of the times when they were children, when she despised her brother—even wished him dead. Try as she would, she could better him at nothing—not at tugging games or puzzles or footraces. She would run until her face was scarlet and her heart threatened to burst from her breast. Theo would run backwards, dance a jig, lag behind, then at the last moment, thrust ahead, to wait for her at the finish line, laughing.

If there was mischief in the house, her mother would place the blame on Karalee, never Theo. If there was a disagreeable task to be done, it fell to Karalee, not to Theo. She remembered well the summer she was thirteen and Grandmother Nolan was ill. It was Karalee who bathed her, fed her, read to her, and put up with her foul temper.

Yet the morning the old woman died, it was Theo she called to her bedside. After kissing him tenderly, she blessed him and pressed into his hand the brooch she had always promised to Karalee. It was her one treasure and had been handed down for many generations. It was finely carved and shaped like a gold leaf.

"You have always been the sunshine of my life, my beloved grandson," Grandmother Nolan whispered. "This is for you to give to the girl you someday choose to wife."

Choking with tears of rage, Karalee had dashed from the house and hidden herself under a wide-spreading hedge behind the outbuildings as she had done when she was a child. Knowing where to look, Theo had found her, and wriggled in beside her, drawing his long legs up under his chin. He allowed her to curse him and to pummel him with her fists.

"I hate you," she said, weeping. "Mother loves you more than she loves me."

Theo said nothing, knowing that she spoke the truth.

"Everyone loves you more. Luck follows you in everything you do. It follows me in nothing. It isn't fair."

"It is true," he said, in the quiet way he had when he was trying to get back in her good graces. He caught her hand, pressed the brooch into it and forced her fingers around it. "But who can say how long my luck will last? You cannot say a man is entirely blessed by good fortune until you follow him to the end of his days and see the way in which he meets death."

Karalee had refused the brooch, saying she did not want it if Grandmother Nolan didn't want her to have it. But her anger against her brother disappeared. Though she fought with him often after that day, she never found it in her heart to wish him ill. Now, as he had predicted half in jest, good fortune had deserted him.

"Is there nothing I can say to change your mind?" She traced the line of his chin with one finger, wanting to memorize the sweetness of his face.

"Karalee, last night they dragged dear Paddy out, the

dear lad who was taken with me, and they flogged him until the bones lay bare upon him. Still they had no evidence against him. So when they finally led him off, we cheered, saying to each other they were to let him go. We rejoiced in his good fortune. His mother stood waiting. Then came the terrible noise. Around the corner where we could not see. But we knew it was the board falling. We knew before the guards came back shouting it. They had hanged Paddy."

"Theo . . ."

"Afterwards, they cut off his dear head, and put it upon a spike." Tears of rage and sorrow flooded his eyes and began to roll down his cheeks. But he did not reach to brush them away. "Would you have me swear allegiance to them?"

"I would have you live. Yes!"

"If I am to live, it will be with honor."

Before she could say more, the outer door clanged and the guard grunted that it was time for her to leave. She started to protest, but Theo stepped away from the bars and into the shadows where she could not see him.

Heartsick at her failure to convince him of the importance of his life, she retraced her steps, keeping her head down and her eyes turned from the poor creatures along her way who would suffer unspeakable tortures at the hands of the inhuman beasts who had caged them.

"It is good you saw your croppy lad this night, Miss," the guard told her as he opened the gate. "He will not be among us tomorrow."

"Where will he be?"

The soldier laughed. "In hell, I'll wager. He goes by chaise for Gort at the rising of the sun. The major waits for him with fresh evidence. All in that cell are doomed. It is why they have been given such generous rations and why they have been removed from the others. I would say it was why you were allowed to visit."

Karalee broke into a run, past the guards and into the gaol. She had questioned a dozen men and searched at least as many public buildings, before she found Phillip in the questioning room above the ale-house, laughing and drinking with two other uniformed men.

"I must see you at once," she cried, gasping for breath.

"This was most unwise of you, Karalee," he told her

stiffly, when the other men had left them alone. "You will give me a good deal to explain."

"I am sorry, Phillip, but it could not wait. Theo has refused the oath. He will not enlist and he will not give testimony."

Phillip nodded gravely. "I rather thought that would be his decision, from what I have heard of him."

"What am I to do?"

He lifted an eyebrow. "I think what you are asking, is not what you will do—but rather what I will do."

She threw herself into his arms and began to sob. "The guard has told me they are taking him to Gort at sunrise. Theo will be facing new charges. Oh Phillip, he will die. I know he will."

Phillip sighed, his anger fading, and began to stroke her hair gently. "There is one thing left. Though it may not be so appealing."

"Anything."

"I can arrive before his escort, and sentence him to transportation on those charges we already have against him. Instead of Gort, he will be sent to Dunraven to serve twelve years."

"Twelve years!"

"It cannot be less or it would be put under study."

"So long for him to be away."

"He would still be a young man when he was released—and he would live."

"Do it then."

"You are sure? Without consulting Theo?"

She nodded. "I think I must make the decision for him. He has been so abused and so heartsick over the loss of dear friends, that he can not think clearly. He seems to relish the thought of dying."

"Then it is done. You must be at the bridge an hour before sunrise. The chaise will stop for you and you can ride with your brother to the crossroads. There an escort will be waiting with Theo's horse and his orders. You must say your goodbyes during your ride and explain to him what has been done."

"I must keep thanking you, it seems."

"Yes, you must. Later, in my quarters." He kissed her gently, then tightened his arms around her and kissed her so deeply she felt dizzy from it. "All against your will, of course. I'll remember."

"You did not tell me how you like the dress," she said, spinning away from him, feeling light-headed from his kiss, and from the hope that Theo would be saved.

"You look lovely in it. Almost as lovely as you look out of it."

There was a knock on the door and a young soldier stepped into the room. "Sorry, sir, but the colonel is here to see you."

"Good." Phillip cleared his throat and extended his fist toward the ceiling. His voice was strange and stern-sounding. "See this young woman out. And the next time you allow a blubbering female citizen in here to disturb me, you will answer for it. Do you understand?"

"Yessir. I do sir. This way, Miss."

Ten

A hare appeared from nowhere and raced for the safety of the hedgerow. Karalee turned toward the sound, caught her dress in the low-hanging branch of a hawthorne tree, and ripped a finger-long gash into its skirt.

She sank onto a shaggy patch of green wanting the relief of tears. But all over her dear land, men were being caged, flogged, hanged, and subjected to unspeakable tortures. It would be sinful to wail over a gown, no matter how soft, or how elegant—no matter how special its giver might be.

She threw one leg over the other and inspected the foot that had been plaguing her for the last mile. At another time and under better circumstances she would have found her way back to the rebel hideaway in less than two hours with little difficulty. She had gone as far often for her own pleasure. But the boy, Jacksy, had done his work well. He had led her and Patrick over and around surrounding hills. He had backtracked more than once, making a crooked trail for anyone to follow. It was almost dark before she found herself in a place she recognized.

Fortunately she had kept her wits about her enough to pick a landmark when she left the hideaway before. She had chosen the round tower, deciding its tall, cone-shaped top would be easily spied at a distance, wherever she might be, even if a heavy mist were to descend.

She despised such towers, and there were many. They were silent witnesses to a history of warring, built nine hundred years before, during the onslaught of the Danes. Whoever had devised such a structure had been wise indeed, she thought, staring up at it. Its entrance was the height of two tall men, toe-to-head, from the ground. Once inside, a man could draw up his ladder, bar the door and be secure from any but a severe or prolonged attack. He could ascend by ladder the five or six stories within until he reached the inward-sloping, slit windows at the top, where he could see out for miles. He could ring his bell to alert the others, and in case of immediate attack, drop heavy stones upon his attackers.

Karalee wrenched her ankle as she dropped to the tunnel floor, but she did not pause to ease her pain. There was little time. Theo's message for Darby had been urgent and she had taken so long to arrive here it could well be too late already.

She began to crawl through the passage, closing her thoughts to the damage that was being done to her new dress. She met the first stone barrier head-first, then eased herself into a standing position so that she could climb over it. As she did, hands reached for her from the blackness and she was dragged to the other side and slammed to the earth.

A wild-eyed man with snarled black hair and beard stood over her, holding a wicked club above his head as if any moment he would bring it down upon her. Another man, smaller than the first, but whose expression was every bit as fierce, stood beside him, holding a clay lamp. Suddenly there was a third face. And a fourth. All strangers.

"Who might you be, girl?" one of them snarled.

"It don't matter who she be," the first man said. "She has found her way in somehow, but she shall not find her way out again."

"And if someone waits for her?"

"I came here alone," she stammered. "I bring a message for Darby."

"And how will you prove the truth of what you say?"

"The girl is the sister of Theo Nolan. Let her be." The woman, Peg, stepped into the light. "She is safe enough."

"She could have been followed," the black-bearded man said. "Coming here the way she did, giving no warning. She is a fool, no matter whose sister she be."

"I was not followed."

"Hah, you say!" The fruit-woman's face appeared from the shadows. "So innocent, you be. Yet I saw you flouncing after your pretty soldier boy. And this morning with such a fancy dress. Tish!"

"Shoneen!" another voice called. "Your British lover cannot help you in here."

"You waste time. I must see Darby at once. Then decide what you will do with me. I am too fatigued to fear you."

"I have said the girl is safe," Peg told them, in a voice that would allow no contradiction. She offered Karalee a hand and helped her to her feet. "Follow after me closely so that you'll give yourself no injury."

The men grumbled behind her, but single file they followed through the narrow, sloping passageway, stepping around the stone traps and ducking where the earth overhead had not been cut away enough for them to stand upright. The sour smell of damp, deep-buried earth caught in Karalee's nostrils, coating her tongue and throat. It was not the same tunnel they had followed when they were with the boy, Jacksy, but it led to the same cave room. Two cook fires were burning and there was the delicious smell of roasting meat.

"Come now," Peg said. "Sit yourself by the fire and tell us your message."

Karalee drew back. "I am sorry. But what I have to say is for the ears of Darby Finnawn alone."

"Hah!" The fruit-woman snorted and spat. "A likely tale she tells."

"Can you say, at least, who it is who sends this important message?" The black-bearded man settled himself on the ground and let his club rest across his lap, but he looked ready enough to snatch it up and use it at the slightest provocation. He was younger than Karalee would have supposed he was when she first saw his face in the yellow glow of the lamp. His eyes were overlarge, dark, and heavily lashed. There was a thick, white streak of twisted skin upon his neck as if he had once felt the hangman's rope. "Or is it a guessing game we play?"

Now that Karalee's eyes had grown accustomed to the dim light, she felt more at ease. She recognized many of the faces she had seen during her last visit—Dermott Bigger, Jacksy, and Loretta Fallon. But Patrick was not among them. Dear God, where was he?

"Who sends us the message?" the man repeated.

"It comes from my brother, Theo."

"I told you the girl lies," the fruit-woman said, her eyes

narrow. "I see the comings and the goings and I can tell you no one has been allowed inside these days. Only those with great influence."

"She has great influence." The black-bearded man waved a paring knife he had been using to dig the dirt from under his fingernails. "A pretty face and a fetching shape."

Loretta Fallon leaned close. "You saw Theo? Has he suffered horribly?"

"He has felt the lash." Karalee tried to shake away the image of Theo's poor, torn back. "But he was able to walk and to speak, and even to smile a little when I saw him this morning. With our prayers, he will stay that way."

"Your pretty British soldier is seeing to it?"

"Yes!" Karalee answered defiantly, matching the fruit-woman's glare.

"Praise our dear Lord." Loretta knelt and extended her hands in cros-figill.

"And Paddy?" someone asked fearfully. "Did you get word of Paddy?"

"Theo told me Paddy had been killed."

"Ochone!"

"What have you done with Patrick?" Karalee asked over the wailing. "I was promised he would come to no harm."

"The lad left early this morning," Peg answered. "He was a wild thing, straining, cursing, worrying over you. Darby would not keep him bound any longer. When you did not come back, the two of them went to search for you."

The black-bearded man let out a yell of rage and leaped to his feet, his fingers tightening on his club as if he were about to brain Karalee with it. "This slip of a girl is the reason Darby ventured into the open with the entire countryside being combed for him?"

Peg nodded. "Darby feared the lad would be cut to pieces if he stormed into town as he planned to do."

"Damn the lad to hell!" He turned his bulging eyes upon Karalee. "And damn you too. The devil's own curse upon you for not returning when you should have. Darby is worth a hundred like you, with the lad thrown into the bargain."

"I did not ask him to search for me!"

"It is not the girl's fault," Peg shouted at him. "Let her be. We will not fight among ourselves."

"Perhaps it is not her fault," he snarled, "But it will be

mine, if I do not try to find Darby and offer him assistance."

"I must go with you," Karalee said. "I promised Theo I would talk with Darby myself."

"The hell you will. Give me your message. I will pass it on."

"I cannot."

"We will see if you can."

Karalee inched away, as the man started toward her, his lips stretched into a terrible smile.

"If you are to help Darby," Peg said, stepping between them, "you must go at once. There is no time to waste."

The man took another step toward Karalee, shook his club, then turned and stalked into the darkness of the passageway.

"I will go along," another man broke in. "Two will be twice the help."

"And I will make a third," still another added.

"The Lord keep you safe," Peg called after them.

"I cannot eat," Karalee told Peg when the woman offered her a bowl. "I mean no harm to anyone, and it seems I harm everyone."

"I know how you feel. It is only that Darby is beloved of all of us. We would be hopelessly crushed by his loss. The British know this and they are determined to take him. If he ever falls into their hands, he will suffer unspeakable torture."

And what of Patrick? Karalee thought. He was a man of heart and of courage, but he had little knowledge of battle. He had never been like the other young men in the village. He shied away from fighting, he had no liking for sports and never took part in the games. Karalee had faulted him for it cruelly. In fact, she had shown him only scorn in all the time they had known each other. It was a marvel he did not despise her for it.

Though he was born in Kilkee, he did not grow up there. Feargul Roe had taken his family to Donegal when Patrick was still a mite. His father had been stricken with a lingering illness, and as the eldest son in the family, it was Feargul's place to stay close, to settle affairs and to see to the unmarried women and the elderly of the clan. The Roes did not return to Kilkee until Patrick was nearly grown.

Had the other girls in the village not raved about his

manly beauty and his wit, had they not all but swooned if he looked at them, had they not clustered about him, giggling and hanging onto his every word, Karalee might not have felt such contempt for him. He was, after all, promised from birth to Theresa. Their families were branches from the same tree. For Patrick to welcome, or even allow the company of so many comely young girls was unthinkable.

She treated his attempts at making friends with her coolly and for the most part kept out of his way. She had no wish to hurt Theresa nor did she have the intention of letting the swell-headed newcomer think she was desirous of his attentions.

Then one afternoon, during fair week, Karalee had just witnessed a hurling match that ended with one of the young men being carried off the field unconscious and another of them losing his two front teeth. Theo had suffered a broken wrist, but emerged victorious. Karalee, unable to bear any more, left the cheering crowds and climbed the hill to take a quiet moment and weep for her brother's painful injury, if she chose, without shaming him.

No sooner had she settled comfortably with her back against a tree and her eyes closed, than she heard the crunch of footsteps. She smiled, thinking it was Rory, who had watched her go.

"Shh. Don't say anything," she whispered. "Sit beside me and listen to the quiet, will you? Is there anything more magnificent to the ear than silence, after all that shouting?" A shadow passed across her face, and he sat down, his shoulder against hers. "Isn't it fine? Just the two of us."

"It is that."

Karalee opened her eyes with a start and looked into the face of Patrick Roe. He was cool and unruffled, with not a hair out of place. "You!"

He touched a finger to his lips and frowned. "Remember the joys of silence."

"Why don't you go back with the others?"

"Why don't you?" He snapped a white clover flower out of the grass and touched it lightly to her arm, moving it back and forth.

She brushed it away. "The games are for the men." She emphasized the word 'men' so that he could not miss the intended insult.

"There is nothing for me down there."

"You don't take part in the merriment. Not ever. You don't fiddle or pipe and I've never heard you sing. Don't you have talents of any sort?" His smile began slowly and widened and she added quickly, "Isn't there any sport you enjoy?"

"My favorite sport involves only two people. No teams. No spectators and no chance of broken bones."

Karalee met his steady gaze with one of her own, willing herself not to blush. "You don't go in for the racing then because you fear a stubbed toe or a bruised shin?"

"If I join the next race, will you line up to bestow the winner's kiss?"

She laughed. "It would not matter to you if I did. You would not be winner to collect it."

Without warning, he closed his mouth over hers and kissed her soundly until there was not a part of her that did not tingle with it. Pushing him away, she rose unsteadily, unable to speak for many moments.

"You see?" he said. "I have saved myself the trouble of the contest and got the prize anyway."

Karalee wiped one hand vigorously across her mouth and twisted her face into an expression of disgust. But Patrick only smiled. "It will do you no good to wipe that kiss away, Karalee Nolan. You'll taste it when you climb into your bed tonight, as will I, and it will keep you from sleeping."

And so it had. That night and many another night after. Later, when she had accepted Rory's kisses—kisses that sprang from his love for her and not merely from his lust, she told herself—and promised herself to him, she had hoped the sweetness of his lips would erase the memory of the other. It had not.

Rory was gone. Would Patrick come to harm too, because of her? She could not bear the thought of it. She had no idea what she should do. Theo had told her the message was for Darby alone. Yet Darby was not here. The man, Harvey Banon, wherever he might be, was an informer. She searched their faces, wondering which of them she dared trust. She had to trust someone. Peg.

"Your love for Darby is in your face," Karalee whispered. "I must put my trust in you. Theo told me that Darby is to be wary of Harvey Banon. That Banon is an informer. That he has been giving information to the British. That it is Banon's fault they were captured at the barracks raid and

87

that he plans to lead the enemy here. When this will happen I do not know. But it could be at any moment. You are all in danger."

"You are sure? Theo told you this?"

"Yes."

Peg's face paled and she made the sign of the cross. "What have you done, girl?"

"I? I have done nothing."

"Nothing? The man we just sent after Darby? That man is Harvey Banon!"

Eleven

According to the old bacach who had come to their door often when Karalee was small, to share their soda-bread and their turf fire, one could see the winds, if one looked closely enough. The wind of the north was black, from the east, purple. From the south, it was white and from the west, pale. Even those between had their colors.

The red wind of the hills was the wind Karalee had strained the hardest to see. It was this which was caused by the furious battling of fairies. It ruined fruit-crops and vegetable harvests. But it also brought home to rest the ashes of Irish people who had been buried on foreign soil.

This day's wind brought with it only a furious rain, which drenched her through, then ceased as quickly as it had begun. She found herself enveloped in fog so thick that buildings, the bridge, even the streets themselves, were invisible at more than a few feet.

She had not been able to find Patrick—or Darby. Nor had she caught sight of the black-bearded informer, Banon. However, had they stood ten feet away from her at this moment, she would not have been able to distinguish them from a pillar or a tree.

She had taken the nearly ten-mile walk from the hideaway to the barracks, only to find that Phillip had been detained for the night at his post. She had not even been able to speak with him since the day before at the inn. Though it was sinful, she missed the warmth and comfort of his arms. She had wanted to ask him about Dunraven, and how it would be for Theo there. Perhaps she could even have told him of her new troubles and asked for his counsel.

Nothing was happening as it should, so until she heard the rattling of the chaise wheels and the clatter of horses' hooves, she feared it might not come.

She cried out and waved her arms frantically, running after it, when the chaise hurtled by as if it would not stop. But with a loud creaking, it shook and jolted to a still at the far end of the bridge, and the uniformed driver grudgingly eased himself from his seat.

"Step quick now. The downpour has made us late." He threw the door open for her, allowed her to climb in as best she could, then leaned against it, to give way to a racking cough. "Nasty day for a man to be dragged into."

Theo was so stunned by the sight of her that until she drew him close and kissed both his cheeks and his lips, he did not say a word or make a sound.

"They did not tell me you would be here. I wish you were not. It only makes the going harder. I had resigned myself to . . ." He took a quick shuddering breath and turned from her, his shoulders trembling as if he wept.

"Please, darling," she said. "Do not begrudge me this chance to look upon you. 'Twill be so long before I see your dear face again."

"Ay, that it will," he murmured.

His black hair was dripping and flattened to his scalp and his clothes were soaked through as if they had kept him standing in the rain. He had grown pitifully thin. It was hard to imagine the way he had looked just this spring at the fair when he had taken on the Cassidy brothers with his faction stick, his muscles bulging through his shirtsleeves. Always before, looking at his face had been almost like looking at a reflection of her own. Now his eyes were sunken and the bones of his cheeks seemed prominent enough to push through his skin.

Someone had left the windows of the carriage open and the seats were soggy. Karalee clung to her brother, not only for the comfort of feeling him close, but to share some of her body warmth. A chill could easily bring him a fever in his weakened state. It was useless, of course. From the Coach House Inn at the crossroads, he would not even be riding inside the chaise. He would be on horseback, behind one of the dragoons who served as his escort. There would be no way her arms could protect him from the weather— or from whatever else was in store for him.

She had always been with him to protect him when they were children, though he was the older. When he had made some mischief, which was often, he would hide, while she went to their father to speak on Theo's behalf, to make his punishment less severe.

"If it begins to rain again," she said, "surely the soldiers will stop at the inn at the crossroads until the sky clears. If not for your comfort, surely for their own."

"I don't mind the wet, my heart. 'Tis dry enough in here."

"But you will change to horseback at the crossroads."

"You keep saying 'the crossroads.'" Theo shook his head. "We do not pass that way, Karalee. We take the road to Gort and it will be the chaise all the way I have been told."

"You have been told wrong. They are not taking you to Gort."

"It is you who are misinformed. Gort is certain. As is the guilty verdict that will be reached at my trial there. I do not fear death. Believe me." He smiled sadly. "Though I would live a year or two longer if I had the choice."

"You have the choice. Theo, I have been promised. Sir . . ." Karalee leaned forward to tap the coat of the soldier who sat across from them, snoring, his hat pulled low on his face. "Where are you taking us?"

When he sat up with a jolt, Karalee was startled to see the same guard who had spoken to her at the barracks gate the day before. "You bother me to ask what I have already answered? Gort. I told you myself. Gort. I am to let you off at the barricade. Say your pretty goodbye words to your croppy while you can and let me be." He slouched down into his seat again, and pulled his hat over his eyes. "Fool woman."

"But there has been a mistake. I was promised . . ."

"I don't give a damn for your promises, Missy. I have my orders and they say Gort and Gort is where we will go."

"You must turn around. Take us back and you will see. Major Shepard has sentenced Theo to transportation."

"Back, you say?" The soldier laughed and folded his arms across his chest. "After me losing a night's sleep already for this ride?"

"You must."

"What I must do is get this Papist traitor to Gort, so that he won't be late for his own hanging."

"Calm youself, Karalee," Theo said, pulling her against him. "There's no use in it."

"It was Major Phillip Shepard himself handed me these orders. They are signed by him. He asked me as a favor, and not for the record, to let you ride as far as the first barricade. I did it because the young major is a good sort and because he hands me a few shillings from time to time. I have done it before and I will do it again."

"He promised," Karalee insisted, still not understanding what could have happened.

"Major Shepard has orders, as I do. He has no authority to sentence anyone in these cases. But—well, the truth of it is, he's tender-hearted and has a weakness for a pretty lady. He cannot bear to see one cry. So he buys her a bonnet or a new frock and tells her what will make her happy—for the night, at least. But he leaves me and some of the others, to explain his sweet lies."

"I don't believe you."

"I care not a damn what you believe, Missy. Say another word like that and I will put you off here, where we stand. This journey is not to my liking. If it were my way, all you Papists, men and women alike, would be hanged where you are taken and have done with it. Transportation? Hah! For the likes of this one?" He jabbed a thumb toward a purplish swelling on his chin. "Put a lump on me, he did, the day we captured him. Spat in my face too. The only pleasure I take in this trip is that of seeing him kick the air at the end of a good stout rope!"

The soldier continued to laugh as he drew a flask from his pocket and upturned it, letting a trickle run down his chin. The horses dashed ahead, faster and faster, it seemed, making the chaise roll and lurch. They splashed through a low spot in the road, where the river had swelled over the bridge, and the muddy water sprayed Karalee through the partly opened window. Still nothing was visible except the grey mist and it was as if they stood still.

She thought of how the fruit-woman had looked the day she talked of burning the barracks, with the soldiers who had used her and lied to her, inside. At that time, Karalee had wondered at the wickedness of such revenge. Now she imagined herself with a torch, running toward the room above the inn, where Phillip sat drinking with his murderous friends, bragging about his conquest of her, the ink still wet on his fingers from the pen he had used to sign orders that would send Theo to his death. She imagined herself laughing as the flames rose higher.

A crushing fear took her breath away, and she clutched her throat to keep from choking. There were smears of blood upon her hands and upon the bodice of her dress.

"Your nose bleeds, Karalee. That is all. Here," Theo said gently. "Rest your head against me."

"I shall not smear you with my blood," she told him, leaning against him all the same. "I am here to offer you comfort and it is you who must comfort me."

"A fair exchange, sweet one, for all the times you did as much for me. Rest now, and think no more of it."

A yellow glow moved back and forth in the road ahead of them and a voice shouted. "Halt. Where are you bound?"

"Again?" the soldier growled. "For you croppies we must set up so many barricades we cannot travel more than ten miles without climbing out in the wet and making a show. I'm for hanging you right off. There'd be no need of this."

The wagon pulled up and creaked to a stop. It leaned with the weight of the driver as he climbed off.

"We'll see your pass," a voice called. "Over here."

There were sounds of a scuffle and a loud thump, followed by a gargled cry. The chaise door flew open and at the same moment there was a shot. Then another. Someone lunged at the guard and yanked him from his seat to the ground below. More shots rang out. Then came the sound of a horse galloping away.

"Dammit, bring him down," someone shouted.

Three more shots zinged through the air, but the hoofbeats could still be heard, growing fainter and fainter in the distance.

Darby's face, grinning, and as red as the dragoon's coat he wore, appeared in the door. "Theo lad, can you ride?"

"Watch me."

"Patrick holds horses for you and the girl. There." He pointed. "The minutes are not for wasting. That rider who escaped us will bring back twenty more with him. The shots were no doubt heard already."

"God bless you, Darby Finnawn," Theo said, slapping a hand to the man's broad shoulder.

"Get along with you," Darby said, brushing him away. "I should tie you to the saddle. I could dig up the bones of me grandfather and he would be stronger to ride hard than you look to be. But you must fly at once. We will ride the chaise a false trail for the soldiers to follow. It might give you enough distance. Patrick, lad, and you too, girl, see that he hangs on. We do not want our Theo dropping off into their bloody laps again." He drew the sleeve of his coat across his dripping forehead. "We will meet later, if the Lord is willing."

Patrick waited, silent, as Theo helped Karalee onto her horse, then mounted his own, swaying to one side, then righting himself. The three watched as the chaise clattered out of sight, then started their own escape.

"Do we go south?" Theo wanted to know.

"South?"

"Karalee," Theo insisted, impatient now, "Which trail do we follow? Didn't you tell Darby they must take their refuge somewhere else? To which place did they go? South?"

"Oh Theo," Karalee wailed. "I did not see Darby until only now. He was not at the souterrain. I told Peg, though, and they were making preparations to depart when I left them. She said they would go to the sea. Does that help?"

Theo pulled up on his reins, stopping, and Patrick circled in front of him. "What is it, Nolan?"

"Who rides with Darby in that chaise?" Theo's voice was full of foreboding.

"A man called Clancy. We had little time to . . ."

"Who else? Anyone else?"

"Yes. Another. A big man." Patrick hesitated, groping for the name.

"Banon? Was it Harvey Banon?"

"That's it."

"God help Darby then and Clancy too. The man is an informer. He only helped to free me to catch a bigger fish. To get Darby into his net. He must be stopped."

"Not by you, Nolan." Patrick grabbed for the reins of Theo's horse. "You could not catch up to a tortoise as you are."

"Still a better man than you, Roe." Theo laughed shortly. "I do not wish to insult you, as you have come to help and your meaning is right enough. But I will not leave Darby's life to a foppish dandy. The man is too dear to me."

"I am a better man than you suppose me to be."

"You would have to be."

"Stop it, both of you," Karalee cried, her head pounding with the noise they were making. She could not bear to hear the men of her heart tearing each other apart with such bitter words. She loved the two of them so dearly. Loved. Yes, truly loved. She had not dared to think of it until that moment. It had not struck her fully how much Patrick meant to her.

The mist had begun to lift and before too many minutes, it would no longer hide them. Streaks of sunlight were already struggling through.

"I will show you the man I am when the time is right, Nolan. But now, be on your way."

"And so we will all be taken while you two gorsoons keep up a foolish quarrel that has gone on since you were wee babes," Karalee scolded. If they were caught now, it would not only be Theo who was hanged, but Patrick as well. "We must ride away at once, while we can. Darby can see to the informer."

"He cannot, if he does not suspect."

"Was the rescue for nothing?" Karalee pleaded.

"Are you to be snatched from the hangman's rope, only to put yourself under it again? I will not have it."

"Think of this, buffoon," Patrick threw at him, still holding tight to the reins of Theo's horse. "I do not know this countryside. Nor does Karalee. I do not know this place near the sea where the others hide and where we will find sanctuary. You do. With me leading blindly, Karalee will surely be captured. How dear is your sister to your heart?"

Theo let his head drop back and stared wild-eyed at the sky. "I must admit you are right. My head is not clear or I would have seen it."

"Karalee must not be taken." Patrick's voice was grim. "Promise me you'll kill her with your own hand first."

Theo nodded. "It must be you, Patrick Roe. Guard yourself. Banon is sly and as strong as three men." He reached for Patrick's hand, clasped it, and covered it with his other. "May the Lord's sweet angels protect you."

Karalee ached to touch Patrick too. She could not let him ride away without letting him know how she cared for him. She wanted to tell him that his life was precious to her in spite of all the devilish things she had said to him. That she would suffer as long as she lived if his blood was spilled. But she could not find the words. She wanted to beg him not to go, but she knew he had no choice.

"Karalee," he whispered, riding close to her, and for a moment it seemed he had sensed her thoughts without her having to voice them.

"Patrick."

For a moment it seemed he would reach for her. She waited, already feeling his lips on hers. But he turned quickly and galloped away.

Twelve

The wicker-work dwelling was hidden deep in the bog. Karalee could have wept for sheer joy when Theo pointed to the thin curl of gray smoke that floated from the center of its rush-thatched roof.

For the last mile, she had felt defeated. Theo lost consciousness repeatedly during their ride, and she slid from her horse barely in time to keep him from falling to the ground. Had he done so, she would never have been strong enough to lift him to his saddle again. Steadying him with one hand, and leading her own mount with the other, she walked blindly, having no idea of her destination. The rain had begun again, battering them mercilessly and leaving the ground soft with greasy mud that oozed between her toes and ofttimes about her ankles. The horses sank in it and snorted, tossing their heads in protest.

None of that mattered now. Inside would be friends. The two of them could warm themselves and rest, while they waited. Or perhaps there would be no waiting. Perhaps Patrick and Darby had already arrived. Karalee had taken twice the time to find her way that she would have with Theo's proper guidance.

Wordlessly, she helped her brother from his saddle. He was feverish and unsteady on his feet. Fresh blood flowed from a temple wound that had been crusted over and somehow torn open during the ride. They fastened the horses in the small square timber house that stood behind the dwelling. Other animals were tethered there, feeding out of the wet.

Theo paused before the door and called the warning slogan through cupped hands. "Boolyah, boolyah, boolyah!"

The girl, Loretta, rose as they pushed through the door, her eyes wet and as round as a child's. Her shawl slid from her narrow shoulders to the floor, but she made no move to retrieve it.

"'Tis a fine greeting from you, Loretta Fallon," Theo murmured. "It has been a hard ride and I expected some show of joy. A faint smile, perhaps."

Suddenly the girl let out a shrill cry, like a bird, and dashed for him. Her arms twined about his neck and her uplifted mouth found his and pressed against it. She squirmed and moved against him until Dermot Bigger came forward to pull at her.

"The lad has no bracht or juice of strength about him, girl. Do not smother him."

Theo caught one end of Loretta's ribbon and yanked, letting her golden hair fall loose and free to her waist. He tangled his fingers in it and drew her to him, kissing her until she went limp in his arms.

" 'Twould seem he has strength enough in him at that," another man said, slapping a hand to Theo's back. Two other men rose, grinning, from their benches and offered Theo their hands.

"The sight of you standing and breathing, is a sight I did not think to see," said the one-armed man Karalee had seen at the clochan that first day.

"Where is Darby?" Dermot asked.

Theo shook his head. "With the help of Heaven he will be here. 'Twould be a curse I could not bear should he sacrifice his life in saving mine."

"But where is he?"

All eyes turned on Karalee as Theo told them what had happened, accusing her, without words, of letting Darby fall into an enemy snare. Peg, noticing it, moved forward, and slipped an arm around the girl's shoulder. "What little I have seen of Patrick Roe, I know he has great courage. Let us feel no fear for Darby."

"We will sail with Darby for Inishmore when he returns."

"Inishmore!" Horace growled through his pipe-clenched teeth. "Nothing but gray rock and howling winds. The only bit of green to be seen is across the sea."

" 'Twill serve us to flee there until they tire of searching for us."

"'Tis you and I who must bear the watch," Peg whispered to Karalee as the two men argued. "My Darby and your young Patrick. Men do not know what it is to wait."

Karalee nodded, biting back tears. Patrick knew nothing of fighting. She had never seen him take part in the wrestling games or the stick-fighting that other young men never seemed to tire of at the fair greens. His eyes had ever rested upon the breeze-lifted skirts of pretty girls. And she had despised him for it. She was not sure he could fire a weapon with any sharp aim. He had killed the two yeomen who had taken her in Galway, it was true enough, but only by creeping up on them in surprise. Face-to-face, he would have stood no chance.

"The lad has great courage," Peg said, as if she knew Karalee's thoughts.

"I know."

"It has always been the curse of women to sit and wait," Peg said again, guiding her away from the others. "You are wet and could well take a fever. The spare dress I can give you is not as fancy as the one you wear, but it is clean and dry and untorn."

"I thank you." Karalee could hardly wait to rip the wicked dress from her body, and along with it, the thoughts of Phillip Shepard and the foolish trust she had placed in him.

Suddenly, there was the sound of horses, and then a thud. Everyone froze.

Before any of them had time to reach for a weapon, a slightly-built man with sandy, fringed hair backed into the room unsteadily, followed by Darby. They carried Patrick between them. His eyes were open, but his pupils were rolled back so that only the whites showed. His shirt front was red with blood.

"A chquid!" Karalee cried. "Oh no, it must not be. It cannot be." She staggered forward, but Peg and Dermot held her upright.

"Silence that woman," Darby ordered. "The lad's life hangs by a thread and I fear that thread will soon be broken. The ride bled the life from him. Let him die in peace."

"You must be as brave as he is," Peg said, her voice hushed and solemn.

"I will not be brave." Karalee tore away from them and

dropped on her knees on the straw beside where Patrick lay. Her stomach churned at the sight of his wet gaping wound and his bloodless face.

"Get yourself away," Darby growled. "We need a bonesetter. Damn McLea for being gone. Dermot, you served as herb-leech. Give him what help you can."

He stood to make room for the other man. "When he hammered down on us and turned on Banon, I thought he had turned traitor. I tried to batter him myself. Lord help me, I did not know. Knocked me aside, he did. Took the ball himself that Banon meant for me. It is in him still."

"Karalee." Patrick's voice was a whisper. His hand fluttered toward her, then dropped to his side.

"I am here, my darling. Do not speak. Keep strong for me. I want you to get well." She clutched his hand and pressed it to his lips, wetting it with her tears.

"I am not a wicked man," he said, his eyes blinking, then settling upon her, clear.

"No, no, of course, you are not or I am wicked too."

"And I am not a dandy."

"No, no."

"In my pocket. The papers. You must get to the ship."

"I will not leave you."

"Theresa cannot see to the babes alone. Help her to raise them, and to know that their father loved them."

"It is you who will raise them. You will show them how their father loves them."

"Mavourneen," he whispered. "'Tis my sad fortune that now you would give your lips to me, and I cannot take them." He tried to smile, but groaned instead, setting his teeth as if he were in unbearable pain. "I love you more than life. I always have."

"And I love you too."

"Go then. Get to the ship before it is too late."

"I will not leave you."

"Darby." Patrick raised his head and fastened his eyes upon the other man beseechingly. "See to her. Give me your oath."

"You have it," Darby answered.

"Take the papers and . . . Kerrigan will . . ." He clenched his teeth again and closed his eyes as if waiting for the pain to subside. Then he opened them and looked at Karalee. "I am not a wicked man." He shuddered and his head fell to one side.

Karalee heard herself screaming, but it was as if the sound came from someone else. Darby pulled her away, gently at first, and then with force. She struggled against him, beating upon his chest. He shook her, cursing, and when it did not stop her screaming, he slapped her a stinging blow, first on one cheek and then on the other. She reeled against Theo who had been aroused by the furor. He caught her and cradled her in his arms.

"God help you," he said. "I did not know you were in love with Patrick Roe."

"Nor did I," she said, weeping, "until it was too late."

Darby knelt, his back to her, and pulled the papers from Patrick's coat. "The papers for your passage. Robert Kerrigan will make arrangements for you with the captain. The lad talked all the way of how important it was to get you to that ship and to that ship you will go, damn you, or I will flay the skin from your body. Take them and go."

"Only let me look at him. Let me sit by him for a moment."

"I said you were to go now," Darby shouted, blocking her way. "The soldiers will be upon us soon and we must all make for the sea."

"Only one last look upon him. One touch."

"To start you screaming again? No." Darby lifted his hand as if he would strike her and Theo pulled her away.

"I will see her as far as the village."

"See her to the village, will you? And be taken, weak as you are? You would let the lad's sacrifice be for nothing?"

"Let me take her then," Peg said, placing a warm shawl about Karalee's shoulders. "No one would suspect two women."

"We are all known," Darby said. "She is not. If she would allow you, or anyone of us to chance being taken again because she will not stand alone, then she was not worthy of the poor lad's devotion."

Karalee took a deep breath, gathering herself, and snatched the papers. "I do not want you with me. Any of you. See to yourselves." She kissed her brother on both cheeks, then glanced toward Patrick. But Darby moved into her way. Desperately fighting back her tears until she could cry them alone, she stumbled for the door.

"God keep you safe," she whispered.

Thirteen

The landing dock at Galway Bay was crowded with ex-iles, who, like Karalee and Theresa, were leaving their homeland not by choice but by necessity. The world that closed in around them was gray and rocky. Even the foaming water looked gray, as if they all stood at the end of the world—and indeed, it was the end of the world for many of them.

Karalee heard snips of this conversation and then that one, but she was too numb with pain to feel deeply for any of the others. Patrick was dead. Dead. She would likely never see Theo again. She would sail because she had said she would. Because she had promised to see Theresa and the babes to safety if she could. Then—then nothing. She could envision no sort of future for herself.

Clumps of people stood about, dreading the signal that would tell their loved ones to board the tiny ship. Old men hugged each other. Mothers clutched their sons and daughters, some pressing hawthorne branches, shamrocks, or bits of sod into the exiled one's hands for remembrance.

"Forget not the land of your birth," was the cry. And others, "When you leave me, I lose the last thing dear to me on this earth."

The sun was falling into the sea and the sky had changed from blue to orange. Now it was graying. The mountains were turning purple. Gulls circled overhead, calling their own goodbyes. Karalee thought of the tale she had been told of good St. Columcile, who had heard that same call as, exiled himself, he had sailed from Ireland, never to return.

"The sound of it will never leave my ears until I die," he had said.

"It will be most difficult—if not impossible." Robert Kerrigan's eyes watered as if he too might begin to weep. "Had your dear father known you and Theresa would travel alone, without a man to care for you—and worse, with two babes to tend, he would never have agreed to it. I should refuse to have a hand in it myself, except that you, Karalee, are sought for information. They want Theo badly. It is no longer safe for you here."

"We will do well enough, thanks to your kindness," Karalee assured him, shifting the sleeping Daniel to her other arm. "It will be only two or three days before we are united in Liverpool."

"Two or three days can be like the same amount in years under such conditions. If only I had money enough to sail with you and still return."

"You have given far too much now and you shall have it back when we are able."

The greedy captain who sold them passage had refused to give back any portion of the sum he had been paid, though only two traveled with the babes, rather than the expected four.

"I take a great chance," he snarled. "To carry the sister of an escaped convict and the wife and children of the rebel who helped to free him. I am too kind-hearted for my own skin. I could have my ship seized from under me and held in dock. I could be heavily fined. I would be right in asking you twice the passage money you paid."

Though their passage on the big ship from Liverpool to Philadelphia included provisions, they had to supply their own from Ireland to Liverpool. Robert Kerrigan's sister, though not a sympathizer, had prepared a bag of journey-cakes, nuts, and a snakelike drisheen. It would be ample for their needs.

"How can I warn you of the dangers you face?" Robert Kerrigan's big jaw was squared more than ever as he fought his emotions.

"I know them, sir."

"You know them! Whisht! You cannot. You are a child. To begin with, you must hold your shawl around your face so that the crew cannot look too well upon it. Better they slight your rations, thinking you a crow, than to have them favor you with double and have their hands upon you. Your beauty will bring you great danger if you do not take care." He adjusted her shawl with gentle hands. "Let the cloth hang loose, so that the provocative lines of your— ah—form, do not show. You must pardon me for being coarse, my dear, but your father is not here to say as much. These men are unlike the men you have known. They are at sea, without the sight of a woman for many months at one time. Then seldom do they see one so fair."

He fumbled with a small package wrapped in burlap that he carried wedged beneath one arm. "I don't want to forget. This is for you, Mrs. Roe."

Theresa stared dully at his offering. "What is it?"

"Nothing, really. Only a few cuttings. Rose cuttings. A bit or Ireland to plant when you get where you are going. To remind you of home. The spirit of a departed loved one is said to live again in a rose bush planted in his memory. I—that is, I wanted you to know how sorry I was about your poor, dear husband. What little I saw of him told me he was . . ."

"Patrick had no fondness for flowers," Theresa interrupted, turning away.

"Thank you, Mr. Kerrigan," Karalee said, reaching out for the bundle.

"Only keep them a little damp," he said. "They'll survive the journey well. They're hardy plants, those roses."

The bell clanged announcing the time to board and the wail about them was renewed, louder than ever. Robert Kerrigan moved with them, tucking an edge of blanket under Daniel's chin, smoothing one of Deirdre's soft curls, pressing his lips lightly first to Karalee's forehead, then to Theresa's cheek. "May the smile of the Lord light your way."

"God bless you too, sir," Karalee whispered.

"Send word of your safe arrival. The mail will take time to reach me but I will not breathe easy until I hear you are with your father. Stand strong aboard that wretched ship or you will be trampled. Two women alone will find many to take advantage. Do you remember where you are to meet your family?"

"The Inn of the Blue Pigeon."

"Ay, at Castle Street where it crosses Dale. Speak to no

105

one. You can find your way. It is very near where you dock. And keep an eye on your bags."

He stood on tiptoe, stretching to see over the crowd which separated them. His voice was lost amid the other voices and with the sound of the sea and of the ship. When Karalee turned to catch a final glimpse, she saw that his lips moved still, though she could no longer hear him.

"At last we are free of that dreadful man's yammering," Theresa snapped, pushing ahead. "You do not know how it has been for me while you were away. He is exactly like Patrick's father, Feargul. Always reaching to touch, feigning such fatherly devotion. But as all men, his eyes give away his lustful thoughts."

Karalee was stunned by the venomous outburst against dear Robert Kerrigan, but she said nothing. Theresa had been silent since hearing of Patrick's tragic death. She had surprisingly taken the news dry-eyed and had simply withdrawn as if she wished to build a wall around herself. Surely, now, her words sprang from the roots of her unspoken despair.

The ship's cargo, which was pigs for the English market, was protected from the weather between the decks. This would leave only half the passengers with shelter. Captain Armand of the ship *Roseanna,* which carried them, had learned, as many other money-lusting seamen had learned during these treacherous times, that spare space could be stocked profitably with human cargo.

The girls were unprepared for the frantic dash for cover. All Karalee's toes were crushed and she was doubled over by the jab of someone's elbow. Theresa was flung against the railing and baby Deirdre was nearly torn from her arms. In the end, they were forced to remain on the deck, with only a tarpaulin to protect them from the stinging blasts of the icy sea. Here they would stay through the voyage. Here they would eat and sleep, if they could, along with old people and other women alone who had no menfolks to fight for their place.

When the first wave crashed down upon them, Karalee was so concerned with covering Theresa and the babes, that she received all of it, and was as drenched as if she had fallen into the sea. There was no way to dry herself. The girls could only cling together for warmth, the babes between them, and pray.

When the waters had calmed at last, Karalee peeled

back a bit of Daniel's blanket, so that he could wriggle more freely. Fortunately, the spray had not touched him. He was warm. He whimpered and reached out, clenching and unclenching his tiny fists.

"He hungers," Karalee whispered, marveling at how like his father he was already—and then remembering he would have no father because of her. She swallowed the ache in her throat. "Let me have Deirdre, so that you can give Daniel his turn."

Theresa frowned as she took the precious bundle. "Never long content, the boy. The Roes are alike. All of them. How I despised Feargul. The one good thing in leaving is that I shall never have to look at his ale-soaked features again. And brother Timothy. May the devil stand in his pathway. How wicked he was to leave us when we had need of him."

"How could he have known what would happen? He supposed there would be Patrick and Theo, as well as my father, to help us."

"He never intended to sail, he told me. Only to see us safe to Galway. The cause has need of him, he said. He could not desert it in conscience. Or the land of his birth. Musha. Timothy's only cause is lusting after some ale-house wench. I know the Roes and their animal desires well enough." She bared her breast and poked it at the babe as if he were the one who were responsible for her troubles. "But Patrick was the worst of them. His place was with me. But little did he care. His sin is what killed him. But it is I who must suffer for it."

Karalee tried not to feel shock at her friend's words. Theresa could not truly feel as she spoke. Her loss had been too great for her to bear without bitterness. A part of Karalee had died with Patrick too, and she knew how it was not to be able to speak of it.

When she ran from the wickerwork dwelling where his torn body lay, she had been able to go only a few yards before her legs collapsed beneath her and she dropped to the earth. She wept until her stomach heaved and until her smallest breath gave her pain, until her eyes were swollen nearly shut and there were no more tears left inside her.

She had thought, I am wicked to love him, but I cannot help my wickedness. Let me lie here until the soldiers find me and kill me too. There is nothing more left for me in this life.

107

But after a time, she thought of her mother and father and how they waited for her. She thought of Theresa and the babes and the dying request Patrick had made of her. That she watch over them, see to their growing up with love and with knowing that their father had courage. Somehow she found the strength to rise and to go on her way.

How much worse it must have been for Theresa, who belonged to Patrick in the eyes of God. She had stood with him before the altar and taken her vows. She had lain with him so many nights, listening to his breathing and to the beating of his heart. Theresa had borne him these two babes, the boy so like Patrick that the sight of his tiny face must surely wrench her heart each time she looked upon it. Certainly Theresa had the right to cry out at the injustice in the world and perhaps even to curse Patrick for leaving her.

As the baby nursed, Karalee looked closer at the narrow string of leather that hung about Theresa's neck. Attached to it was a three-cornered stone, carved with the sign of the cross. It was the amulet she had seen many times hanging about Rory's neck, given to him by his father, and his father before him. It was the amulet that hung about his neck as he lay in his coffin, and Karalee supposed he had been buried with. Theresa caught her stare and adjusted her bodice to cover it, but not soon enough. When the girls' eyes met, Karalee's held a look of stunned surprise. Theresa's held only contempt.

Fourteen

"Please sir, we were told that when the ship docked in Liverpool we were to go directly to the Inn of the Blue Pigeon. At Castle Street where it crosses Dale. You see, it was written down." Karalee uncrumpled a small square of paper and held it out to the man who stood behind the desk. "This is the Inn of the Blue Pigeon, isn't it?"

"I have told you that it is and the sign that hangs before my door has told you so. I have also told you that the family you mention—ah, the Nolan family—has left."

"But they could not have sailed. They would never have left us behind." Karalee followed the innkeeper from behind his counter through a door that led to an ill-lit cooking room. A black boy of about twelve sat scrubbing a copper kettle and a woman with orange hair hustled about, stirring one after another of her steaming pots. "Please try to remember what they might have said. Perhaps they mentioned where they were going."

"See to this at once, Sophie," the man barked, slipping out of his brown velvet coat. He pointed to a brass button which dangled by a thread from his sleeve.

The woman wiped her hands on her apron and skittered to take the coat, and to help him into another exactly like it. He pulled at each of his sleeves, as if by doing so he could lengthen them, and adjusted the saffron-hued ruff at his throat.

"You ask me what they said?" He laughed. "My dear girl, they were nothing more than names on my list. I never see faces. I only know they were here because I have

109

drawn a line through the entry. I am sorry, but your story is like a dozen or more I hear every day."

"But surely you could . . ."

"And now, please." He lifted an eyebrow and touched the side of his finger to his nose. "I would appreciate it if you would see to that dreadful wailing. People are trying to rest."

One of the babes had begun to cry, and Theresa, tired and uncomfortable herself, was making only a half-hearted attempt to comfort it.

"There are soldiers in the street," she whispered, when Karalee had come close enough to hear. "They are looking for us. We cannot go outside."

"Nonsense. They are not searching for us in Liverpool," Karalee assured her, though she was not entirely certain it was true. "Besides, they could never pick us out of such a throng. Our only fear is in not finding the others."

"I remember the four you seek."

Karalee was startled by the voice of the orange-haired woman at her elbow. She had not realized that the woman had followed her from the cooking room. "You are sure you remember them?"

The woman leaned closer, and shielded her mouth with one hand as if she feared the innkeeper would hear. "The children—a boy and a girl—were most unruly. Poking each other and sticking out their tongues. The woman was too worn herself to correct them. Mostly I remember the man. Such a gentleman. He stooped to pick up my broom for me when I dropped it—tired as he was. I heard him say he was worried about his daughter. You, I suppose. He said the name 'Karalee' several times. It struck me because it is my own mother's name and not so common these days."

"Did you see where they went?"

"They stayed on two nights. The price had already been paid before their arrival. But they could stay no longer. The man said he had not the one shilling a day it costs for bed and meals."

"So much?"

The woman nodded. "A man-catcher pounced upon them. Said he could arrange a bed for four pence and they followed him. I know the man well. He waits here for poor families, such as yours, and tries to dally me to while his time." She patted her cap and tucked in one stray curl that

110

had escaped at the nape of her neck. "He leads most poor souls who cannot afford to pay much, to a lodging house owned by a man named Titus Lean. Gets a portion of whatever they pay for dragging them there."

"Where can I find this Titus Lean?" Karalee asked, her hopes rising.

"On Tithebarne Street, stuck in between the spirit vaults, you will find a row of such lodging houses—if you can rightly give them that name. A sign hangs in front with his name and the painting of a white swan upon it. Inside, besides the regular guests, there are always twenty to thirty unfortunates sleeping upon bare boards in a damp, reeking cellar. But it is better than the streets, I suppose, for those who can afford no more."

Karalee thanked the woman and took the baby Daniel from Theresa to cuddle him, before starting off.

Liverpool was indeed a wondrous town, she thought, away from the multitude of beggars, the cursing seamen, and the squalor of the docks. The buildings were of brick and stone, magnificent with pillars and arches and gateways of twisted black iron. The Town Hall was crowned by a splendid blue dome, and a statue was set atop that.

Karalee had never seen so many coaches, painted with green or red and designed with swirls of gold. One seemed to clatter by every few minutes from one of the inns. They were driven by coachmen who wore velvet coats and cocked hats and kept their narrow noses turned into the air. Even more elegant were the sedan chairs, lifted by poles, a man stationed at either end. Sheer curtains rose and fell over the windows, so that whoever rode inside could see out, but could not be seen unless they wished to be.

A half-dozen school boys in ankle-length blue coats stood in front of the bakery shop window, watching wide-eyed as the baker carefully arranged his trays of pastries and tarts. He shook his fist at them and they darted, one of then pausing to wiggle his thumbs in his ears first in a show of defiance.

Theresa had been right. There were soldiers everywhere. Still, there was no need for them to fear. Liverpool was a busy port and always kept well-protected. It carried on over half of the English slave trade and was harbor for nearly a thousand home ships. The war of the revolution was at its highest point, and thousands of French prisoners were being held captive, many of them in the dungeon of the cruel gray tower that Karalee had seen as they docked and could still catch sight of from almost anywhere she stood.

She had heard it said that the gaolers received no salary for their work, but lived off whatever money they were able to squeeze from their unfortunate charges. Thus, the imprisoned men were forced to beg through the barred windows of their cells to get enough to keep themselves alive.

Karalee paused to wonder at the beauty of a girl who swished past them, giggling, hanging on the arm of a soldier.

Casually, Karalee's eyes brushed those of the young soldier and she nearly froze to the spot, as his flashed recognition. It was Phillip Shepard. With great effort, she yanked Theresa aside, pretending to inspect a window display of pottery.

"Shh," Karalee whispered, as Theresa started to object, keeping her head low and well turned away from Phillip and his beautiful lady. "I will explain later."

"I care nothing for your explaining," Theresa snapped. "I only wish you would stop your foolishness and let us go somewhere to rest."

Karalee waited as long as she dared, expecting that any moment a magistrate would tap her shoulder and march her away to the gaol. Of course, she would pretend not to be acquainted with Theresa. She would say that she had only held the babe as a favor to a stranger. Would Theresa show surprise and deny it? However would the girl manage without her? What would happen to the babes? No, she must not be taken.

She peered out of the corner of her eye and saw Phillip at the end of the next street, just as he turned the corner. Karalee was bedraggled and unkempt from her exhausting journey and the coarse, gray dress Peg had given to her hung upon her like a sack. Perhaps Phillip had not recognized her after all. Or perhaps he was no more anxious to admit their acquaintance than she. Still—he could be merely seeing the lady home, before he took action. He might alert his soldiers at any moment and send them after her. She had to be certain.

She stationed Theresa on an iron resting-bench near the fountain and hurried to the corner where she had lost sight of Phillip. She flattened herself against the brick wall of a watchmaker's shop when she saw that the two of them had paused on the steps of the Dragon's Head Inn. Phillip was talking, and the girl was laughing and tossing her head as if he had said something amusing. He was smiling—the same smile Karalee had seen the day in his quarters—the smile that had melted her heart. How she despised him now!

At last, Phillip kissed the girl's hand, and signalled for a carriage. He saw her into it and waved as it moved away. Then he went inside—unhurried. Had he bought the girl her exquisite gown? Karalee wondered. And what promises had he made to her that he did not intend to keep?

No matter. At least he was making no move to alert his men. She and Theresa were safe.

The innkeeper, Titus Lean, was bored with Karalee's story. He merely shook his head and grunted, then turned away. His spectacled clerk held out a ledger for Karalee to examine.

"You see, ma'am. There it is. Nolan. Two full- and two half-prices. They were here. But they have sailed." He snapped his book shut and smiled as if he had solved everything.

Karalee shook her head. "My father would not have sailed without us." She drew out her own papers and unfolded them on the desk in front of the clerk. "We were to sail together on the same ship, the *Black Star*."

The man leaned close to the papers and squinted. "This explains it, ma'am. See the date there? Your ship sailed two days ago."

"I know the ship sailed. It is only the people I am asking about. Where might they have gone when they left this place?"

The man clasped his fingers behind his head and tipped his chair to lean against the wall. "My advice is to go to the shipbroker. The man who was paid for your passage. He may have made other arrangements with them. His name is there. S. Wolcott. Wolcott Shipping. He will be able to tell you more than I. It's at the end of Water Street."

"Obviously your ship sailed without you, young woman," the man at Wolcott Shipping told them. "It is simple. Space was set aside for you, but you did not arrive when you should have. You forfeit your passage money."

"But my mother and father . . ."

"Surely they sailed with the ship. Could they afford to forfeit their own passage money as well? I can set aside space for you on the next ship that leaves for Philadelphia and I'll wager you will find them waiting for you there."

"But they would not have sailed. They know I have no money. I have no friends and nowhere to go. What am I to do?"

The man slapped his pen onto his desk and leaned toward her. "Am I to be responsible for all who arrive destitute on our shores? You Irish are the worst of the lot. Why don't you stay in your own land? It sickens me. Go to the workhouse. They will feed you and give you a bed if they find you deserving. Move along now. Next!"

"It is not for myself I ask. The girl with me has two little ones who . . ."

"Next!" the man repeated, louder.

"I can help you, little dove."

The woman who beckoned to her was about fifty years old, but her tight-fitting gown revealed a youthful, alluring figure. Her skin was smooth and dark, but she wore an elaborately curled wig of palest gold.

"I have contact with people who would gladly pay your passage to the colonies. In return you would be bound to stay in their service for an agreed period of time. The work would be easy and you would be treated well." The woman reached out a gloved hand to smooth Karalee's hair. "Black as a raven's wing, and like satin. I can hardly wait to dress your hair for you. And with a suitable gown, you will not recognize yourself."

"How very kind you are." Karalee could not believe her good fortune. She had to suppress the desire to kiss the woman's hand. She had heard of such arrangements many times. Friends of her parents had traveled as a couple to America and had been bound the same way and in the same house. It had worked out well for them. "I must be honest with you, though. I have never worked as a housemaid. But my stitching is good and I can cook simple food. I learn quickly and will try doubly hard to make up for my lack."

"How innocent you are." The woman's laugh was clear and musical, as if it were well practiced. "My dove, you would not be called upon to scrub or to mop floors. You would offer only decoration and companionship."

114

"Companionship? I read only a little and am not educated in social graces. I . . ."

"It will not be necessary for you to read. An education would be a drawback, in fact. No, no! Ragged as you are, I can see that you were born for the life I offer you. It would take little time to teach you everything you would need to know. How to please a man."

"Oh." Karalee could feel her face warm as she grasped the meaning of what her duties would be. "I see. You are very kind, ma'am. But I could not."

"What else is there for you, child?" the woman asked, not unkindly. "You said you have no money and no friends. All you have is the face and the body of an angel. A face and body that could bring you more riches than you have ever imagined."

"I would rather work as a cook or a housemaid. Do you know of someone who would pay for those services?"

"My dove, it has been my experience that the woman of a house prefers her maids plain-featured and straight-hipped. Few are foolish enough to parade someone so fair before their husbands day after day. I'm sorry."

"There must be somewhere I can . . ."

Karalee turned away, weak with disappointment, ashamed of the tears she knew she could not long keep from shedding.

"Wait, my sweet." The woman placed a hand upon her shoulder. "I cannot leave you here. Your friend looks as if she will drop and her little ones are pale and wan. I want you to come with me. Both of you. But only for this night. Perhaps when you have rested and eaten your fill, you will be able to view your situation more realistically."

"I will not change my mind."

"Perhaps. Speak with your friend. There is a frailty about her that some men find attractive. I would likely be able to find a place for her too. Though the little ones would present a problem." She smiled brightly, and Karalee realized she must have been extremely beautiful herself once. She would still be, if she were not so painted, and if her hair were done in a shade more fitting to her tanned skin.

"Come, come now," the woman said, clapping her hands together. "Let us be on our way before I change my mind. There are many other girls I could choose. Perhaps they

would not be so lovely, but they would be more willing—
and ofttimes willingness is the greater attribute."

"We are not going with that painted woman," Theresa
said through tight lips. "Whatever are you thinking of? Do
you know what people will think if they see us walking
with her? Do you know what sort she is?"

"I know she is kind," Karalee whispered, hoping the
woman had not heard Theresa's insult. "I care not what
anyone thinks. She offers us help when no one else does.
She will give us food and a place to sleep. She is an answer
to our prayers. Come along."

"Prayers?" Theresa gasped. "Shame on you, Karalee
Nolan, for thinking of her as being sent from our Lord.
May He forgive you." But she handed Daniel to Karalee,
bundled Deirdre more closely, and followed anyway.

Fifteen

The two-story house was built of square gray stones, a web of fine ironwork showing against its front like lace. Fluted columns stood on either side of the door and lantern-holders with link extinguishers were set into the front railings. The curved inside hall was lined with bright wall hangings and portraits in gilt frames. The panels of the half-domed ceiling were decorated with graceful paintings and a winding staircase with lyre-shaped balusters led to the upstairs bedchambers.

What most took Karalee's breath away was the square court at the rear of the house where, down two steps and along a gravel path, she found the garden. There was a shimmering fountain, surrounded by marble statues and beyond it, two stately lines of lime trees, scattered tubs of orange trees and a terrace of magnificent roses.

On the terrace, the girls were served plates of delicate steamed fish, floating in a rich cream sauce, tiny herbed potatoes and three different kinds of vegetables. A basket sat upon their table which held an array of fresh fruits such as Karalee had never before seen. Afterwards the woman, who insisted they call her Madeline, showed them the bathing-house where they might refresh themselves, and then their tiny attic room with its soft tent-bed.

"If there is anything you need," she told them, opening the glass doors that led to a shallow balcony overlooking the garden, "pull the fringed cord at the side of the window and summon one of the housemaids. There is water in the pitcher and there is a chamber pot under your bed for your convenience. But you must not creep about in the corridors, and you are not to come downstairs under any circumstances, unless I send for you. Understood?"

She smiled when Karalee nodded. "I do not wish to make prisoners of you, my doves, but we entertain many people of great importance here, who do not wish to be known. Discretion is vital."

The babes slept contentedly in boxes, fitted for them with pillows and soft blankets. Karalee could easily have joined them in their napping, had it not been for Theresa, who stayed on her knees for a quarter of an hour, praying loudly, then lay upon her bed, weeping into her pillow.

"I shall never feel clean again. Can you imagine what has happened upon this very bed? What is happening in this house now—at this moment? I cannot rest for thinking of it."

"Then do not think of it."

"I cannot help myself. Listen to the disgusting noises about us, everywhere. It is too terrible."

Once Karalee was made aware of the sounds, they seemed magnified. There were creeping pairs of footsteps in the outside corridor. There were giggles and guffaws, glasses clinking, moans, and creaking of bedsprings. Someone was playing the harp and singing in a squeaky, drunken voice.

"It will not be for long," Karalee said. "Surely in two or three days there will be a ship bound for Philadelphia that will have room for us. I will think of some way to arrange our passage."

"Two or three days? That woman said we could stay only one night."

"I feel sure Madeline will allow us to stay longer if we do as she asks and if we stay out of the corridor."

"Nothing could drag me out there," Theresa wailed, covering her head with a pillow. "I wish I could die."

"That is one wish you will not have." Karalee sighed and slipped into her dress. Its dull gray color did nothing for her face and its straight lines hid her figure. But for the errand she planned, her appearance did not matter.

"I shall not be gone long. If Madeline returns, tell her I am out seeing to our passage."

Theresa sat upright, her eyes wild. "You cannot leave me here alone."

"I must."

118

The girl began to wail again and Karalee sat beside her and took her hands. "Do you remember when we were children and used to play in the castle near Killaloe? How we pretended we were soldiers fighting against the English? You said you wished you were old enough to join the fighting. Well, this is a kind of battle too. We must find courage."

"I have no more courage in me," Theresa said. "And we are no longer children. Dear Rory is dead and so is Patrick. We are all alone."

"That is it, Theresa. We are not alone. We have the little ones to watch over. We cannot cart them around with us. One of us must stay with them. It must be you. You are too exhausted to walk another step. You wish to sail, don't you?"

"Have I a choice? But what would I do, if you did not return?"

"I will. I promise. Sleep now, before the babes wake to tire you further. All will be well," she said as she stepped out into the corridor.

The idea had struck Karalee as she lay listening to Theresa's wailing. She had no reason to fear Phillip. He would not dare to report her. His dallying would come under the scrutiny of his superiors, she thought as she ran through the streets of Liverpool. They might well suppose he had a hand in Theo's escape—the escape that had left two of his own kind dead and two others seriously injured. Phillip would, in fact, have every reason to want her out of the country.

Phillip showed no surprise when he threw the door open and saw her. He was dressed in full uniform as he had been the first time she had seen him and she was again struck by the handsome cut of his features. He looked as if he had planned to leave just as she arrived.

"So it was you I saw, after all. I have seen your face in every other face lately, so I was not sure."

"Is that all you would say to me?" She kept her hands knotted in the ends of her shawl so that their shaking would not be noticed. She wanted to appear full of confidence.

He lifted an eyebrow. "I can think of a great many things to say to you. I missed you, Karalee. I was afraid I had lost you."

He reached for her, but she moved away, turning her

119

back to him, so that he could not see her eyes. "I need money for passage to the colonies."

"I see. And you have come to me for it? I am not a rich man."

"I come to you because you owe a debt to me."

"A debt?"

"A promise that you did not keep. This will be your chance to make it up. Have you forgotten already?"

"Karalee, I did everything possible to save your brother. I had almost managed it. But as they brought him out, he broke away, kicked a guard in the belly and gave another such a punch that he lost two of his teeth. He made many enemies. I had not realized how important a prisoner he was. It was out of my hands."

"You did not seem to think so when I was in your quarters."

"It is true that I wanted your gratitude, Karalee. I wanted you." He took her shoulders gently and turned her to face him. "But all I have said to you is truth. I waited for you that night so that I could explain what had happened. I wanted to tell you that things did not look good, but that I had not yet given up. That I planned to ride to Gort to speak to someone of influence on your brother's behalf. But you did not come to me as you promised."

"I could not."

"As I could not do what I promised. Please believe me. You have not been out of my thoughts."

Karalee did not want to believe him. It would be easier for her to live with her hatred of him. "The soldier who rode with us told me of your promises. It seems that I am not the only woman who has heard them."

"Chalmers! It was he who lied, Karalee. The man is full of hate. He has hatred for the rich and for all who rank above him. But he has even more hatred for Papists."

"I care not for any of this," she managed. "The fare is three pounds, ten shillings. I have need of three times that. My friend, Theresa, makes two and her babes count together as a third."

"In the morning I will go to the shipbroker and arrange your passage. Will that convince you that your welfare is important to me?" Phillip replied.

"I would rather you gave me the money, so that I could arrange it myself. When I have settled in America, I will return every shilling to you. I want nothing from you."

120

"Perhaps not." Slowly he removed her shawl and tossed it onto the bed. "But I want something from you."

"I see." Karalee stiffened in his arms, tightening her lips against his kiss.

He growled and shoved her from him. "Your passage money does not depend on your giving yourself to me. I had no idea you found my lovemaking so distasteful. It did not seem so."

"Then I may have the money?"

"No, damn it, you may not have the money," he shouted. He crossed to the window, where he pulled aside the curtain and looked out as if he expected someone. "I have told you I would arrange your passage. I will not have you wandering alone near the water." Without looking at her, he made a sweeping motion with one hand. "Get out of my sight. Go. Come back at noon tomorrow."

Karalee did not move. "How can I be certain you will do as you say?"

"You little vixen." Phillip clenched his fists and tore away from the window so quickly that he nearly pulled the curtain down with him. He raised one arm as if he would strike her a blow and she tensed for it. But he gathered himself. "My word is good! Do not look at me disbelieving. I will not have it from you."

"I can judge you only by what I have seen."

"Stay then," he said, pulling her into his arms with a violent jerk. He brought his mouth down hard to cover hers, pressing more and more as if he were trying to crush her lips with his own.

When, at last, he released her, they both stood, unspeaking, as they recovered their breath. Phillip removed his coat and folded it carefully across a chair. His breeches were of a knit material, very snug-fitting, and the line of his aroused manhood was evident.

"I have changed my mind. Let me be what you think me to be. My broken promise will pay for one passage. But you still must pay for the other two." He waved one hand toward her. "Take off your dress. Quickly. I have an appointment."

"As you wish," she said strongly, vowing not to weep or beg or show any sign of shame.

As she slipped her dress over her head, he took it from her and held it at arm's length, examining it, as if it were sewn of fine silk.

121

"Lovely," he said. Then he ripped it in half, and in half again. "How sad." He feigned an expression of sorrow. "Your beautiful gown is ruined. What a pity! But it will better serve as cleaning rags for the housemaid." He tossed the torn pieces of cloth into a corner and waited, his arms folded across his chest. "Come now. All of it."

She removed her skirts and the rest of her undergarments and with a glare of defiance ripped each of them in half as Phillip had done and tossed them into the corner with the ruined dress.

She stood before him, naked and shivering, though the afternoon was warm. He studied her from head to toe, circling her and frowning, as if she were an animal he expected to purchase and had found flawed. She yelped as his fingers pinched the flesh of her rump.

"You are scrawnier than you were the last time. I must see that you are better fed."

"I am truly sorry I do not please you," she snapped, keeping her head erect.

Phillip laughed shortly. "You manage to hold onto your arrogance even as you stand bare as a babe. We will see how much longer you can do it."

He seized her off her feet and flung her onto the bed, where after tearing off his own clothes, he fell upon her. He was not gentle, as he had been the other time. Without a kiss or a caress he worked her legs apart with his knees, guided himself into her with rough fingers and thrust— again and again—until he was finished. Then he rolled onto his back next to her. The weight of his body upon hers and his quick frantic movements had awakened her own desire. But he had not stayed long enough upon her to spend it. Now she squirmed, burning with frustration.

"Who was the other man?"

"I do not know what you mean."

"When I asked if I would be the first, you told me I would not be. Who was he?"

"His name was Hugh." She was surprised that she remembered the man's name, or that she had even heard it said. She found herself telling Phillip about the Galway marketplace and about the two yeomen in the filthy boxstrewn room. It was not until she had finished her story that she realized she was cradled in his arms, making his chest wet with her tears. He was stroking her hair, now and then touching his lips to her forehead.

"Poor little waif," he said. "And I have been no better than they. I took the same advantage of you. I do not know why it should be, but you can build the fires of anger within me as no one else has ever been able to do. Perhaps it is that I want to be a hero in your eyes, yet I fall short. I do not imagine I could be in love with you. Love builds with time, with memories shared and twined together until two people are fastened as one. But I know I shall love you one day. And you will love me."

"There is no time for love."

"There will be. That is why I'll expect you to repay the passage money. When you write, I will know where you are. At the beginning of next year I will be in Boston, seeing to some unsettled properties from an uncle's estate. Nothing will keep me from you then."

"I cannot think so far ahead. I must consider immediate problems."

"Such as your passage money?"

Karalee giggled. "Such as my clothes. However will I leave here without them?"

"You cannot. At least while I keep my appointment I can be sure you won't run away." He rolled to his side, and propped upon one elbow. "When I return, I will bring you a dress. What color would you like? Yellow this time? No—green, I think. To match your eyes."

"If I accept another dress from you, I insist on paying for it when I send the other money."

He shook his head. "I do not intend to buy it. I shall steal it. My appointment is with a sister who lives in Liverpool. She has a closet packed with more dresses than she will ever be able to wear. She is about your size too. Though there is a little more of her—" He stooped his head to kiss the tips of Karalee's breasts "—Here—and there."

"I cannot refuse," she told him.

"I promise not to touch you again tonight," he said gravely. "I have misused you badly. In fact, I will never touch you again until the time comes that you want me to. Now—to keep my mind off lovemaking, we will go out tonight. Have a fine dinner and attend the Royale Theatre. There is a presentation of Hamlet, I believe."

He touched a finger to her lips as if he would kiss her. Instead, he moved the finger down her chin, along the length of her throat and down between her breasts. "But again," he whispered, "as long as we are already here—unclothed—perhaps . . ." His hand slid down her belly and found the warmth between her legs, where his fingers moved, exploring. "Perhaps one more time would not count against me."

This time Karalee longed for him.

He slid into her easily, moving gently, and she felt no pain, only the comfort of his body, the warmth, and the ecstasy of fulfillment.

When she awoke to a tapping on the door, she ignored it at first and tried to drift back into her comfortable sleep. But the sound persisted. Phillip was gone. She slipped into the dressing gown he had left across the foot of the bed, and crept to the door, wondering if she should answer.

"Who is it?"

"Jocelyn Shepard."

Karalee puzzled, still not jarred completely from her sleep. The name meant nothing to her.

"Please open the door, dear. I have something for you."

It was the girl Karalee had seen hanging onto Phillip's arm that morning on Dale Street. She wore a morning dress with a short-fitted jacket of brown velvet this time and a darker wig with a line of ringlets across her forehead. But her smile was Phillip's. She was surely his sister.

"May I come in? Please do not be embarrassed. Phillip has explained your misfortune and I wish to help." She opened a large box on the bed and brought out a dress of green calico, with a wide attached collar of white, like a shawl, and panniers of white draped toward the back, falling to the hemline. "I can see why Phillip insisted on green. It is lovely with your eyes. This dress is not elegant, but I felt it would be more in keeping and less perishable for traveling."

"It is beautiful, thank you."

"But not right for the theater," the girl said. "And so I brought another, though I was not sure how much room you would have in your luggage box. I have heard it said that it is unwise to carry too much. You find yourself guarding it against theft and are not free to move about."

The second dress was red with embroidered designs of black upon its fitted bodice. The neckline was low and the sleeves were much like those on the dress Jocelyn herself had been wearing that morning, long and slashed at the wrist to expose black lace.

"The rest is undergarments. I hope everything fits."

"I do not know how to thank you."

"Then I will tell you how," the girl said, still smiling. "You see, my brother and I were not born into wealth. While our blood line is noble, our father lost his fortune through unsound investments. Thankfully, we have an uncle who is most generous. We want for nothing."

"I do not see . . ."

"Phillip has not my good sense when it comes to affairs of the heart. Three years ago, he found himself penniless—disinherited because he fell in love with a girl of low birth. She was beautiful—quite like you, as I remember—but oh, so common! Any trace of loveliness vanished, as far as I could see, when she opened her lips to speak and displayed her lack of breeding. When she discovered Phillip had no fortune of his own, she ran away with a silk-merchant from London. It nearly destroyed my brother. It is only of late that my uncle has reconsidered—softened toward Phillip. He is no longer young and has no son of his own. He has given my brother another chance. I will not have you ruin it."

"I would do nothing to hurt Phillip." Karalee could not believe what this woman was saying. What had Phillip told his sister?

"Ah, but you would. Phillip is more than taken with you. There have been a great many other women, of course. Women who meant nothing to him. Women he treated shabbily, trying in some feeble way to make them pay for what the girl, Constance, made him suffer. But you are different, I fear. I see a light in his eye that signals danger when he speaks of you."

"You have no need to fear me," Karalee told her. How she wished she were in a position to toss the girl out, or at the very least, to speak up for herself! She had never been one to take insults without returning in kind. But her debt to Phillip was too great. She would make no trouble for him. "I leave for the colonies in a few days. Tonight will likely be the last time I ever see your brother."

"Until he follows after you. And he will—unless we do something to disillusion him. To let him know you are undeserving of his trust." The girl fluttered a delicate ivory fan before her face. "It is warm—so very warm. I must leave. I find it hard to get my breath. Perhaps it is these stays."

Karalee crossed to the door and opened it. "Thank you again for the dresses."

"I shall ask you not to go to the theater tonight. You would not enjoy it. The audiences are rowdy and prone to riotous behavior. Rabble, turning from their own countries, waiting for a ship that will make room for them. Why, I read in the *Monthly Mirror* just last evening that they had to evacuate several of the theater boxes at the Royale. The worthless wretches above were urinating from the gallery and soiling those who sat below. No, I do not think it wise to attend."

"I shall see what Phillip has to say," Karalee replied quickly.

Jocelyn lifted an eyebrow and picked a bit of imaginary lint from her sleeve. "I thought I made it clear. There is no need for you to see Phillip. You will be gone by the time he returns. I sent a manservant to the docks to arrange your places on a packet ship—the *Gallant Lady*. It leaves in the morning."

She withdrew a large envelope from her bag and held it toward Karalee.

"I will not take it. I must see Phillip."

Jocelyn smiled. "You are living in the house of Madeline Aumont, are you not?"

"Yes. She was kind enough to . . ."

"I am sure. You would be a great asset to her—her establishment. There is a demand, I understand, for a certain look of innocence such as yours. I do hope the woman pays you well. Such sweetness of expression is fleeting when one goes about making a living in such a sordid manner."

"You do not understand. I . . ."

"I know everything about you, my dear. After Phillip told me your story—poor trusting boy, he believes everything—I made inquiries. Pretty as you are, you did not go unnoticed. You left a path quite easy to follow. I would imagine Madeline Aumont has already made up a waiting list of those gentlemen eager for your company."

"I have done nothing of which to be ashamed."

"There is an oddness about Phillip, Karalee, which you have evidently failed to notice. He appears worldly and sophisticated. He is not. He is quite proper. When I tell him you are in the employ of Madeline Aumont—when he hears that you are living in that house of sin—the sight of you will turn his stomach."

126

"I will explain to him. He will not think badly of me!"

"Ah, Karalee," Jocelyn shook her head sadly. "You make it necessary for me to threaten you. If you are still here when my brother returns—if he so much as lays eyes upon you again—I will immediately report your whereabouts to the port authorities."

"You would not."

"I sincerely hope you do not force me to prove it. You are sister to an escaped traitor. You are wanted for interrogation and possibly for aiding in that escape. Undoubtedly your friend is wanted also. I realize my actions might get Phillip into some difficulties, but they would save him from worse."

She held out the envelope again and Karalee took it. She paused at the door. "Have a pleasant voyage, my dear."

She blew a kiss and was gone.

Sixteen

As the *Gallant Lady* set sail, there was merriment. Fiddlers played—others tapped their feet and sang. No one shed any tears as Liverpool grew smaller and smaller in the distance. But then the ship was caught up in the ocean swells and the singing of the joyful turned to the groaning of the seasick. The day's ration of water had not been doled out yet and tongues were thick with thirst. As the weather turned stormy, the hatches, which had been the only source of fresh air and light, had been battened down and all those below rolled and tumbled against each other, smeared with each other's vomit.

For want of something to divert her mind, Karalee had counted the passengers as the roll was called. Nearly three hundred were packed into steerage, huddled in near darkness, wallowing in their own filth. Only one man seemed unaffected by the closeness, the stink, and the movement of the vessel. His clothes were sooty rags and his hat, the same gray, shapeless upon the back of his head. His eyes were close-set and round—the whites, so white they seemed to glow. He stood in a half-crouch before them, as if it were his place to entertain them. But for the most part, no one listened.

"Rode in all alone, he did, that day," the man was saying, "on the very horse he stole from Pad O'Geary. Hammered upon the door hard enough to bring the cottage down around him.

" 'I have come for the pigs,' says he."

The storyteller stepped to one side, straightened, and

pitched his voice higher, as if it were another who spoke. " 'We got no pigs left, sir. They up and died with fever, they did.' "

He stepped back into place, half-crouching again, a fierce scowl on his face and his voice thunderous. " 'Your cows, then. Where are your cows?'

" 'Alas, you would not believe the sadness of it, sir. But the cows is dead too.'

" 'You are right when you say I would not believe it. We will see if they are dead. I will be back within the hour with my men. If your pigs have not then been resurrected, we will batter your cottage to the ground. If not then, we will batter your neighbor's cottage. And if not yet—the next, and the next. There will be nothing of your village but rubble.' "

"Och, leave off it now, Brodie," a woman groaned from a dim corner. "Your mouth has not stilled since you left your mother's breast. Leave us to our misery. We have heard your tale."

The storyteller did not appear to have heard the admonition. He went on, his voice rising.

"Then he wiped his feet on the doorstep, looked around him and laughed. Imagine, if you can, a human soul laughing at the prospect of seeing old women and children homeless! So busy laughing, he was, he did not notice how we had closed into a circle about him. We yelled, loud, as if we were but one voice, and leaped upon him. We battered him with fists and sticks and kicked him until he was nothing but blood and pulp upon the ground. Then we jigged around him and it was us who laughed."

"But was it worth it to you? Having to run off—to leave all you love behind?"

The man was silent and the glow left his eyes. But the silence lasted but a moment. He slapped his palm onto the knee of the man who had asked the question.

"Damn right. Damn fool right, it was worth it. And I am a hero now, you see. The magistrate rode in and wanted to know who had committed the killing. He would know, he said, or all would suffer for it. We talked and it was decided I would take the blame all to myself. My woman is dead these three years and my only son with her. So I was free to be their hero. They took up a collection in a hat for my passage."

"And what of your immortal soul?" Karalee was sur-

130

prised to hear Theresa pipe up beside her. "You took part in a murder."

"Bah," the storyteller answered. "Live a few more years, before you ask such a question."

"'Tis the child's love of traveling packs her among us in this hell's pit," someone added. "It could not have been a sniveling land-grabber. If it were, she would know it is not murder when the one who lies dead is a landlord. Owning property changes a man. It rips the heart and soul from him."

"Ay." The storyteller giggled as if he were being tickled and the others joined in. "They fancy calling the poor Irish lazy and filthy because we choose to live as we do. Pigs in the kitchen, they say, and a dungheap before the door. The roof full of holes and weeds growing among the turnips."

"But what happens if we fix things, eh? If we nail our roofs and whitewash our walls? If we plant flowers and hang curtains?"

"I should know what happens," a sour-faced woman who sat next to Theresa said. "Did not it happen to me and mine? The landlord rode in and says the place is too good for us now. He ups the rent so we cannot pay. He puts the land up for cant. Finds another who will give him more for such a fine house and throws us off. Hah! 'Twas not murder at all."

Theresa was about to say more, but Karalee stopped her with a warning look and a poke in the ribs. "We must have no trouble here," she whispered.

"I cannot hold my tongue against such sinful talk."

"You must learn."

"As you have learned? And I should do as you do?" Theresa snapped. "Perhaps get me a fine dress as you did?"

"There are two dresses. You are welcome to wear either of them."

"I would sooner walk unclothed than put on garments which you degraded yourself to own."

"Theresa, that is not fair."

"No mind," the girl said, turning away. "It is not my place to judge, nor is my forgiveness to be asked. It is His forgiveness you must beg to receive."

"Whatever it was you did, it was well worth it. You look splendid in the dress."

Karalee had not noticed the young man who sat beside her. Now she turned her eyes upon him to put him in his place, but found she could not. It seemed foolish, packed together as they were—all suffering the same. His expression was not that of a leering lecher, but rather that of someone trying to make the best of wretched conditions.

His peaked brows were the same dark rust-color of his waving hair and his eyes were those of a small child who had performed a feat of daring and wanted applause—though from the lankiness of his limbs, Karalee could see he was well past the growing stage, as well as exceedingly tall.

"Thank you," she said.

"I am Jeremy Treacher. Peddler. This will be the seventh time I have crossed this ocean and it becomes no easier with the getting used to, I fear. I suppose I could ride above, but I would rather put the same two hundred-fifty dollars into saleable wares, than into passage money. And your names, ladies?"

He waited, and when neither Theresa nor Karalee replied, he leaned closer. "Druscilla, you say? Druscilla Wiggenbottom? Lovely name. And your friend? Ah yes, Hortense Beanblossom."

Karalee giggled behind her hand at the thought of Theresa with such a flowery name, but Theresa made a clicking sound of disapproval with her tongue.

"If you are a gentleman, Mr. Treacher, you will leave us alone."

"If I were a gentleman, I would surely do that. But as I have told you, I am a peddler, and that allows me considerably more leeway. Besides, we will be at sea for many weeks. It will hardly be possible for us to remain strangers."

"I would like to try," Theresa answered.

"I watched you board and admired your courage. But the worst is yet to come. I would like to suggest that you pretend you are traveling with me. It would be safer."

"With you?" Theresa snorted. "If you respect our wishes, sir, and leave us, we will do well enough."

"Will you? Wait until you try and cook your meal. They have set up less than a dozen grates upon the main deck to serve all. You will find yourselves standing from sunrise to sunset for your turn at the fire, only to be shoved out of place by someone stronger, and in the end, you will eat your food raw. Are you aware of what raw oatmeal does to the stomach?" He made a comical face. "You will run for the privies and you will find another line. Without a man to guard you, you'll be mixed with male passengers and find little privacy. Sometimes the crew will turn the hoses on you for sport."

"We will manage." Theresa stiffened, her cheeks reddening from the candor of the peddler's remarks.

"If you are thinking to use your chamber pots in some dark corner and avoid the privies . . ."

"Sir!"

"If you are, you will be disappointed. On every voyage I have taken, the captain has the ladies in tears. He goes about collecting those vessels and tosses them into the sea. He says they are filthy and spread ship fever."

There was a clanking above and shouting and at last the hatches were removed. The weather had settled. Daylight streamed in, and Karalee flung one arm over her eyes to protect them from the sudden glare. Sailors in black-ribboned, low-crowned hats, clothed in striped shirts and bright neckerchiefs, raced down the ladder carrying buckets of tar.

"Up you go, the lot of you," the first and burliest of them snarled. "Water rations on deck. Step lively or you'll go thirsting."

The other seamen set down their buckets and began to jab red-hot irons into the tar to fumigate. "They could swoon from the stench of ye all the way to Boston. It's like a bloody cesspool down here."

Each passenger was allotted three quarts of water a day to meet his needs. This water had to be used for cooking and washing as well as drinking. Not a drop could be spared, and so often, even among the dainty, washing was all but abolished. It was murmured that the seamen who pumped the water into the cans used a false measure and so cheated each of at least a half-quart. But Karalee had noticed that one man who was foolish enough to suggest this was cursed and brutally kicked, so the others kept still.

When Theresa moved up to her turn at the barrel, the mate grinned and gave her a wink. "Such a little lass to be toting such a burden. Is there no man with you?"

Theresa wrinkled her nose in distaste and kept silent.

"Too fancy for a rough sailor, are you?" He scowled and raised his hand, ignoring her empty water-can. "Foul weather ahead. No more water today. Get below."

"We'll have our water," came the anguished cry from

those who had not yet been served. "We thirst. Give us our due."

"You have no right to deprive us," Theresa said. "I have little ones besides myself to nourish."

"Found your voice now, have you, my lady?" the mate sneered. "Too late. Move away."

"We want our water," the cry continued.

The other sailors moved forward, brandishing their weapons.

"Below. I'll not tell you again," the mate barked. "Or I'll rope's end the lot of you."

"Sir." Jeremy Treacher, though he had already received his ration, stepped back into line. "There are at least two dozen souls who have not received their dole. We all have human needs."

"I said no more water today."

"Our contract ticket says we are to receive . . ."

He got no farther. He was clubbed from behind by one seaman and kicked to the deck floor by another. When he fell, sprawling, his eyes rolling as if he were unconscious, he received another sharp kick in the belly that he was beyond feeling. The mate stepped over him and lashed him back and forth with a knotted rope, cursing with each blow.

"You live by the law of the sea and you will take orders. You are walking freight—all of you—no more!"

Karalee could stand no more. She rushed forward and caught the mate's arm. "Please. You will kill him. Let me take him. Please."

The sailor yanked his arm away and puffed up his huge chest as if he planned to blow her below by the sheer force of his breath. But when he saw her face, his fierce expression faded and he let his arm drop to his side.

"You may have him, little Missy," he said, his black eyes sliding over her body, down to her toes and back again to her face. "Tell him how fortunate he is to have a comely wench to speak for him. Tell him also to hold his tongue the next time—or nothing will save him from finishing his passage in irons."

Karalee felt a shiver from the touch of his eyes, but she forced herself not to show revulsion as she stooped and slid her arms around Jeremy Treacher, trying to budge him. It was no use. He was dead weight.

"One of you." She looked over her shoulder at the other

passengers who watched in horror. "Won't someone help him as he was trying to help you?"

No one moved, each afraid to be marked in the wicked mate's eyes as a comrade of the fallen one. Suddenly an old woman pushed her way through and knelt beside Karalee "Perhaps the two of us can slide him along," she whispered. "Though if he is badly broken inside, it could harm him."

"Out of the way, Granny." Red-faced, one of the men stepped away from the others and called to the man who stood behind him. "Lend a hand here, James. You too, Sweeney."

He caught Jeremy under the arms. Another man took the unconscious man's knees and a third supported his backside. Together they carried him below.

The mate, still undressing Karalee with his eyes, seemed to have forgotten he had ordered an end to the water doling, and continued pumping. He muttered something under his breath that she could not hear and the sailors around him laughed raucously. She took her place in line again and waited until her own container was filled. Then she held Jeremy's measure out for his ration.

"His was spilled when he was knocked to the deck," she explained.

"It could as well have been his blood spilled," the sailor answered. But he filled the second can and grinned, watching, his head cocked to one side, as she climbed down the ladder that took her below with the others.

Seventeen

The *Gallant Lady* had not been built as a passenger ship.
In other times she had, as many other such ships, arrived
in Liverpool with cotton from Boston or lumber from the
forests of Canada and had returned in ballast. Now that the
value of human cargo had been realized, hasty changes
were made to accommodate passengers.

Bunks were hammered together of rough planks—four
rows of them, in three tiers along the sides of the ship on a
level between the main deck and the hold. Two more tiers
were fashioned over the rows of water casks that were
lashed amidships along the between-decks. Each berth was
six-foot square and meant to sleep four persons. That gave
each only eighteen inches—or about what they would find
in their own coffins. Men and women—often strangers to
each other—slept side by side. Married couples engaged in
lusty love-making, their movements brushing and tumbling
them against the mortified, single young women who were
often forced to berth with them. While there were parti-
tions of sorts, they were only four inches high and the piles
of bedding brought all up to the same level. Everyone lay
together in a tangle.

Karalee managed to undress herself for bed beneath an
improvised tent—a blanket she had Theresa hold around
her as a screen. But Theresa refused to do the same.

"I shall not disrobe while so many men stare at me. It is
indecent."

"It is dark. Besides, they can see nothing under the blanket."

137

"It is indecent all the same. I will sleep as I am. I intend to sit up all night anyway—as should you. We can sit with our heads resting upon our folded arms in our laps."

"Who could sleep in such a position? Theresa," Karalee pleaded, "we will be sailing for many weeks. We would die of exhaustion. Only think now. Deirdre and Daniel will lie on one side of you and I will lie on your other side. What could be amiss in that?"

"And you will sleep beside the peddler?" Theresa gasped.

"There is no other way. Things could be worse for us. Imagine if we had not met Jeremy? We could well be bunked with one of those rum-reeking creatures who boarded alongside us. Or someone who had not washed himself for a month. Or a ruffian who would take advantage."

"It is not decent."

"I thank you for your words of confidence," Jeremy whispered, lying next to Karalee. "But it does put me on my good behavior, doesn't it?"

"I only meant, broken up as you are," she told him, "you are quite harmless."

"I am not so broken as all that." Jeremy rolled his eyes and folded his arms across his chest. "A goodly part of me is painfully aware that someone soft and curvaceous shares my pallet."

"We should not have sailed," Theresa wailed into her hands. "I was foolish to listen to you. Your parents are wandering about Liverpool looking for us. What will they do when they do not find us? And what will we do when we reach the colonies and no one meets us?"

"My parents will be waiting for us in Philadelphia," Karalee insisted, wishing she was as certain as she sounded. "Their names were crossed off the list. I saw it."

"Then it was a cruel and dreadful thing they have done to us."

"They had no choice. Had they waited, they would have lost their passage money and there was none to spare. They presumed we would have male protection and that we would follow. Please now, do not think of it. Come to bed."

"She will sleep when she has grown tired enough," Jeremy said. "There are always women determined to sleep sitting up throughout the voyage rather than to lie next to a man. But their eyelids grow heavy and their backbone weakens and before long, they would curl up beside Satan himself."

"It is sleep you are needing too," Karalee whispered, grateful that he was well enough to joke. "Are you feeling all right?"

"I have felt better and I have felt worse."

Karalee's body ached with fatigue, yet she could not sleep. During the daylight hours she could usually force Patrick's image from her mind and concentrate upon other things. But with the silence and the blackness that came with the night, his face stayed before her. If only she had refused to do as her mother asked that morning. If she had not gone to fetch Theo. Patrick would be here now—alive, and sailing with them. Dear God, would such thoughts ever stop torturing her?

Jeremy's companionship was a comfort to her and a joy. He was full of stories that could draw smiles from her even through her most dismal hours. When some of the water casks began to leak and passengers were put on reduced measures, he donated a part of his cheerfully for the welfare of the infants. When food rations were not distributed due to rough weather, he pulled some extras from his own stored provisions and shared them. He had a way with the infants and could extract a burp from Deirdre or a toothless grin from Daniel when all else had failed. He stood beside them and helped them to hold their places in the interminable lines. Still Theresa did not warm to him. He was always "the peddler."

"I am welcome as sunshine wherever I go," Jeremy told them. "Imagine, if you will, a poor family—up before the sun, working their hands into blisters, trying to hack a living from the barren ground. No sign of civilization have they seen for many a month. No faces other than those of their own. All at once they hear the toot of the peddler's horn from the river where he has tied his raft. They drop everything and run. The oldest of them is a child again."

"What sort of goods can you carry in that small trunk of yours?"

"You would be surprised at how many pins and needles, spools of thread and scissors, knives and forks, cups and plates can be squeezed into one such trunk. But I have two larger ones in baggage."

"There are few who would find happiness in such a wandering life as yours. Have you no home?"

"The river is my home. My customers are my family. And how happy they are to see me! They sit me down with a cup of cider and they gather around as if President John Adams himself had come to pay a visit. It is not only for the toys and the yard goods and the cooking utensils I bring, you see. Just as important to them is the news I carry. Who has married, who has died, who has given birth, whose wife has run off from him? After a bit, I comment on how grand the smell of their roasting meat or their apple pie is, and I am invited for a fine supper. I remark how comfortable they are by their fireside and I am given a soft bed for the night and then again breakfast in the morning. I can steal kisses from many a pretty woman, without having to bear the nagging of a wife. It is a glorious life!"

"And what of the time you must spend sailing on such ships as this one? Can you truly say that part of it is glorious?" Karalee asked, wondering if he was as happy as he seemed.

"I do not mind it. True enough, most others in my line dream of the day they will no longer have to go out themselves. But that is not for me. No, I will continue to pole up the river and float back twice a year and take my own time—do whatever I please during the between-times."

In spite of Jeremy's good humor and the attempts of some of the others, who told tales and sang to lift sagging spirits, time grew heavy and each day more difficult than the last. Tempers flared. Arguments turned into fist fights. Horace Brodie, the man who had told his tale of the slain landlord on the first day of their voyage, repeated the story at least twice a day, and when he was yelled down, he only yelled louder until he had finished.

Most emigrants had no clear idea of the distance they would be traveling, or the time it would take them to get there. One aged man stood erect most of the time, staring, expecting at any moment to see the shores of the new land. When weeks passed and still there was no sign of it, he began to grumble, then rave, and finally he shook his fist and cried that they had been cheated.

"It is not America they take us to," he shouted. "It is a black lie we have been told. We are being shipped far away to be sold as slaves among the heathens. See how they lock us below like unfortunates in a slave ship? We must rise up and take over before it is too late."

His fears took root in some tormented minds and others

took up his cry. A handful of them rushed onto the deck to be beaten back and kicked by the seamen until they returned below where they fell in heaps, bleeding and sobbing out their helplessness.

It was said that April and May were the best months to make the voyage. July and August were to be avoided at all costs and it was easy enough to see why. Southwesterly winds plagued the ship constantly and made passage tedious. During one of the more severe storms they encountered, several of the water casks broke loose. One man was killed outright. Jeremy's leg was slashed from kneecap to upper thigh trying to reach him and another man's arm was so badly crushed it had to be amputated. He died three days later.

But the greatest dread was ship fever. Many had been ill when they boarded. A medical examination was required by law before anyone was allowed on board in Liverpool, but Karalee learned it had been a pretense. One man inspected the nearly three hundred passengers in little over an hour. He told them to stick out their tongues, and then he asked, "Are you well?"

Who, wishing to sail, would have said otherwise?

The pitching of the ship, the fetid atmosphere, the lack of fresh water and adequate nourishment did nothing to ensure good health. More became ill each day and some died. Their bodies were sewn into a cloth weighted with stone. Karalee could not watch as they were thrown into the sea.

When Theresa grew listless and her appetite failed, Karalee was certain, at first, it was part of the girl's homesickness and dissatisfaction. But she became alarmed when she noticed Theresa's feet were swollen and discolored. There was the same puffy discoloration in her cheeks.

"My dear lady," the doctor told Karalee without a change of expression, "I cannot descend into that hole of pestilence. What would occur, if I, the only medical man aboard this ship, were to become ill? If you wish me to examine your friend, you must bring her here."

He prescribed a sugar cube with peppermint for seasickness and sent Karalee on her way. Jeremy let out a roar when he heard the diagnosis and bounded up the ladder in spite of his injured leg. When he returned, he had the doctor in tow.

"I only promised him a few playful rounds of fisticuffs in some dark alley when we dock," he explained.

The medicine, which cost Jeremy sixpence, seemed to relieve Theresa's discomfort so that she slept soundly for a time. But it did nothing to check her fever. Karalee lay awake that night, now and then changing a dampened cloth she kept on Theresa's forehead, listening to the labored sound of the girl's breathing.

When she was finally able to drift into sleep, she was haunted by fitful dreams. She was a child again, playing with Rory and Theresa, running through the fields of heather and bounding over walls and hedges.

Their favorite game had been the story of Moira O'Glanny and her sweetheart Aran Roe, who had lived over six hundred years before. Theresa always insisted upon being Moira and she would become furious when Rory and Karalee giggled behind their hands and did not take it as seriously as she did.

Moira had rushed to the water to meet her beloved bridegroom, only to find him covered with blood from battle and lying with fifty brave warriors who died by his side. After weeping, Moira laid him on his barge, surrounded him with all the fine things they were to have shared at their wedding, and painted his face and the faces of his men with gold, so that they would have eternal youth. She placed a sword by his hand and a bronze shield upon his chest. Then she covered the barge with dry rushes. When the moon rose after seven days of mourning, she drank poisoned wine from a jeweled goblet, set fire to the barge and lay down beside him.

Except now, in Karalee's dream, they were not playing. The blood was real, as was the fire. The face of Aran Roe, painted with gold, no longer belonged to Rory—but to Patrick.

She woke with a start, to the sound of Theresa's voice, stronger than it had been since before she had been taken ill.

"Are you awake?"

"Yes, yes, I am."

"I have not been a good friend to you, Karalee."

"Foolish talk."

"Why must girls grow into women? We were dear companions once. We truly loved one another. What happened to that love?"

142

"I still love you, Theresa."

"I have not loved you. I have not loved you for ever so long. There is meanness in me."

"Do not say that."

"I tried all I could to turn Rory from you."

"Do not speak of such things now."

"I did. And I have not loved Patrick either. I told him as much and I made him unhappy. I made up stories about you to him—so that he would think you were wicked."

"It does not matter."

"Nor have I loved my little ones. Now it is too late. They will die when I die. There will be no milk for them."

"Stop your talk of dying."

"Would you have hated me, had I grown to be more beautiful than you?" Theresa did not wait for a reply. "No, you would not have. There is no meanness in you, Karalee. May God forgive me."

She died in her sleep an hour later, holding fast to Karalee's hand. Jeremy, who had found a woman willing to nurse Daniel in return for a sack of sweets and nutmeats, did not tell Karalee until the next morning that Deirdre had become ill and died that night too.

Eighteen

"Take the blame upon yourself for the tempest we're having and for the water casks that broke loose while you are about it," Jeremy said, cradling Karalee against his chest. "And the poor soul who lost his arm and died. Was that your doing?"

"Deirdre did not seem to be ailing. She was always so good—never complained or felt in the least feverish. But I should have watched her more closely. I should have . . ."

"It was sudden, Karalee. It is the way with little ones sometimes. There was no way of anybody telling."

"And Daniel? Will he be next?"

"If we can judge by the strength of his lungs, the lad is fine."

"And you, Jeremy? Will you be fine?" Karalee's head throbbed with a grief she was too weak to vent. She had not even been able to shed a tear at Theresa's passing. Her inner agony was too intense for weeping. "You would be wise to stay clear of me. I carry a terrible curse."

"Hush now," Jeremy whispered against her ear, tightening his arm around her. "I take no store in your foolish superstition. But some around us would love to find a place to lay the blame for their sufferings. They would jump at the chance to name you a Jonah."

"I care not what they think."

Oh my sweet Patrick, she thought. I have failed you. Your wife is dead and your darling little girl—and after you entrusted them to my safekeeping with your dying breath. They are with you now. I take some comfort in

145

that. But there is still Daniel. If you can hear my thoughts, hear this. Nothing will happen to your son. I promise it. Nothing.

"Cockroaches?" someone was saying. "You think the cockroaches aboard this ship are big? You should have seen those that swarmed out when we landed from the Indies. Long as a man's hand they were, and when you stomped one under your heel, it made the crack of a pistol shot."

"To hell with cockroaches," another voice rasped. "It is the cursed lightning and the wind. A few more waves like the last and this wooden box we call a ship will be split in two."

"Ay, when I visited the privy, I heard them call all hands to pump."

"For God's sake, does that the mean the ship is leaking?"

"What else?"

"Merciful heavens," a woman shrieked. "The ship is leaking. We're going to sink."

"There is not a ship on the sea that does not leak," Jeremy cried so that the others could hear. "Some leak a little, and some a lot. And there is not a ship that does not call hands to pump at least once every twenty-four hours. Stay calm."

"Stay calm, you say? We have been sailing these eighty days with no sign of land and the entire voyage was to take but forty. And you say to stay calm? No sleep any of us will get this night."

The silence that followed was more ominous than the conversation had been, each passenger forming his own mental picture of their fate. Jeremy, in spite of his attempt at light-hearted confidence, tensed with the dash of each wave.

Karalee had never imagined the wind could make such a sound—like the howling of a human being in mortal agony. Instead of calming, the storm had only increased in its fury. For three days now and three nights, the vessel had threatened to split its seams, quivering and shaking, rocking as breakers crashed against it. It would be lifted high as if upon a mountain of water, held aloft for a moment, then dashed downward again with savage force.

"Mrs. Cleary," Karalee whispered. "Is Daniel sleeping?"

It was too black a night to make out the opposite tier of

146

berths, where lay the woman who had agreed to let Daniel suck along with her own babe. But Karalee knew he must have had his fill by now and she needed the security of feeling his warm nuzzling against her again.

"Ay, he is," the woman answered good-naturedly. "The little piggy eats twice as much as my own Franklin. He will grow to be a big fellow one day."

"I'll take him then. Thank you." When Karalee stepped down, she found herself ankle deep in icy water. "Jeremy!" she cried.

At that moment came a terrible jarring and a sickening crunch. People were torn from their bunks and flung into the slowly rising water as the ship swung about, shivered and struck again—again, then again, as if it were sliding along a jagged shelf of rock. It jolted to rest, then careened to port.

"On deck, save yourselves," came a call from overhead. "Get into a boat if you can. Grab a plank. Whatever will float."

"Daniel," Karalee screamed, reaching out, unable to see anything in the pitch-blackness.

"I have him," Jeremy cried at her elbow.

Hundreds fought to get onto the deck at once, clogging the passageway so that it was nearly impossible for anyone to move. The sound of shrieking, cursing human beings as they shoved their bodies against each other was as deafening as the sound of the vessel breaking up and that of the foaming billows of sea that rushed through the gaping hole in its side, carrying dozens away.

The scene topside was more appalling than anything Karalee had imagined. The ship, after being ripped open, had rolled onto its side, grinding along, until it was caught between two gigantic rocks and could not slide free. It was being battered to bits by powerful waves twenty and thirty feet high. The port lifeboats had been smashed and the others were dangling out of reach. The rope holding the jolly boat had snapped and it fell into the water. Some seamen jumped after it, but wreckage fell on top of them and they were swallowed up. The other crew members, who had not deserted, dashed about, leaving the passengers to help themselves, as they hurled everything they could get their hands on into the sea to lighten the craft.

Karalee could only watch, horrified. There seemed to be no possible escape from their fate. Those who threw out

147

broken timbers and cargo and jumped after it in the desperate hope that it would float them to safety, were soon pulled under and gone. Those who stood still and did nothing were trampled by their fellows, crushed by falling debris or swept overboard. She felt Jeremy pushing her upward, forcing her to climb, though she had no idea why, until she felt him lashing her to the crosstrees above the reach of the waves and Daniel with her. She wanted to protest that there was no use in it, but she knew her voice would not be heard. Then he went down to help Mr. Cleary with his two children and with his wife, who was too fat to make the climb easily. When they had all been safely fastened, Jeremy lashed himself.

"Pray to God she holds together until morning," he shouted, "so we can see where we are."

"I heard the call of land shortly before we struck," Mr. Cleary cried, holding tightly to his wife, who prayed at the top of her voice that they would be killed quickly and without pain.

"Your call of land was right enough, Albert," she wailed. "And we have struck atop your land. We are doomed. Let us prepare to meet our maker."

"We'll not be meeting him this day," Albert assured her, as if the strength of his words would save them.

"Someone, please," came a terrified voice from below, and Albert Cleary, despite his wife's protests, undid himself to climb down. Before his fingers could touch those of the poor woman who reached to him for safety, however, she was carried away. Mr. Cleary would have been pulled along with her, had not Jeremy loosened himself and caught the man back in time by his trousers.

Karalee had never been so cold. Even with Jeremy's long arms wrapped around her, she shook from head to toe, and she could feel him shivering too. Poor little Daniel, whose cries had gone unheeded and even unheard through the sounds of the wrecking and the scramble for life, had given up and was sleeping. She couldn't tell if he was feverish, or even if he was dying. Perhaps she was dying too. She thought ruefully of all the romantic tales she had pored over and the ballads she had heard telling about drownings and death at sea. Now she knew there was no romance in it. Only cold, and pain, and waiting. Waiting.

When at last the first gray streaks of dawn appeared, the churning water had not settled—nor would it. The air was still biting and raw, but the rain had ceased, if there was any consolation in that. They could see that the ship was wedged broadside before a gigantic cavern that had been hollowed out by the splashing and beating of waves over a long period of time. Towering walls of granite rose upward on either side and to the rear was a narrow ledge along the otherwise smooth cliff face. Between the ledge and the ship lay jagged rocks set into a boiling sea.

"The captain is abandoning us," someone screamed.

It was true. The jolly boat had been cleared and was floating away, carrying on it the captain and some of the surviving crew members. Half mad with fear, a few of the men called after it and some dropped into the sea in an attempt to swim after the departing craft. One made it and was dragged aboard, but the others were tossed by breakers and sucked under.

"Wait. We are not being abandoned. Look there!" Albert Cleary pointed where in the distance could be seen a harbor and tiny ships. "The captain is only going for help. We will be rescued if we hang on."

"Too late," Jeremy muttered under his breath. "Even if he makes it through that churning sea to shore, it will be too late for us. Come. We must climb down from here before we are thrown down."

They reached the deck just as a violent wind struck. The foremast crashed and then the mizzenmast.

"You are right in that, lad," Cleary said. "It will be worse before it will be better, I fear."

There were no more than twenty-five survivors from the hundreds of passengers who had boarded at Liverpool. They gathered, shivering, in the roundhouse, which was for the moment intact, to discuss the likeliest method of escape and to receive water-soaked biscuits and a ration of water that had been salvaged.

"I see no reason to escape." The young man who spoke wore a trim moustache and shoulder-length dark hair. He held a protective arm around a girl Karalee had talked with many times during the voyage. The two of them were newly married and going to begin their life together in America. The girl's eyes had sparkled with the love she felt for her new husband, and with her eagerness to see the land of opportunity she had been told so much about. Now her eyes were dull, her face was ashen and she looked half-drowned, as Karalee knew she herself must look. "We are within sight of land. The captain is on his way to shore. We need only wait it out here."

"I agree," another man said. "We are well wedged between these boulders, protected by the cliffside from the worst of the wind. I have seen ships more damaged than this one survive nearly a week before rescue arrived."

"And if rescue does not arrive?" Jeremy persisted.

There was silence for a moment as everyone looked toward the shore, hoping to catch a glimpse of the boat that had carried their captain on his mission. They could see nothing.

"Our worst enemy is panic," the young man said. "Rescue will arrive. Besides, man, there are passing ships. We must encourage hope. Especially with the women and children."

"Our worst enemy is not panic, but false hope. We cannot wait. If the storm begins anew and the wind with it . . ."

"What do you suggest?"

"I am not certain yet. But my guess would be—we try for the ledge."

For a moment there was shocked silence. Then everyone flew at Jeremy at once. "You can't be serious."

"Could anyone survive, without being battered to a pulp in that water?"

"The strongest of us could never reach the ledge. What of the ladies—and the children?"

The ledge. Karalee stared at Jeremy's face and then at the tiny ledge he thought could save them. Poor Jeremy, she thought. He was trying so hard to survive. No. That wasn't true. He was not a man interested only in his own survival. If he had been, he could have deserted the ship at the beginning. He was trying his best to help all of them survive. He may have been impractical and foolish and a little mad, but he was heroic, and she was proud to have known him, if only for a little while. Whatever he decided to do, unbelievable though it might be, she would go along with it.

Daniel stirred against her, and opened his eyes. She could feel the strength in his little arms as he struggled against his uncomfortable wrappings. Karalee looked at Mrs. Cleary and the woman, calmed now, took him to her breast.

Only a handful of the men were in agreement with Jere-

150

my's plan. They followed him outside to study their chances. One of them fashioned a noose and tried to hurl it onto a spiral of rock that rose from the waters close to the ledge. But he was unsuccessful. Each tried in turn and each met with failure. Jeremy fared no better than the others.

"I think I can make the swim." The lad who stepped forward was red-bearded and stripped nearly naked by the force of wind and water. His arms were long and thin, but hard-muscled, and his narrow face wore a look of cocky assurance he could feel only if he were a lunatic. "I am a strong swimmer."

"No one is that strong a swimmer," Jeremy answered. "I cannot allow it."

"And who has named you captain?" the boy snorted. He hurled a piece of mast into the water and leapt after it before anyone could stop him.

His head bobbed up like a cork in the black water, then disappeared. A cry of despair went through all who watched. But then he reappeared, clinging to the mast and there was a wild cheer. All eyes were fastened upon him as he sank and rose, in turn, moving forward, only to be tossed back, until at last, he was flung against the rock. He recovered, letting loose of the piece of wreckage and pulled himself up onto the ledge, where he lay, lifting one arm in a wave of victory.

After a dozen tries, he caught the end of the rope that was tossed him, tied it securely and called for the second, which he caught and fastened also. The other men prepared a halter, while Jeremy hurried back to the round-house with the news. An old woman was leading a prayer, her voice shrill and wailing as if it were part of the wind's cry.

"We each have the right to decide for ourselves," the young man with the moustache announced. "And you also, my sweetheart. You will have your say in it." He lifted the quivering chin of the girl who clung to him. "Those of you who wish to try the ledge, go now, and good luck to you. Though I must tell you I cannot see how you would be as well off standing out there in the wind and wet, as you are in here. Those who wish to wait for help with us, may do so also."

The girl said nothing, but fastened her arms more tightly and clung to him fiercely. Only the Cleary family and three other men moved forward to join Jeremy.

"You cannot mean this," Jeremy cried in despair. "If the gale is renewed, as it certainly will be—look at the sky, will you—the roundhouse cannot hold together. Its seams are bursting apart already. Reconsider. Please."

"You speak your opinion, sir," the young man said. "That is your right. No offense intended, but do not try to force that opinion on us. We have made our choice."

"Only come and see what we have rigged," Jeremy pleaded.

But none would hear.

It was two hours later before all twelve had managed to reach the ledge safely, and though none had fallen into the water, none were certain they were the better off for their decision. The ledge was slippery and little wider than the length of a man's foot. There were no handholds and the wind was rising. When the tide changed or if the tempest were renewed, all would be washed into the sea. Already the sky was black, the rain had begun and the breakers were crashing toward them as if the sea were something alive and vengeful.

"We should have stayed aboard the ship," Mrs. Cleary began. "The others were wise. The captain will bring help and it will be too late for us to receive it. We cannot even seat ourselves here and I cannot stand much longer. What is to become of us?"

At that moment there came a terrible cracking sound as if the earth were split asunder, and a foaming black wall of water slapped the pitiful remnant of ship they had abandoned. It carried away the roundhouse as if it were a child's toy, rolling it over and over until it sank with an agonizing whoosh and was gone. The shrieks of those within could not even be heard above the wind.

No one spoke for a long time.

"I'm going to follow the ledge to the end," the red-bearded lad said when he had recovered himself. "From where we stand, we cannot see what lies around the corner. Whatever it is, it is better than what we have here."

"What lies around that corner is sheer drop. The ledge tapers off to nothing, can't you see?" said one of the other men.

"We cannot be sure."

"Take care," Jeremy told him. "The rock could be brittle and break off underfoot."

"Perhaps the rest of you can balance yourselves on that

inch of rock," Mrs. Cleary said, as the boy worked his way into the shadows and out of sight. "But there is twice as much of me and I cannot. I care not if he finds all of London over there."

"It is wider on this side," the boy called, only his head appearing around the corner. "And I think we can make a climb to the top—to safety—if we can use the ropes. Come on. All of you. But take care. It's slippery."

"I will not budge from this spot," Mrs. Cleary insisted, hugging her babe against her breasts.

Her husband's eyes widened, and his face, already reddened by the biting cold, reddened still more as he gathered a bit of her dress bodice in one fist and drew her to him.

"In the twelve years of our marriage, Bertha Anne, I have never struck you to cause hurt—though there have been many times I would have paid a month's wages for the privilege. But if you do not follow me now and still your tongue, I will beat the living daylights out of you."

The big woman blinked and her mouth opened and closed, but no sound came from her. Her husband took the babe and handed it to another man who lashed it to his chest with a sash and flattened his back against the cave wall. He inched his way sideways, forcing himself not to look down, moving so slowly it seemed that he did not move at all. He tottered once when the babe let out a wail, but righted himself and went even more slowly. No one dared to breathe until he had disappeared. Mr. Cleary went next, his oversized two-year-old daughter tied to his own narrow chest, his lips moving in silent prayer. He too worked to the end and disappeared. In a moment, he was in sight again, his hands clear. He moved back along the ledge for a few feet and reached an arm toward his wife.

"Now, Bertha Anne, only think. You are trim and dainty—flat-rumped as you were the day I married you. Remember how you used to dance, your tiny feet in those satin slippers? Come on now, my girl, my little darling."

The woman squealed as the man behind her, impatient with her hesitation, jabbed her in the small of her back with his finger.

"Do not look below, precious," her husband coaxed, as she began. "Only come to me. Come and get yourself a big kiss. Come, my darling."

The man behind her started after her, ready to steady

her if she needed it. They too disappeared around the corner and a loud cheer went up. Karalee was next, her knees quivering as if they could not support her weight. Then Jeremy, with Daniel, who screamed in protest. Finally they all found themselves on a wide, flat stretch of rock, slippery with slime and sea life, but wide enough to rest themselves and high enough to be out of reach of the spoon drift.

The Clearys fell into each other's arms, blubbering like babes. The tall sailor, who had prodded Bertha Anne along her way, swung Karalee off her feet and kissed her with a loud smack on the lips. Then he hugged Jeremy and each of the other men in turn, dancing and singing as if he were full of rum. Jeremy pulled Karalee to him, the babe between them, and began to kiss her cheeks, her forehead and the tip of her nose. They laughed, trembling against each other, weak with exhaustion and from the cold. At least they were on solid ground. For the moment, no one gave a thought to what would await them now.

"Halloo down there," came a call from the red-bearded lad, who had climbed the rocks ahead of them and now stood far above. He was leaping and waving his arms frantically. "There are houses! Did you hear me? Houses? And people. There will be firesides and warm blankets. Food. Hot tea. Hurry along. We are saved!"

Nineteen

"There is a farm in Reedsville, a town not far from Philadelphia—rolling hills and fertile land. It awaits me, surely enough, and I see it before me when I lay myself down to sleep each night. But I have lost the money that was to have made it mine. It sits in the stomach of some fish or perhaps at the bottom of the sea." Albert Cleary huddled beneath his blanket, grinning as if the loss of all his possessions mattered little. "Therefore, I see no urgency in getting to the colonies. What would I do there? America is no kinder to the destitute than our own England. And so Quebec will serve me as well. A man can make a fine living for his family there. I see no earthly reason to make the long, dangerous trek."

"But the friends you have said are awaiting you in Philadelphia . . ." Karalee argued.

"Let them wait."

Bertha Anne reached over to squeeze Karalee's hand. "We have grown fond of you, my pet, and of your young man. The baby, Daniel, is as one of my own. You, too, should remain in Canada with us."

"She is right, my dear," Albert Cleary offered. "The way is arduous. What is it—three hundred miles?—of river with rough waters and rapids, and yourselves only in a canoe? And the portage? However will the two of you manage it? Walking through stinking bogs and tangled forests, thick with savages—and with a child!"

"My family waits in Philadelphia. My father would die of grief if I did not arrive."

155

"Ah, the confidence of the very young," Albert Cleary said. "How do any of us survive it?"

The inhabitants of the settlement they had stumbled upon were mostly Frenchmen who spoke little English. The only women who lived there were their Indian wives. But there was warmth and food and the language barrier mattered little. The sprinkling of cabins had been hastily built, with dried mud filling the chinks between the logs to hold out the wind. The floor they slept upon was packed earth and only a blanket served for a door. But it had been months since Karalee had felt so snug, and sleep came easily. She woke with the first rays of the sun to find Jeremy propped on one elbow, looking down at her.

"I have it figured," he began, when he saw her eyes opened. "I can take work in Quebec and save until we can afford to take a proper ship to America."

Karalee swallowed the ache in her throat. "Hundreds have walked. I can do the same."

"But I have it all in my head. From Quebec, the fare for the three of us would be . . ."

Karalee touched a finger to Jeremy's lips to silence him. "The three of us, is it? Poor Jeremy! What of the freedom you treasure? Now you are willing to take a job—for me?"

His answer was an urgent kiss that sent streams of warmth through her entire body and robbed her of her breath. He would have kissed her again, had she not turned her head away. It was not until that moment that she realized there was a danger here. What would she have done had she not found Jeremy? What would she do if he were not here? Yet she could not—would not—hurt him. He was too good.

"I am not ready for love, Jeremy," she managed. "I am not sure I ever will be again."

He looked as if she had slapped him. But then he recovered himself and grinned. The only hurt remained in his eyes.

"What is this chatter of love? Is it love that has caused me to kiss more girls than I can ever count? Girls whose faces I cannot even remember?"

"Would you go to Quebec and take a job if you were not tied to me and Daniel?"

He groaned. "Of course not."

"What would you do?"

156

He scratched his head. "I would take a canoe if I could get one—or build a raft, if I could not—and float where there was water, and walk where there was not. I would get to Philadelphia where I am known and borrow from men who trust me. Enough to buy a little from the sailors at the docks for peddling. It would not take me long to begin again."

"And so we will walk together. I am strong."

"I would have thought as much when I saw you first. But there is much less of you now. There are bones where there were nice cushions of flesh. A good wind would send you skyward. You have not the strength you imagine you have."

"If fat means strength, you would blow away with me," she said giggling.

Jeremy had been thin when he began the voyage, but now his chin was a point and his legs were long pipe stems in the leather breeches their rescuers had supplied to him. His weather-tan had faded, his face was drawn, and he looked years older. Only his blue eyes held the same boyish twinkle.

"I imagine you regret you ever introduced yourself to us that first day aboard ship," Karalee said solemnly. "You would have found the way much easier alone."

"I have many things to regret in my life, Karalee. But gazing upon you will never be one of them. No matter what troubles come from it, I will always feel the same."

Suddenly, Jeremy's face turned grim and Karalee realized with a start that he was jealous. Jealous of a man who was dead. She wished now that she had never told him about Patrick.

Twenty

They had traveled more than fifteen miles as far as Jeremy could calculate, before they found the village they had been promised would be only ten miles away. And a sorry-looking village it was. Most of the houses had been nailed with boards across their fronts and leaned as if the slightest ripple of wind would topple them.

Only one man stood on the shore. Unshaven, with filthy, tattered clothes and muddy rags wound about his feet for shoes, he watched, hollow-eyed, as Jeremy brought in the canoe and secured it. Another man, dressed even more shabbily than the first, appeared in the clearing, a rifle in his hands. A third—an Indian—rose from his squatting position in front of a dying fire. His hair had been shaved off, except for a narrow strip in the center, which was fastened with the rattles of a snake. Karalee's heart sank as she looked about her. But when she heard the bleating of a goat, none of the desolation mattered. There would be milk for Daniel.

The man with rags for shoes laughed and pushed away the colored beads Jeremy offered in exchange for a portion of milk. "Do I look like a damned Injun to want such pretties as that? Save your treasures for those savages you will meet along your way. They might save your scalp. Though I doubt it."

"I did not mean to insult you," Jeremy explained. "It is only that I have nothing else to offer in return for your hospitality."

It was true enough. The canoe, which Jeremy had bought at the settlement in exchange for a pocket watch he had saved from the shipwreck, along with a few trinkets, such as the beads, were their only possessions. The canoe was lightweight—made of white birchbark, gummed with resin and sewn with tree roots. A green bear and a vermilion sun along with the face of a devil were painted upon its sides, and other symbols Karalee could not comprehend. The Indian who had made the trade had worn his head shaved in the same manner as this one. Jeremy explained that the strip of hair—the scalp lock—was a courtesy, left so that the one who was victorious in a battle could claim it as a trophy.

"You are welcome to your milk," the man said, "though it will do you little good. You are a madman to bring a child of that size on such a trip. And the woman? I have seen Iroquois braves shed blood to win a woman with the face and udders of a cow. This one—with her beauty—could set off a full-sized battle. If you must continue on with her, dress her in skins. Breeches. Chop off her hair or tuck it beneath a hat. Though I doubt it would fool any of them. I would wager they have already picked up her scent."

Jeremy cleared his throat uneasily. "I was told there was a peace made with the Indians here. A treaty."

"A treaty?" The man's smile showed jagged yellow teeth. "Why should the poor savages keep a white man's peace when the white man does not keep it himself? This peace you speak of is a fragile thing."

"But the tribes have scattered. We were told there were only a few left."

"How many does it take to lift your scalp, lad?" The other man moved closer and began to scrape at his teeth with a knife blade. "Let us say there are enough of them to do the job.

"The nations in this part of the country are unlike many of the others. The women have great power. Though they do not sit in the longhouse council, they have a big say in the decisions their men make."

"Ah, there is a peace," the first man said. "But the peace is made by chiefs. Young braves will listen more readily to their women who call for vengeance than they will to the words of their leaders."

He dug an elbow into Jeremy's ribs. "It is so with men of any color, is it not? Look how you, yourself, risk your scalp to lie beside this woman and receive her favors. I am Isaiah Pershoff—and not at all the bounder you take me to be. I am kin through marriage to a cousin of Ethan Allen. This here is Seth Small. Green Mountain boys, we were, if you know your history. We learned enough of these forests in those days to move about in them with our eyes closed if we had to. We cut down timber and built the very ships that won the war of freedom. Still, we know to keep eyes in the back of our heads where Indians are concerned. We keep our muskets handy."

"Why do you remain here if you must live in fear?" Karalee asked.

"I did not say we live in fear—only that we are wary and trust nothing as a certainty. That is the secret of keeping alive as long as I have, no matter where you choose to make your home."

They feasted on lyed corn fried in grease and dried strips of pemmican over rice. The berries that had been pounded along with the beef and then dried were what gave it the agreeable sweet taste, Karalee was told, and she was well-satisfied as she lay down to sleep, watching the mist gather over the water. There was a chill in the air that warned of an early winter, but it did not reach her skin through her blankets. She had never heard so many night noises: the chirp of the cricket, the shrill laugh of the loon, the rushing water along the dark bank and the night scream of the wildcat. But with Jeremy so close she could hear his breathing, she was not afraid.

She would have given in to sleep easily, had it not been for the devil mosquitos that feasted upon her and left a mass of swollen bites. Isaiah, fortunately, supplied her with a small square of netting, sufficient to keep them from getting to Daniel, but Karalee was unable to rest for the itching.

"Here, little lady." Isaiah squatted beside her and held out a sheet of bark which contained a blackish-looking paste. "Rub this well into your skin."

"What is it?"

"Gunpowder and high wine mostly. It will help. Take it."

Karalee accepted it with thanks and, in spite of its foul smell, did as she was told.

They arose before the sun to the smell of Isaiah's breakfast on the fire, ate hurriedly, clasped hands in goodbye and pushed off. The canoe scraped its bottom along the pebbled shallows until it floated free, rocking slightly as it moved toward the center of the lake, where some young gulls, trying their wings, fluttered for safety.

The autumn had begun to rob the green from the land. Seed heads had formed on the goldenrod and the woods were rusty. The vines that crawled along the forest floor were reddening, the birches were yellowish and maple leaves had begun to fall. Would they make it through this savage country, Karalee wondered, before the frost came? Before the ice and snow? Would they make it through at all?

So far things had gone well. The goat's milk had not given Daniel colic. But if they were unable to find a fresh supply tomorrow, she would have to try the mash an Indian woman at the settlement had prepared for her. It was made from pulverized butternuts and dried meat, pounded into a powder, to be mixed well with boiling water. Indian babes, left without their mothers, thrived on it, the woman told her. It was to be poured into a dried bear gut with a bird quill tied to one end as a nipple. The whole thing could be opened out for rinsing clean and for airing. But Karalee was not eager to try it. Poor little Daniel had been through enough changes already.

They spent the night in a friendly Indian village Isaiah had told them about where the waters rushed, then shallowed and the banks almost touched, as if a giant hand had pinched them together. Jeremy traded the chief Karalee's dress, ragged and dirty as it was, for a pair of scarlet leggins and a blue smock shirt Karalee could wear with a string looped at the waist. As Isaiah had suggested, she braided her hair after washing it in the stream, and tucked it under a squashed hat the Indians gave her to go with it.

Jeremy doubled over with laughing at the sight of her. "I will have to keep you looking this way, so that I do not find myself yearning for you." He dunked one finger in a puddle of mud and drew a line down the center of her face. "That completes the picture."

They sat on a mat under the sky where a pot of corn was passed to be scooped out by handfuls. Karalee's wooden dish was filled for her when she appeared too timid to serve herself. There was fish, leaf bread, squash, wild peas, and mushrooms.

"Esa dekoni," the chief said, jabbing his thumb at Karalee's plate when she had pushed it aside, too full to eat any more.

"He is telling you to eat," Jeremy whispered to her.

"But I cannot. There is not room in me for another mouthful."

"It is a terrible insult to them not to eat what you are given. Try."

"Esa dekoni," the chief repeated and all eyes were upon Karalee as she forced spoonful after spoonful into her mouth until all of it was gone.

"Niawe," Jeremy said when the meal was through, poking Karalee in the side so that she would say the same.

"Niu," said the chief's wife, smiling as if what they had said pleased her.

"But they gave us twice as much as they took themselves. How could they expect us to eat so much?"

"They have learned from their dealings with the white man that he is a glutton. Their own people are taught from the cradle to stay always a little bit hungry. This way they are better able to withstand the hardships of famine."

Karalee liked the early mornings, when the waters were often calm, with hardly a ripple—clear green changing in places to a dull, reddish brown. She could catch glimpses of a white-tailed deer feeding upon the shore or a fat bear drinking his fill along the curved sandy bank. The little canoe would sail past a dense fringe of rushes and then into a place where the branches reached out to them, overhanging the stream, dipping into the water. In the warmth of the early day's sun, it was difficult to imagine how chilly the nights had become.

But sometimes the river would run a frothy blue and there would be rapids and they would have to pole their way to shore. Here, they were forced to carry the canoe, moving only a short way before setting it down and going back for the provisions and for the babe. Then they would carry it again, set it down, and return for provisions. Light as it was, the canoe was a burden for only the two of them. Jeremy had to take most of the weight, but still Karalee's knees would buckle and her back would feel as if it were about to break before a long portage was finished.

Sometimes the wind would rise and the blackening sky would not warn them of the coming of a thunderstorm before it was upon them. By the time they were able to bring their canoe to shore and turn it over their heads for shelter, they would be drenched. They clung together, shivering in their discomfort. Karalee would take Daniel up and rock him, tickling his chin to make him laugh and often scolding to quiet his wailing.

"Let the lad be," Jeremy would tell her. "He is speaking my feelings exactly."

Karalee would find him staring at her, his eyes burning and his lips dry, and she knew that he was not talking about the discomfort of the cold and wind. He would rise abruptly, his chin jutting, his expression fierce, and he would stalk away to stand by himself until his feelings had passed. When he came back, he would try to pretend all was well, but he would be short-tempered and snarl at her, which was not his way.

This day had been their hardest yet. Their walk had taken them through an icy bog which had risen up around their ankles and they had been forced to remove their moccasins and wade barefoot. Karalee's eyelids were swollen and they twitched and burned. She woke repeatedly, crying out in her sleep.

The morning's light had not touched their encampment, yet Karalee lay awake and she could feel that Jeremy, who lay close beside her, was awake too, though his eyes were closed. A loon broke the silence, its voice like an evil, taunting laugh. It sounded again, more ugly and shrill than before, as if in answer to the call of the first and Karalee felt Jeremy stiffen.

"I despise that . . ." she began, but his hand covered her mouth before she could finish.

They had cut a line of bushes the night before and set them along the shore as a screen and so it was difficult to make out any forms in the still-dim light, but Karalee could hear the soft pulling of paddles and the movement of a canoe, perhaps two of them, through the water. She crawled to one side and stretched her neck so that she could peer through a parting of branches. Then she saw them. Indians. At least ten of them. But they did not look like any of the others she had seen. They were painted with stripes of black and red—on their faces and their arms.

Some of them had skulls of white drawn upon their chests.

Suddenly there was the crack of a rifle and a moan. Jeremy pushed Karalee down and rolled onto his stomach, his rifle cocked and ready to fire. Then came the sound of twigs breaking. Someone was crashing through the brush toward them.

Jeremy yanked Karalee to her feet, snatched Daniel into his arms and they began to run, deeper and deeper into the forest until the trees grew so close together the branches slapped and stung them, jabbed at their eyes and tore their clothes. They crawled on their bellies under some of the fallen trees and climbed over others. At last they fell to the forest floor, gasping for breath.

When Jeremy stirred, Karalee caught his arm. "Surely it is too soon to go back to the river."

"Go back?" Jeremy shook his head and pointed through the trees. "We cannot go back. We must travel by land."

"But the canoe? Our food and blankets?"

"We will have to manage without them."

"You really are a madman," she cried. "The sun is on us now, but by nightfall it will be bitterly cold. How will we warm ourselves?"

Jeremy's answer was a lift of one eyebrow.

"What will we eat?"

"Berries, nuts, bird's eggs."

"And Daniel?" she asked. "Can we feed him these things?"

"If we have to. But there is a chance we may find a village of friendly Indians or a white settlement. Then all your worry will be for nothing. Now we must move."

"I cannot."

"You would be surprised what you can do when you have to." He grinned. "Remember Bertha Anne Cleary and how she walked the edge of that cliff as if she were as nimble as a mountain goat?"

"If I were Bertha Anne I would be smart enough to have stayed with the others. Oh, how I wish I had."

"It is too late for wishes, Karalee. Up with you now."

He pulled her to her feet and for a moment held her crushed so tightly against him that it seemed with only a little more pressure he could break her in two.

"Should one of these Indian braves get his hands on you," he said, "he will not hold back his desire for you as I

165

have learned to do. I am not sure you fully appreciate my strength of character. I am not sure either how long I can . . ."

There was the sound of snapping twigs and Jeremy spun around, throwing Karalee behind him. But there was no use in it. They were surrounded by Indians.

Twenty-one

The Indian women gathered along the oozy bank to watch as Karalee stripped off her mud-caked leggings and smock and stepped into the icy stream, gritting her teeth so that she would not shiver and show weakness. The men were, she had been assured, all in the longhouse, in Council, and so would be until the sun was high. There were many things of importance for them to speak of.

The women giggled and pointed at her, rocking back on their heels and hugging themselves with glee. "Your skin white as belly of fish," one of them explained.

None seemed to know what she meant when she asked for soap and so she bathed herself without it. She was brought a scarlet smock that reached almost to her knees—worn, but clean, and closer fitting than the one she had discarded. Next she was given dark leggings, tied at the knees and for her head, a small beaded cap. A little girl knelt at her feet to help her on with her new moccasins and another stepped forward to place a string of colored stones about her neck.

She was about to study her reflection in the water when she saw an Indian brave standing only a few feet from her—so still that she had not noticed him before. He wore only skin-tight buckskin breeches laced up the sides. The bare skin of his chest and arms shone as if polished with oil. His black hair, unlike that of the other braves, was left flowing and his eyes were the same light copper color of his skin. He stared at her, unblinking, as if she were still unclothed. It was an expression she had seen on other men, and one which did not need voice to interpret.

Karalee felt a hotness through cheeks. "Why is that one not in the longhouse with the other men?"

"Tonaoge not sit in Council while shadows fill his dreams."

"His dreams?" Karalee echoed. "He seems very much awake."

"His dreams truth," the woman said.

"And is he allowed to watch as the women bathe?"

"He not see. His thoughts with spirit messenger."

"No—no, please," Karalee cried, running toward the old woman, Osinoh, who had begun to unwrap Daniel for the same icy dunking she had been subjected to. "He will become ill."

Osinoh laughed, her face crinkling into a hundred narrow lines beneath her eyes and down her cheeks. "Water not make sick."

"It will if it is too cold."

The younger women who had been watching, laughed along with the aged one, until she lifted a hand to silence them. "When Indian born, he washed with snow if land is white. We do each day to harden him. He grow strong."

"But Daniel is not used to such cold, you see. Only let me warm it for him a little." Karalee eased the babe gently from the woman's arms. As she took him, Daniel let out a howl, punching the air with angry little fists.

The Indian woman hooted. "He cry much."

"All babes cry."

"Indian babes do not. We swaddle on cradle-board. Safe like inside mother. All time. He cry only when unwrapped."

It is no wonder, Karalee thought, if unwrapping meant an icy bath. But she said nothing. As if Daniel could be bound onto such a board. He was no longer content merely to lie on his back and play with his toes. He was able to roll over now and crawl on his knees and in the last few days he had begun to pull himself to his feet. He would be harder than ever to confine.

"When will I be allowed to see Jeremy?" she asked the old woman, who seemed to have rule over all the others. "They have kept him locked away since we were brought here."

"Ha, oneh!" the woman said, touching her fingers to her lips.

"But I must see him. To know that he is all right."

"Not for me to say."

"Where is he?"

The woman backed away and the others closed around her so that Karalee could not follow.

"One of you must know where they have taken Jeremy, the man who was captured along with me. Won't you tell me?"

When none would answer, Karalee turned to the brave who still stood beneath the white birch tree, watching.

"If the women are not allowed to speak of it, won't you tell me then?"

There was a flicker of understanding in his eyes as they slid from her face to her feet and back again. Still he said nothing.

"He not hear your words." The girl who spoke was very young, shorter than Karalee, but with full breasts and wide hips. Her skin was a smooth light-brown and her eyes bright—tilted slightly upward at the corners. She would have been extremely beautiful had her face not been so round and her figure so plump. She wore her hair parted in the middle in sleek braids that hung over either shoulder.

"I can tell he understands me," Karalee argued. "It is clear from the way he looks at me."

"He not hear," the girl repeated.

It was no use. The women who could not speak her tongue were not able to answer her questions and those who could speak, would not. There was nothing for her to do but wait until the Council meeting had ended. On the first few days of her capture, she had been confined in one of the houses, its door barred. She had been given food and water, but no one would speak to her. Now they had evidently decided she would not try to escape, as she was allowed to roam freely, except for the longhouse and another windowless cabin set apart from the others where she had decided Jeremy was being held. She had ventured near it once, but two young men, their arms smeared with red paint, had barred her way and she had not tried again.

The village was a scattering of log houses, some small and some very large, in the middle of a pleasant meadow. On all sides were fields of corn, ready for harvesting.

"The great bear is in the heavens," she had heard them say.

She had watched the women as they walked down the rows, tearing off ears of corn and throwing them into harvest baskets, which when filled were emptied into huge piles in front of the lodge. Old women stood over steaming iron pots, cooking a thick corn soup, which Karalee had been served that morning, and every morning since her arrival. She had found it delicious.

At night the old men sat before their fires until very late, smoking pipes and telling what must have been tales of adventure, judging by the excitement in the eyes of the young boys who sat around them listening. Women sat upon the ground, chattering, their eyes dancing, as they stripped down husks of corn and braided them. Many of the young braves, though it was not expected of them, sat down with them to help, simply for the pleasure of the maidens' company. How Karalee envied them the pleasure they took in their simple chores! It reminded her of the harvesting and the barn-raisings young people took part in back home and she began to lose all her fears.

Today all work had ceased. The women had bathed themselves in the stream and Karalee had been brought outside with orders to do the same. It was the beginning of their Corn Harvest Festival and preparations were being made for a celebration of thanksgiving that would last four days. Its details were the reason for the meeting in the longhouse.

Anxious as Karalee had been to be admitted to the Council so that she could ask about Jeremy, her courage left her when the door opened and a grim-faced brave, his shoulders draped with a blanket, beckoned for her to enter.

The elm-bark walls and roof of the longhouse were lashed together on strong poles. An opening in the roof let out much of the smoke from the firepit and from the pipe tobacco, but not all of it. Karalee's eyes burned so that tears came into them, and rolled down her cheeks.

Iron pots and strings of braided corn hung thickly from horizontal beams and a high shelf held cooking utensils, weapons, clothing, and furs. The men sat cross-legged along two walls, except for the chief, a giant of a man in fur robes, who stood before the firepit.

"Spirits of our forefathers do not call for revenge against you," he said. "When Harvest Festival through, Dark Bear

170

will lead you to your people. Village two days down river. You not come back."

"I will not come back," she assured him. "And Jeremy? Where is he?"

There was no answer.

"The man who was taken with me. Where is he?"

"Man die."

The room blurred and Karalee felt her knees buckle, but somehow she managed to steady herself and find her voice. "How did he die?"

"Tonight. When moon rise. He die by fire."

Karalee drew in her breath. "Then—he is not dead yet?"

"He walk. He talk. But he die."

"Why? What has he done to you?"

"He die by fire when moon rise," the chief repeated, widening his eyes. "Da neh hoh. Sah Nee Wah."

"Enia ehuk," the seated braves murmured.

The chief's eyes were very black and close set. He wore a ring of silver in his nose and others hanging from his ears. A black cap of skins sat upon his head, decorated with bits of silver and bright feathers. His countenance was so fierce that Karalee wanted to run from him. But she could not.

"May I see him?" she asked.

Certain the chief would refuse her request, she was preparing an argument in her mind, but he clapped his hands together solemnly, and the brave who had brought her into the longhouse beckoned again for her to follow.

"Honio," he grunted, pushing her into the cabin she had not been allowed to enter.

There was greased paper upon the windows and with the door closed, there was little light. She could not, at first, force herself to meet Jeremy's eyes. She could only wonder, miserably, if it would be her lot again to watch someone she cared for die—and by the horrible death that burning would bring. She would rather die herself.

"Who in hell are you?"

The man who squinted up at her from his seat on the packed earth was not Jeremy.

Twenty-two

"You aren't an Indian." The man rose to his knees, leaning forward to get a closer look at her. His hair was light-colored and cropped unevenly as if done quickly with a dull-edged knife. A mud-covered bandage lay across his forehead and over one eye. He sat back again and let his head rest against the wall. "If you are supposed to be a gift those savages have sent to while away my lonely hours, sweetheart, you will have to come back later. My head is pounding."

"Who are you?"

"Helmut Tiebout, if the name is what you want. Trapper, if it's what I am that concerns you. I would guess you are the one who put me in here."

"I? I do not understand."

"Your canoe. All that bright paint on the side of it. It was yours, wasn't it? Even pulled beneath those boughs, who could miss it? I had run as far as the bend and nearly into the thick of the forest without being spied. They would have missed me. Paddled right on past. But they spotted that damned canoe and shot at the first thing that moved. Me." He touched his bandage gingerly.

"It was you who cried out."

"Hell yes. I'm no Indian. Shoot a hole as big as a fist into an Iroquois and he'll grit his teeth and smile at you. Me? I don't stand up to pain well."

"There was a man with me when I was captured. Do you know what they have done with him?"

He shook his head. "That bullet put me to sleep—who

173

knows how long? But unless he has committed some horrendous sin against them, I wouldn't worry about him. These people have 'sat under the great tree of peace,' as they say. They aren't as bloodthirsty as most of their kind. In a day or two, they'll let me out of here. The Great Chief, Ayendes, will flare his nostrils and shake turtle shells at me and yammer about how I have angered the spirits of his forefathers. They've gathered in the longhouse to decide what will be done with me. But I don't worry. If they banish me forever from this part of the country, I'll find other places for my traps."

"Then you do not know?"

"Know what?" He lifted an eyebrow.

Karalee hesitated, remembering what the man had told her about not standing pain well. There was no use in causing him hours of anguish by telling him so soon what had been planned for him. She was nearly certain now that the burning the chief had spoken of was for Helmut Tiebout. Not for Jeremy.

"Nothing. I only wondered what you could have done to offend them."

"I told you. They are not bloodthirsty. And it's true. Unless there is a dream of it. They believe that to deny a dream is to sin against the Great Spirit who sends his prophecy as a gift. As we might ask, 'What did you do today?' they ask, 'What did you dream?' When a man awakens, he is required to act on his dream—whatever it might be. You're from Ireland, aren't you? I like the soft way you Irish slur your words, and the way your voices rise and fall as if you are singing. You've a wild kind of beauty, quite like one of these savages. I had an Irish—that is, I knew an Irish girl once. Her hair was black and flowing, like yours. Not twisted and powdered and . . ."

"What did you mean when you said a person is expected to act on his dreams?"

"Dream you are bathing and you must strip yourself and jump into the river to do so. No matter if you have to break the ice first. Dream you are being burned, and you must roll yourself through flames until you are cooked to whatever extent you were burned in your dreams."

"What was it that you dreamed?"

"Me? Little sweetheart, do you suppose I would be foolish enough to repeat such a dream if I had it? Hell, no. It was not my dream. That is, not a dream I actually

174

dreamed—but rather one I made up. You see, there is a brave among them who has a special gift. He's a kind of village dreamer. Something goes wrong with the harvest, or one of them becomes ill—" he snapped his fingers. "Tonaoge disappears into the forest and does his best to dream about it. Though I would suspect he sneaks off to a nearby village for a little—what they call 'gaknowehaat'—with a pretty squaw who is willing. Then he returns to tell of some dream he has had. His dream is acted on and all is well—no one the wiser. Or perhaps I judge him by what I might do myself in such a case."

"I saw Tonaoge," Karalee said, remembering the penetrating stare of the brave who had watched her bathing. "His dream concerned you then?"

"Not directly. You see, he has a little beauty of a squaw. She is—" he paused, as if trying to phrase his description so that Karalee would not be offended. "She is comely. Very rounded and soft. Perhaps too rounded for some. But that is how I like my women. There must be something substantial I can squeeze with both hands. I do not like to lie upon bones." He slapped his hands against the sides of his buckskin jacket. "I don't suppose you were given a little tobacco for me?"

She shook her head.

"Only a pinch would do me. But they wish to make me suffer, I suppose. They know I love my tobacco. There is a special blend they have with sumac leaves . . ."

"Finish your tale, please. They may come for me at any moment."

"I watched Desiio grow and ripen. My traps had brought me among these people for years. It got to be more than I could bear. I had to have her. You understand. No—I suppose you don't. When Tonaoge went away this last time, I had my own dream all made up. I told Desiio that in my dream, a spirit had appeared to me in the form of a bird. The bird told me that Tonaoge had been vexed by dark spirits while he was in the forest—great believers in witchcraft, these Indians. I warned her that she must lie with me to protect herself. That she must not allow Tonaoge to enter her, unless I were to enter her first. Protection, you see. If she did not, she would be vexed by the spirits of darkness too, and any babe who came from their issue."

"Ochone! Such wickedness!"

Helmut grinned and patted the ground beside him. "Sit

here, won't you, sweet? I can talk better if I do not have to bend back my head to see you."

"No! Please go on."

He frowned. "I've told you all there is to tell. Except I did not realize that to their way of thinking, only the dreams of a red man can spring from good. The dream of a white man may be truth, but it comes from evil. Whoever has a dream that pretends to foresee the future, is in the power of the faceless ones." He began to laugh as if it were a joke.

And so they planned to burn him and his evil spirit along with him, Karalee realized. "I do not think you should take this so lightly, Mr. Tiebout."

"I would do it all over again," he said, setting his teeth in a wide smile, his eyes shining with a strange light. "When Desiio lay with me, she was quivering inside with fear and that made it all the more exciting. You understand? There is nothing to touch making love to a woman who fears you. Nothing. Is there any man you fear, sweet? I doubt it. You would stare the devil himself down to his heels."

"Mr. Tiebout . . ."

"Strange about women. Mindless creatures. Desiio. Who would think I should have to caution her to keep it our secret? When Tonaoge returned, damned if she didn't run to meet him with the tale of how she had saved him and their future children from the spirits of darkness. I could not believe it. I headed for the trees as quickly as I could. Didn't even wait to pick up my rifle."

"There must be a way you can escape. You are not heavily guarded. Perhaps when they open the door . . ."

"Why did they send you to me?" he asked, studying her.

"They did not send me."

"Is it true that a woman comes a poor second to whiskey in the passions of an Irishman?"

"Mr. Tiebout, you would do well to consider your predicament."

"I know these people. Now that the heat of Tonaoge's anger has cooled, I do not fear him—or any of them."

"Perhaps you should."

Karalee disliked the man intensely. There was little doubt he deserved punishment. But certainly not death. She could not allow him to sit calmly, believing he was safe, giving him no warning of his terrible danger. She was about to tell him what she knew of the decision in the long-house, when the door flew open and the brave who had escorted her here motioned for her to leave.

"You go."

"Only one moment . . ."

The Indian gripped her shoulders, not roughly, but with a firmness she could not wrest herself from, and led her out.

"Mr. Tiebout," she cried, "you must try. Believe me, you must."

The door slammed between them and the brave stood in front of it, his arms folded across his chest.

"You go now," he said.

Twenty-three

Karalee threw aside the bearskin that covered the opening of the log shelter and drew in her breath, throwing her hands to her face. "Praise be to Heaven. You are safe."

"I am more than safe," Jeremy said, extending a spoonful of the soup he was eating. "I am warmed, rested, my belly is full to bursting, and I am as refreshed as a new babe."

"I can see that."

The two young girls who had been bathing him let their cloths drop into their basins of water, and backed from the room, giggling.

"Have you tasted this soup?" Jeremy asked.

"I have." Karalee clenched her fists against her sides.

"Is it really so tasty, or is it only that I have tasted nothing palatable for so long?"

"Jeremy," Karalee cried, unable to contain her anger any longer. "Where have you been?"

"Why, right here. Where did you suppose I had gone?"

"Have you any idea how worried I have been? When they told me the man who had been captured with me would be burned, I . . ."

"Yes, I heard about that. The poor wretch."

"I thought it was you who were to be burned."

"Nonsense. Why would they want to burn me?"

"But I have not seen you since the day we were taken."

"I have not been allowed to leave this room. My leg. It's been so bound up that I could not walk on it. They bathed it with water hot enough to boil my blood, they soaked it in such a foul-smelling brew, I could hardly stand to breathe in the same room with myself, and they packed it with mud and leaves until I wanted to hack it off and say, 'Here, take it.' But would you believe it is beginning to heal?"

Karalee threw back the covers and gasped at the puckered line, jagged and enflamed, that ran halfway up his thigh.

"Dear Sainted Mother," she said. "You did not tell me your leg had not yet closed properly. You did not even complain as we walked ankle-deep in that bog. How painful it must have been for you."

"It did not tickle." He caught her wrist and yanked, so that she sat beside him on his cot. "And so you were concerned about me, were you?"

Jeremy's face was red and raw-looking as if he had been freshly shaved and not too expertly. A knick on his cheekbone showed a narrow trickle of blood. Karalee wiped it away gently with a bathing cloth and brushed back a wiry strand of hair from his forehead. She bent to plant a firm kiss upon his brow.

How anguished the thought of losing him had made her feel! And how good it was only to touch him now. Perhaps what she felt for him actually was love. She could no longer tell. Too much had happened—too much was yet to be. There was no time to waste in prattling or in examining her feelings.

"Of course I was concerned about you." She stood and moved away from him. "As I am concerned about Mr. Tiebout now."

"About who?"

"The man they plan to kill this night. Jeremy, there must be a way to stop them."

"The two of us—and me with only one good leg?"

"I was hoping you could think of something."

"I can only think that you are safe—and Daniel—and I. In a few days we will be on our way again and before long we will have reached our destination. I am sure of it now. I feel it in every inch of me. Then I will take care of you for the rest of your life. A wonderful life it will be too. Not like some. Where a man and woman live together so long that they stay married only because they have no heart to begin fresh with someone new. You will never be sorry."

"Jeremy, a man is going to die. I must do what I can to stop it."

"How many good men and women died aboard the *Gallant Lady*—and children too, Karalee? How many are dying in the land you have fled? There is nothing we could do to save them and there is nothing we can do to save this man. But there is a great deal we can do to hurt ourselves. These people have beliefs that you and I cannot understand. This man sinned against them. In their eyes his death is right and necessary. Defend him too strongly and we may end up alongside him."

"I must try."

"I am not sure the man is worth saving."

"Is it for us to judge?"

"I am asking you—no, I am telling you—to stay out of it. Go to your cabin and remain there until it is over."

Karalee stared at him in disbelief. "Will you be able to lie upon that cot, Jeremy Treacher, and listen to his screams of agony? I know that I will not. For if I do, each time I look at you throughout that wonderful life you speak of, I will look at him. We will, both of us, go on hearing his screams forever." She pushed aside the bearskin at the door. "I am sorry."

Twenty-four

The sun had turned the ripples on the lake a bright copper. Swallows and purple finches flitted noisily from tree to tree, as if they had much to accomplish before settling into their nests for the evening. The air was heavy with the odor of pine, roasting corn, ripe wild berries, and with the logs of sumac which burned continually upon the great fire.

Young men in the garb of women had done the Women's Dance, their arms laden with corn, while other men chanted hymns of thanksgiving. Now came the Gagosa, the False Face dancers, who would drive illness and witchcraft from the village. Osinoh had explained to Karalee that there were only three things that caused illness. The first, of course, was injury, wounds received in battle. The second was a wasting away which came from desire—of dreams unfulfilled and not acted upon. The third was from witchcraft, and it was the duty of the Gagosa to drive it out.

The hideous masks the Gagosa wore had been carved from a tree as the tree still lived, and so when cut away, remained alive. Each was a representation of a spirit seen in a dream by the one who carved it. What horrible dreams they must have had! The faces were shades of red and black, with bulging eyes, twisted noses, distorted mouths and long swollen tongues protruding from them. These masks were polished and hung carefully when not in use, coddled and even fed with gruel, as if they were beloved children.

Now the sick were brought before the great fire. Those

who could, walked. Others were carried. The Gagosa blew ashes into their faces, chanting, "Yowige, Yowige, Yowige."

They cooed and gobbled, stomped and crawled on all fours, banging windows and rattling doors, shaking huge turtle-shell rattles.

Karalee had tried again and again to see the Great Chief, Ayendes, to plead on Helmut Tiebout's behalf, but she had been stopped by a brave who made it clear, in spite of the few English words he knew, that she would be locked away if she persisted. Jeremy had been right. There was nothing either of them could do.

Through the trees, well away from the noise and the merriment, she spotted Tonaoge, sitting by himself on a fallen log. Osinoh touched a restraining hand to her shoulder as Karalee started toward him.

"Not speak to Tonaoge now."

"I must," Karalee said. "Perhaps he can save Mr. Tiebout."

"White man die. It is good. For many years we had no harvest. White man burn corn and fields. Fields and fields of corn. In our village. In all villages. They chop our trees. Our children cried with bellies empty."

"Osinoh, it was not Mr. Tiebout who burned your fields."

"Long Knives all as one."

Karalee knew how the woman felt. She, herself, had hated all British and would have gladly seen any of them dead. It was only during her last months she had learned that each man must be judged on his own merit. She knew that there would be no way she could explain this to Osinoh, who had seen so much killing and had felt so much pain.

"Please, let me go to Tonaoge," Karalee begged. "Only let me try."

The woman dropped her hand to her side, and without another word, walked back to the great fire.

"Tonaoge," Karalee began, when she had reached him. "Helmut Tiebout is not a good man and he was wrong in doing what he did. I cannot ask you to forgive him. But how will it help to kill him? Other white men will only come to your village to seek revenge and then what will happen to your peace?"

Tonaoge did not speak. His eyes burned into hers, but

there was no sign in them that he understood. She was not certain he knew any English words.

She dropped to her knees on the ground in front of him. "I do not even know this man, Helmut Tiebout. I saw him for the first time only today. But he is a human being the same as you and me. Please. Have him sent away. Order him never to return. But do not kill him."

Tonaoge was silent.

"I fled from a land far away where blood flowed as freely as it has in the battles you have seen. I have watched men and women and even children tortured, beaten, and starved. I have seen many people I loved die. I left because I thought it would be different in this country. But it is not. Oh dear God, it is not." She reached out with her hand to touch him, but he drew away.

"I cannot bear to see another person murdered. I cannot."

Karalee got to her feet, weeping. She stumbled through the trees, past the great fire, to the log shelter where she had slept since her capture. She threw herself upon her cot, covered her head with the bearskin blanket, and sobbed.

Twenty-five

The drums stopped and so did the chanting. Karalee sat up, listening, waiting. She had never heard such silence. Against her will, she pictured them dragging Helmut Tiebout from his hut. Would he be bound? Or perhaps he would come willingly—smiling and joking, unaware of what was in store for him. Each moment she expected to hear his scream. She gasped, startled, when the blanket at her door flew aside and Osinoh entered, followed by two young maidens.

The old woman clapped her hands, then raised them above her head. "Yeo Ye wayei."

"Why have the drums stopped?" Karalee asked, fearing the answer.

"You dress and come," Osinoh said.

"If it is part of your chief's pleasure to make me watch what he plans to do, he will be disappointed. I refuse to be a witness to murder. You may tell him what I have said. Tell him they will have to bind and carry me."

Osinoh looked pleased. "It is well. Then white man die."

"You mean . . ." Karalee was on her feet. "Osinoh, do you mean there is a chance Mr. Tiebout will be allowed to live? Tell me, is there?"

"Tonaoge have dream. He dream of Tarachiawagon."

"Of who?"

"Tarachiawagon. He-who-hold-up-sky. Tarachiawagon say Tonaoge to take white woman to his hut for one moon. To lie with her. White woman will be as fire. Burn evil from him."

187

The maidens giggled and nudged each other. "Yeo, gak-nowehaat."

"And if I will not go to him?"

"They not force you." Osinoh folded her arms across her breasts. "Then all will be as should be. White man die by fire."

Karalee allowed herself to be washed and rubbed with perfumed oil. She tried to sink into a trance-like state, so that she could imagine this was happening to someone else. Her hair was brushed by each of the maidens in turn, and then by Osinoh, until it was gleaming and her scalp tingled. She thought of Theresa suddenly, and how they as girls had brushed each other's hair, dressing it, pulling it up, then twisting it back—pretending they were fine ladies preparing to go to a ball. She wondered what Theresa would say now if she knew what Karalee was planning to do. She could almost see the girl's horrified expression and hear her voice, scolding.

Osinoh watched glowering, as the two maidens dressed Karalee in a loose, ruffled shirt of scarlet which left her thighs bared. Then they laced her into scarlet leggings which reached only to her knees. A square, beaded cap of the same bright red was set upon her head and three scarlet feathers were stuck into it.

"Tarachiawagon say spirit of fire live inside you now. You must be color of flame," Osinoh explained.

The blanket at the door moved aside, and the beautiful, but too plump, girl Karalee had spoken with that morning entered the room, smiling. She held out a string of elderberries which she placed over Karalee's head.

"This you take off and put on Tonaoge when you alone in hut," she explained. "Then Tonaoge put string of berries on you."

"What is your name?" Karalee asked gently, knowing the answer before it was given. The girl's appearance matched the description Helmut Tiebout had given of the girl he had taken.

"Desiio," the girl said, stepping back with the others.

"Why do you not tell them that this does not make you happy?" Karalee asked. "Tonaoge is your husband, is he not? Cannot you refuse to share him with another woman?"

"Tonaoge dream truth," the girl said, deep dimples forming in her cheeks when she smiled. "Tarachiawagon most

188

wise. He make victor in battle. He make corn grow tall. He bring beasts to hunt. He say you go to Tonaoge."

There was a rumble of angry voices outside the hut, then a shout. Jeremy burst in, his eyes wild, his face as scarlet as the clothing Karalee wore.

"Ye gods, look at you, naked as a heathen," he stormed. "Is it true? Have you agreed to lie with that savage? To give your body to him? To let him gaze upon you and put his hands upon you? Have you?"

"Yes."

"I did not believe it when they told me. I had to see for myself. I still do not believe it."

"I do what I must."

"A harlot's excuse. A decent woman would not even consider what you are about to do."

"Then I am not decent."

"Does this filthy trapper mean more to you than I? Do you care that I love you? Does it matter that I have made plans for us?"

"It matters very much."

"Then tell them you have changed your mind. We will not wait for my leg to heal. We will leave immediately. Before—it happens."

"I cannot do that."

"Damn you. I am not a handsome man, Karalee. I know that. I am not rich. I only felt my religion now and then when it suited me. You were so beautiful and so fine and good. I could not believe my good fortune in finding you."

"Jeremy, please . . ."

"I used to lie next to you aboard that ship, burning with what I felt for you. Dear God, how I wanted you! I told myself again and again, wait until the time is right. When the two of you are man and wife and the good Lord will smile upon your union. And again, night after night in the forest, only the two of us. Never knowing if we would ever reach civilization. Never knowing if we would live to see another day. Still, I held off, though it was nearly more than I could bear. A little longer, I told myself. Only a little longer."

"Jeremy, please . . ."

"Damn you. I should have ripped off your clothes and taken you. I should have used you again and again, as this savage will do. Because now it will be too late for us."

He walked to the door and stood, silent for a moment, his back to her, as if waiting for her to say something.

"Because when this is over," he said at last, "when he is through with you, I will not want you. Nor will any man worthy of being called a man."

Tonaoge was seated before the fire when Karalee entered, but he rose swiftly and walked to her, his eyes bright in the orangish glow of the coals. He wore only a leather breech cloth about his narrow hips and a thick chain of hammered silver around his neck.

The drums began again, with a slow muffled beat, and there was singing—very close—as if whoever it was, stood just outside the door. Karalee remembered what Desiio had told her and, determined to fulfill her bargain, she removed her elderberry necklace to place it upon Tonaoge. He caught her wrist and shook it until the berries fell to the ground and scattered.

"You not Indian," he said. "And I say you not maiden."

"What makes you say that?"

"My dreams tell much."

"Yes, I know of your dreams."

"You have great love for white man?"

"If you mean Mr. Tiebout, I told you, I hardly know him."

"Then why you come to me to save him?"

"I told you that too. I will not see a man die if I can stop it."

He circled her. Then, standing before her again, he yanked at the strings which held her shirt together. The more he twisted them, the more they knotted. He muttered something Karalee could not understand and dropped his hands.

"Take off shirt. I want to see you."

Karalee did as she was told.

Tonaoge drew in his breath and studied her, bending to take a closer look at her breasts. "You very small, like buds which are not yet flowers."

"Your dream did not tell you that?" she managed.

Tonaoge glared. "I beat women with sharp tongue. Take off all you wear." He pointed to her leggings.

"If I do, then there will be no flame color upon me. Osinoh told me I am to be the spirit of fire." Karalee met his glare and returned it.

Tonaoge grunted and one corner of his mouth lifted as if he were suppressing a smile. "Truth in that," he said. "Take off all you wear."

He knelt before a square, lidded basket and brought out a tiny jar, which he opened and dipped into with two fingers. They emerged a bright red, dripping with paint. Karalee stiffened as he touched his fingers to one breast, circling it with color. He did the same for the other, then dipped his fingers into the jar again and made another figure, like a bolt of lightning, upon her belly. He turned her around and drew more lines upon her back and her buttocks. Then he wiped his fingers on a cloth, folded his arms across his chest and studied her.

"Now you color of flame. Dance for me, as flames dance upon great fire."

"Dance?" she protested. "Oh, Tonaoge, I do not know how to dance."

He wrinkled his forehead. "Not know how to dance? I call someone to show you." He started past her, but she caught his arm. It would be too humiliating to stand naked before another of them.

"Wait. I will dance."

"Ah!" Tonaoge nodded and sank onto the thick rug of animal skins which lay upon the floor close to the fire. Karalee began to sway, feeling very foolish, very conscious of her lack of clothing. She raised her arms slowly over her head, keeping in time with the drums as best she could, swaying from side to side. She stomped her feet and turned, then swayed her hips again. Tonaoge began to laugh and reached his arms for her.

"You speak truth," he said. "You not know how to dance. I will have Desiio show you." He swung her so quickly that her feet left the ground, and she landed with her back against the rug. "Tomorrow."

Tonaoge stood, tore off his neck ornament, and then his breech cloth. He stood over her, his body hard and very muscled, wide-shouldered and narrow-hipped, and for a moment he looked like a statue carved by a people many hundreds of years ago. A statue of an ancient pharaoh or at the very least, a king.

"I call you Dancing Flame," he said, and sank to his knees.

He pressed his mouth against her mouth deeply, more deeply, and yet it was not a kiss, even when his tongue

191

found hers. It was more as if he were tasting her, as if he were trying to breathe in some fragrance which emanated from her. He brushed her hair back from her forehead, pressed his lips there too, then curled a long strand about one finger, letting it fall, then catching it up again, to study it closely in the red glow from the fire.

He buried his nose against first one ear and then the other, nuzzling and breathing into it. His body was hot as if he had been roasting himself a long time before the fire during the time before she came to him. As he continued his inch by inch scrutiny of her, his tasting and flicking of her with his tongue, he began a rhythmic movement of his lower body, hardly noticeable at first, then stronger, catching up the pulsing beat of the drum outside their tent.

"Tonaoge," Karalee whispered, almost frightened by the spell that seemed to have come over him, as if something had taken over his body to make him twitch and move so.

He jerked his head up from her breast, slapped his hands smartly against her hips and frowned. "Woman not talk with tongue. Talk with body. So." He began the movement of his hips again and caught his hands beneath her, forcing her hips to move along with his. "You. Now. Talk with body."

Karalee did as she was told, churning her body to the drum beat as Tonaoge had done. "No stop," he said, pulling back to touch his tongue between her legs so that she would move against it. He sensed when her movement took a life of its own and was not of his direction, and rose to his knees, watching her. He laughed, caught up her hand, opened it, and brushed his lips across her palm. Then he lowered it, nodded, and indicated that he wanted her to take the lead. That he wanted her to guide him into her.

He settled against her and their bodies were as one. It was as though they truly were flames, dancing higher, with greater and greater intensity, until it was over and she floated high above the place where she lay, entirely spent.

"Tomorrow in our tongue mean more than in tongue of white man. Tomorrow mean sometimes a year."

His mouth found hers again. "Or longer. I will keep you very warm through the nights. We will need no fire or blanket. Should we lie together in snow, you and I, snow would melt around us."

And he was inside her again, moving his hips in rhythm with the beat of the drum.

When at last he lay quiet, Karalee found her voice. "Tonaoge, did you truly dream that Tarachiawagon ordered you to take me to your hut? Did he truly tell you that you must lie with me?"

"You sleep," he grunted.

"Did you?"

"I beat women who ask many questions," he answered, pulling her head to his chest. "You sleep."

In the morning, Karalee discovered that Jeremy had gone.

"He said I was to see you to Philadelphia," Helmut Tiebout told her. "Damned if it isn't two weeks out of my way."

"I am sorry to be such a trouble to you," Karalee said, shocked by his ingratitude.

"I know what you're thinking, sweet. But you're wrong. I told you, Ayendes would have done nothing to me. He only wanted to throw a fright into me."

"Then perhaps I should tell them I have changed my mind. That I will not stay out my time here."

"We both know you won't do that, don't we?" He winked. "You're only getting what you wanted all along and I gave you a good excuse to get it and feel noble all at the same time."

"You are a wicked man."

"How is it with an Indian brave, sweet?" He threw his head back and laughed, an ugly high-pitched laugh that shook his whole body. "I hear that women, most of 'em, once captured by Indians, never want to go back to their own beds. Not once they get a taste of . . ."

Karalee slapped his face, but she was off balance, so was able only to catch him with the tips of her fingers. She turned away.

"Dancing Flame," he called after her, still laughing. "That's what your Indian brave calls you, I hear. You must be a hot little wench. Dancing Flame."

He was right in a way. Much as Karalee wanted to leave, much as she needed to reach Philadelphia quickly and find her parents, she knew she would not be wise to leave yet. She was still weakened to the point of becoming ill from her long journey, and her feet were sore and swollen. Daniel needed the weeks of rest from travel, where he would have a cozy bed, warm milk, and a place to crawl and exercise his growing skills.

He was round-faced and healthy, and Karalee had put back most of the weight she had lost by the time they were free to go. Tonaoge arranged for plenty of provisions and a canoe, as well as for a trusted brave to accompany Karalee on her trip, so that Helmut Tiebout would take no advantage of her. But when she looked for Tonaoge to tell him goodbye, he had disappeared. She and Osinoh found him in the same spot he had been sitting the first day she spoke to him.

"Tonaoge," she said, "I wanted you to know that I have grown fond of you and that I will think of you often with joy in my heart. You have been gentle with me when you could have been harsh. Desiio is fortunate indeed to have such a husband."

Tonaoge said nothing.

"He not hear," said Osinoh. "He have dream."

"I see." Karalee blinked back a tear and pressed his hand to her lips before turning away.

When she looked back for what would be her last time, she saw that he was watching her.

Twenty-six

"Goodness me, so you are the daughter, are you? Eliza, will you look here? This is the girl of that poor Nolan family. The girl they supposed had drowned in that shipwreck."

The woman who sat knitting in a sunlit corner near the window raised her eyes briefly from her needles, and smiled a smile that disappeared as quickly as it came. Her cheeks were as red as if someone had dabbed a bit of paint upon each of them, and so they must have, as the rest of her face was as grey as bread dough. "So it is."

"I can tell you exactly when they arrived," the boarding-house keeper, Jacob Whittaker, went on. "It was the last of August. I know because it was the same month that yellow death visited Philadelphia again. So I had rooms for begging. I let these poor bedraggled souls—your family—have two of my best for the pittance they paid. Why not? There was no one else to use them. The town was a ghost. Coaches would not even pass through. They found new routes around Philadelphia. Had we been dependent entirely on what money we took into our pockets from this lodging-house, we would now be destitute."

"My mother and father—my brother and sister. Did they look well?" Karalee asked fearfully. "They were not touched by this yellow fever, were they?"

"No, no. At least not while they were here. But people were falling in the streets. Everyone who was able, fled. The few pedestrians bold enough to venture out held wads of cotton gauze to their noses—so they would not have to breathe the poisoned air."

Jacob Whittaker stopped to rest his short, plump forearms on the handle of his broom. His round face was red and wet with perspiration, more from the excited manner of his speech than from the effort of his sweeping. "And when two of them met, it was most comical to watch the way both would dance about—as they made a pretense of polite conversation. Each trying to get upwind of the other."

"You may make jest of it, Jacob," the woman reprimanded him, her lips drawn together so that they seemed to disappear. "I lost my only brother and two dear sisters that one month. I remember August well and so I always shall."

Karalee allowed them to continue, impatient as she was to know more of her parents.

"The death bells tolled night and day," her husband went on, "until town officials decided that their sound was too disheartening and put a stop to them. There were so many buried in St. Mary's churchyard alone, that there was no time for proper burial. They dug shallow graves, dumped corpses in, and covered the lot of them with hundreds of tons of earth—all at once."

"Where did my family go when they left here?" Karalee asked, when the boardinghouse keeper stopped to take a breath and she saw her chance to interrupt. Daniel was fussing, wriggling in her arms, wanting to get down and crawl.

"Who can say where they went? I was only surprised they stayed as long as they did."

The woman grunted. "And I was only surprised when they left. With a free roof over their heads and food to eat without a penny of cost to them."

"Every few hours the death wagon would rattle by to collect the dead—a sound to chill anyone's bones. It was not many wanted the job of driving one. They used Negroes. Negroes are known to be immune to yellow fever— still it was grim work. There were not enough wagons or drivers to collect all the dead at one time, and so many would have to wait—rotting in the streets. The stench of the dead and dying was unbearable."

Please let him stop speaking of it, Karalee prayed silently. She had not eaten since morning and she felt light-headed, as if she might drop into a faint at any moment.

"The child," the woman said, putting aside her knitting, as if she felt it was expected of her in the name of hospitality. "Let me take him and give your arms a rest. A boy-child?"

"Yes. His name is Daniel."

"There were two infants, were there not?"

Karalee swallowed. "The little girl, Deirdre—died—aboard ship."

"I lost two babes in their first year," the woman said. "Both girls. Then I bore six fat, healthy boys. 'Tis a hard world for women. I told myself it was a blessing when the Lord called them home before they had lived long enough to suffer. And still . . ."

She blinked several times, then stopped speaking. Karalee followed her gaze to the framed sampler, done in colored worsteds, hanging opposite the fireplace wall. It said, "God Bless Our Home." Daniel began to pull at the woman's earlobe, but she did not appear to notice.

"The *Gazette* printed letters advising people how to survive the fever. We were ordered by law to put out our rubbish on the streets Wednesday and Saturdays, instead of merely throwing it into our backyards or into our basements to become putrid."

The woman snapped off a length of yellow yarn and rolled it into a tiny ball for Daniel to play with. "They have learned the true cause of it, but they will not act to remedy it. It is the seeping of juices from those mid-city cemeteries. Polluting the water we drink. They use no lime on the dead, to make the danger less certain."

"Finally, the cold weather came and the fever left. There are only a few cases remaining in the entire city."

"I have traveled so far," Karalee whispered, wishing one of them would invite her to sit. Her many times wet-and-dried moccasins were weather-blackened now and stiff. Her bare toes protruded in several places. "I must find my family soon. Then all will be well."

The man shook his head. "I cannot help you in that, child. They stayed here, as I have said, waiting for their daughter—you—who became separated from them in their homeland. It is a sad story, to be sure, but there are a thousand stories exactly like it. Pick up any newspaper.

You will find heartbreaking letters, begging readers to write if they have any information as to the whereabouts of William Smith or John Jones, who sailed from Liverpool or from Dublin, or from any one of a hundred places on a certain date and on a certain ship. Sometimes the sailing was four or five years ago. Husbands, wives, fathers, sons. The tragic end to most, I would say, is that they never find each other. I would set about, if I were you, beginning your life afresh. Making a home for yourself and for the boy. You have each other."

"I will find my family. I must."

"The man—Mr. Nolan—went down to the Delaware each morning, early, to see the ships that had come in and to inquire of the passengers that arrived on them. My housemaids and serving girls had run off to avoid the fever, and so I was able to give the woman—Mrs. Nolan—work. There was plenty of it with only Eliza and me. And Eliza was not feeling herself, due to the loss of loved ones. I could pay no salary, of course. But I gave them their rooms and the food for their mouths."

"That Mr. Nolan!" The woman made a clicking sound with her tongue and shook her head. "Never lifted a finger to do his share. Once he had the excuse of hearing your ship went down, he spent all his waking hours in those foul places on Race Street and in Jones Alley. The Pewter Platter, the Crooked Billet, the Bull's Head. He kept blubbering that your drowning was all his fault. That he should never have agreed to leave without you. He would come home late, only to stagger up to his bed. My heart went out to the poor brave woman, with two young children to raise—and impudent, wild ones at that—as good as alone."

"Please try to think of something they might have said to you. Something that would hint of where they might have gone. It is so important."

"I have told you." Eliza straightened and wrinkled her nose. "We saw little of the man. I suppose he was afraid we would find honest work for him to do if he stayed about. The woman did little speaking. She was even unfriendly, you might say, considering how good we were to them. Though I did not fault her too much for it. She had a hard lot."

Jacob Whittaker sniffed and wiped his nose upon his sleeve. "They left most unexpectedly. The other man appeared one day and took them off."

"Other man?" Karalee felt her heart leap inside her. "What other man?"

"He was quite young." The boardinghouse keeper touched one finger to his lips and closed his eyes as if trying to form a picture of the visitor. "His hair was dark."

"Black, like yours, and curling," the woman added, her expression softer than it had been before. "Handsome as a young prince, he was. But oh, so thin. Pale as if death itself sat upon his shoulders."

Theo, Karalee thought. Oh, Theo. There was hope now, wasn't there? And comfort in knowing her brother had escaped the British soldiers and that he was with her family—that she might even be able to see him soon. That they might be a family again after all, in spite of where they were and what had happened to them.

"It must have been my brother, Theo," she said. "Was there a young woman with him also?"

She could not imagine Theo fleeing Ireland at all. It was not like him. But it was impossible to think he would have left Loretta Fallon behind. Karalee had seen the way the two had looked at each other—as if only death could separate them.

"He brought no young woman here. Only himself. He broke down and wept—standing right where you are now—when he was told you had perished."

Karalee caught her lower lip between her teeth, feeling what Theo must have felt. To have been subjected to so much pain, to have made such a voyage, and then to find tragic news awaiting him. She was more frantic than ever to be reunited with her loved ones now—to let them know that she was alive and well. But how? Jeremy was somewhere in the city. Despite his anger toward her, she was certain he would help her. But she had no idea how to find him either.

Jacob Whittaker began his sweeping again, but his movements were half-hearted and hardly raised dust. "A woman weeps and I feel pity for her. But I have seen the tears of a woman enough to have become accustomed to the sight. Eliza, for instance, cries if her pudding is not a success, or if her needlework ravels. But the weeping of a man—a strong young man—can wrench the heart from you."

The blazing fire made the room extremely warm, but Karalee had felt so much bitter cold of late that she was comforted by it and by the sparks and crackling noises it made. It was a reposeful room, if not grand. A green frieze sofa sat along one wall before the front windows, with a bright-colored patchwork throw spread over its back. Two deep armchairs stood on either side of the Franklin stove. A round, dark, marble-top table held a shaded kerosene lamp and next to it lay a much-read Bible. A glassfront bookcase—locked—contained many volumes. Karalee could make out only a word or two. Wedged in one corner was a tiny nook-shelf, holding glass bottles, china figures, shells, and a dainty white fan—perhaps a memento of Eliza's girlhood. Had she ever been a girl? Karalee wondered. The woman seemed to have been born with a dour, heavy-lidded expression and tight lips.

"The young visitor told your family through his tears that they were his family now and that he wanted to work to take care of them, if they would allow him to. Then they all wept together, packed up their few rags and they were off."

With a wrinkled nose, Eliza Whittaker stood suddenly, holding Daniel away from her skirt. "This babe is soaked through and me with him. Do you not have anything proper to change him into?"

Karalee felt a flush of embarrassment. "No. We traveled so far today. There was no time to . . ."

Eliza plopped Daniel into her arms before she could finish her sentence and began to brush furiously at her full skirts.

"Young woman." Jacob Whittaker set his broom against the wall and sat heavily in one of the chairs, his fingers twined together in front of him. "Where do you intend to go when you leave this house?"

"That is none of your concern, Jacob," the woman said, throwing him a warning glance.

Karalee thought a moment. She had been so certain she would find her family easily once she located the Whittaker Boarding House on Front Street, that she had made no alternate plans. "I truly do not know."

"You wear the garb of a savage, but Eliza might be able to find an old dress in the attic you may have. So that much can be solved. But your speech. There is no way you can disguise the fact that you are Irish."

Karalee wasn't certain she had heard him correctly. "Why should I wish to disguise it?"

"For the sake of finding employment. True, good help is

200

scarce these days in Philadelphia. There are many openings available for domestic workers—cooks, serving maids. But most advertisements state clearly that Irish need not apply. French, English, African, Dutch, most of them read, but no Irish."

"Why should that be?"

"And I take it you are Catholic?"

"Yes." Karalee felt a fluttering in her stomach. Surely the hatred for the Irish Catholic could not have followed her here, to the land that was said to be a sanctuary for any and all who needed it.

"Impossible! You see, my dear, we have religious freedom in this country. We do not imprison or torment those of the Catholic faith here. Oh, on occasion, a few of our feisty young men will find themselves fired with rum and decide to set flame to one of your churches." He smiled broadly. "But other than that—you are not molested. You must realize we have our freedom too. The freedom to hire whomever we choose to hire."

"I see."

"I do not suppose you could renounce your faith—that is, only pretend to renounce your faith for . . ." He stopped mid-sentence as if warned by Karalee's expression that he should proceed no further.

"Had I been willing to do that," she told him, wanting to twist his nose painfully and push him over backwards, "I would not have had to flee my own land, nor would any of us."

He sighed and scratched the tip of his nose as if her thoughts had set it to itching. "I find I am often too generous for my own purse-strings. But I cannot send you away. I am willing to offer you employment."

"Jacob!" Eliza took a flurry of steps toward him, forgetting the stain upon her skirts which she had been fussing over. "She can easily go to the poorhouse. Or—isn't there some society for Irish relief?"

"I believe we can use her services in this house."

"But she will not be able to give us an honest day's work and care for the child at the same time. He seems already to be most unruly. He will be creeping everywhere. Digging his little fingers into our things. Breaking . . ."

"She must watch that he does not."

Eliza gave Karalee a scathing look. "I mean no offense, my girl, but we do not know you."

"We know her people."

"That is no recommendation of character. What of the savage clothing she wears?"

"She explained that her journey here after the sinking of her ship took her down Lake Champlain and Lake George—through Indian country. Her own dresses were ruined."

"Yes—she explained that." Eliza raised one thin brow. "And the journey took her a very long time, did it not? Very long. With no other woman to guard her and care for her."

Karalee hugged Daniel closer to her, trying not to listen as the two discussed her as though she were not a human being, but a length of soiled dress goods they might purchase and trim to their liking, because its price was cheap. The Karalee Nolan she had been once would not have tolerated a word of it. She would have upset their spindly little tables and chairs, pulled their throw rug out from under them, and tongue-lashed them as they had never been tongue-lashed before. She would have left them with a reason to despise the Irish Catholics. That Karalee was dead. She had died in a dank and dismal cave in Connemara.

"Karalee—that is your name—is it not?" Jacob asked. "We bear no malice toward you because of your origin or because of your religion. Our country was formed as a refuge for people such as yourself, fleeing to avoid persecution. I have found Irish scrub women and serving maids to be as hard-working and as virtuous as many of other origins and of non-Catholic faiths."

"We cannot say as much for your men-folks," Eliza added quickly.

"If you agree to stay on, you will earn your keep. There are rooms to be scrubbed, there is washing to be done, and there are meals to be cooked. Besides, we are short of other servants. Most of the work will fall upon your shoulders. You will be paid two dollars each week to spend or save as you wish. You will be allowed an hour or two of freedom each day, provided you finish your duties beforehand. This will be so that you may conduct a search, of sorts—make inquiries about your family. It might serve to ease your mind, though I believe you will discover it serves you little. Can you think of anything else, Eliza dear?"

"Yes. If you stay, my girl, I insist that you visit the public bathhouse first and scrub yourself clean. You will find it only three blocks away and the use of it will cost you fifty cents, I have been told."

"I have no money at all."

"We will give you enough for the bath," Jacob offered, reaching into his pocket. "And then deduct it from your wages. After this first time you may use our own bathtub. But now—well, you understand, we cannot be too careful."

Karalee would have sacrificed six months of wages for the privilege of telling them what she thought of their employment and of their superior attitude toward her and those of her faith. Still she could not afford pride. Not with Daniel to care for. No. She could not lay it all upon Daniel. She, herself, was exhausted. Should she attempt to leave in a huff of righteous indignation, she would probably be able to get no farther than the hallway before collapsing.

"I promise to work very hard, sir," she managed, straining to keep her voice light and her manner humble. "And you, ma'am. You will never be sorry. Thank you."

Twenty-seven

Philadelphia was a city of colors. Women wore crisp bonnets and shawls of every hue imaginable, and dresses with skirts so wide that some of them had to walk through doors sideways. Men wore coats of emerald green and of mulberry, with nankeen waistcoats and breeches of still another shade.

The streets were cobbled. The sidewalks and gutters were brick, with strong poles every fifteen feet or so to protect those who walked from galloping horses and carriages. Glass lanterns sat upon posts, waiting to be lit when the sun disappeared, and secretly, Karalee longed to be allowed out after dark—just once—to see the lines of them, all afire.

Most houses were of two stories with an attic and with benches set on either side of their doors for sitting during warm evenings—though there was little use for them this winter. The shutters of the ground floor were usually green and those above were white. Many of the fronts were painted too, with white sills and trim and white lines drawn between the bricks. The white stone steps leading up to the porches were temporarily wood-planed, to prevent slipping during the icy spells, and rose bushes were dressed with ashes at their base. But Karalee could imagine how lovely it must have been in the spring, with the stately elm and poplar trees lining the sidewalks with bright green, with purple wisteria in bloom, and honeysuckle and roses.

But what fascinated Karalee most was the marketplace. The market building, made up of stalls, was pillared and nearly a mile long. A separate section was set aside for the selling of meat, another for the selling of vegetables, still others for fruit and for dry goods, for shoes and for trinkets. There was no yelling or quarreling, no dancing fools or beggars to pull at the sleeves of those who shopped. Policemen, handsome in their immaculate uniforms, walked first in one direction, then in the other, making certain all was as it should be, settling spats and seeing that none were cheated. If a woman complained that her meal had been weighed short, for instance, the meal would be weighed again in the policeman's presence. If it were indeed short, it would be confiscated and given to the poor.

Karalee's favorite day was Wednesday, when she was allowed to do the shopping—and usually alone. Eliza disliked crowds and chilled air gave her headaches, so she preferred to remain indoors. Karalee could watch the skaters on the Delaware for a time, if it were iced over, and she would chat with other housemaids she had come to know.

George Washington was in the city, it was whispered. He had come to speak with Hamilton on the possibility of war with France and to appoint officers, if they were needed, who might be popular enough to encourage fighting men to re-enlist under their command. He had even paid a visit to the debtor's prison to dine with his friend, Robert Morris, who was incarcerated there, and to ask his advice.

The house on Market Street where George Washington and his wife, Martha, had lived while he was the president, was pointed out to Karalee in reverent tones and she was told how in those days he had strolled through the market ways promptly at noon as any common man might do, dressed in his black velvet suit, setting his watch by the chronometer and pausing to converse with many who saluted him.

One day there was a flurry of excitement and people crowded together along the street to watch a cream-colored carriage clatter past, cupids and wreaths painted upon its sides. Although the glimpse Karalee caught of the white-haired man inside was not enough that she would recognize him if she were to see him again, she was told that she had seen Washington himself.

When the Whittakers had told Karalee they were short of help, they had not exaggerated. Their only servants were an aged cook, Anna, whose eyes were so poor that she nearly had to be faced in the direction of the cooking stove before she could begin a meal, and a boy of seventeen, Orson, who was strong enough, but who had the mind of a child. He tended the stove, chopped wood, and shoveled snow, but he was dreadfully slow in his other tasks. Karalee would find herself doing Orson's work too, to prevent him from being punished.

Anna was short-tempered, and seldom did a day go by that she did not swing her heavy cane at the boy, who only stood and blubbered as the blows fell upon his back and shoulders. He slept in a dim, unheated basement room, upon a creaking cot. He was given his meals there too.

"The filthy little beggar throws his food into his mouth as if he were a beast," Anna explained, when Karalee asked why the boy was not allowed to eat at the kitchen table with them.

"How will he ever learn the proper way to eat, if someone does not teach him?"

"If you admire his company, Missy," Anna said, sniffing, "You are free to carry your own tray down and eat with him."

And so Karalee did on many occasions, which so infuriated the old woman that she would have loved to use her cane upon the girl's back if she dared. But Karalee's manner must have warned her it would not be wise to try. So she contented herself with muttering about the Irish.

"You people are used to eating and sleeping with your pigs, so it matters little."

It didn't take too long for Karalee to become hardened to the taunting. She had almost learned to feel pity for those who were so small-minded they had to find others to look down upon. She was safe now, wasn't she, and warmly dressed? Daniel was well fed, happy, and growing as a healthy boy should grow.

Her sorrow lay in her loneliness. It was a deep and growing sorrow—more unbearable with each passing day. Each time she ventured out she found herself looking into the faces of those around her, thinking, "Surely today I will see Jeremy."

She'd spy a lanky man ahead with a gait like his, and she would run to catch up, only to be disappointed by the face of a stranger.

And Phillip Shepard. He had told her he would be in Philadelphia this time of the year. Where was he now?

Would she see him? Had he only a moment before passed this way? Had he just turned that corner? Had she only just missed him?

It was as if the ground had opened up and swallowed her family. There were four Catholic churches in Philadelphia, but none of the priests could remember listening to a confession, or even seeing any member, of the Nolan family. St. Joseph's Catholic Church was wedged into an alley between Walnut and Third Streets. It was much like an ordinary house, with hard benches and an ancient-looking organ. But on one wall was an oil painting of a ship being battered by a savage storm. Above was the Virgin Mary and with her, her son, Jesus, holding the vessel safe. Karalee often walked blocks out of her way, only to gaze upon that painting and to pray.

Weeks passed, and she was about to admit to herself that Jacob Whittaker had been right when he told her a search would be futile. Then hope sprang before her unexpectedly.

A woman in the square was chattering about how her husband drank up all he earned in a place of sin called the Quiet Woman. One of his drinking companions was a man named Micheal Nolan.

The woman's husband confirmed the story when Karalee begged to be taken to him. "Nolan never has a coin in his pocket, but we all throw together to see to his thirst. He's so full of jolly tales he could extract a belly-laugh from a corpse."

The physical description seemed to match too, from the bushy gray sideburns to the slight limp and the jaunty way he pulled his cap low over one eye. The man had to be her father.

It was not easy to slip away from the Whittaker home at such an hour without being seen by anyone. Karalee knew they would be scandalized should she even suggest going out after dark for any purpose. She might even be dismissed. Daniel must have sensed her anxiety, as young children often will. He dawdled over his supper, then refused to fall asleep when placed in his crib. Eliza called for hot tea and biscuits to be served in her bedroom. When Karalee hurried the tray up to her, she caught her foot in a rug and spilled all of it upon the staircase.

That meant another trip to the kitchen for more tea, and a scolding from Anna for her clumsiness. It meant she had to mop up the mess and then wait for the cup to be emptied, so that she could return it to the kitchen, rinse it, and hang it away.

Somehow, she managed to arrive at the Quiet Woman slightly before eight o'clock—the hour she was told Micheal Nolan never failed to appear. She stood beneath the swinging tavern sign, with the painting of a headless woman on it, her back turned against the icy wind, blowing on her fingers to warm them and praying her wait would not be in vain. She searched the face of each man who entered, and each time turned away, disappointed.

"Go on with you, Nolan, it never happened that way at all," she heard someone say. She spun toward the voice.

Her heart seemed to stop beating within her. Neither of the two men who were heading toward the tavern was her father. One had grayish sideburns though, and he walked with a slight limp. He wore a cap pulled low over his forehead.

"Sir, would you be Micheal Nolan?" she asked, after tapping his shoulder, hoping his answer would be no.

"Waitin' for me, are you, darlin'?" The man caught her about the waist and began to dance in a circle, doing a jig step. His breath was already strong with spirits. "You see, do you, Haney, how the ladies seek me out wherever I go? Do you suppose it's me great beauty?"

"It is more likely your purse, Nolan," the other man snorted. "This wench takes you for a man with two dollars to spend in return for fifteen minutes of pleasure."

"Is your name Micheal Nolan?" Karalee tried again, wanting to be certain.

The other man staggered close, leaning as if he would lose his balance if someone were to breathe upon him. "You look like the little piece what lured me into Jones Alley last week and had her friend waiting to tap me on the head and steal my poke."

"No sir, I only . . ."

"It was you right enough. I remember now."

"You are wrong. Believe me." Karalee backed away.

"Believe you, eh? You sweet-faced ones are the worst of the lot. I'll have my poke back. The money you stole from me."

"I do not have your money, sir."

"Then where is it?"

The man's eyes were misty and his drunken voice was so

loud that passers-by stopped to listen. A carriage pulled to a halt in front of the tavern and the man and woman inside it leaned from their windows to hear.

A stern-faced policeman pushed through the crowd and caught Karalee's arm. "All right, young woman. Come along. You've been standing here most of an hour. I knew you were up to no good."

"I was waiting for my father, sir."

The people laughed. "She wants her father," one of them mimicked.

"Does he look anything like me, sweetheart?" another asked, making a kissing sound with his lips.

"Disgraceful."

"One moment, officer."

The carriage door swung open and a gentleman stepped out. He wore a finely tailored tan suit, a tall brown hat and a greatcoat of a darker brown, with a brush of soft fur about the collar. There were ivory-colored gloves on his hands and he carried a gold-knobbed cane. He was perhaps thirty-five years old, with pale, gray eyes and a sprinkling of freckles over his face which gave him a more youthful appearance.

"I'm sorry you were disturbed by this, Mr. Philbrick, sir," the policeman said, taking a tighter hold of Karalee's arm. "But the young woman will be seen to immediately."

"I think not, officer," the man said. "The young woman you speak of is the daughter of an acquaintance of mine. He was delayed and asked me to fetch her home. I'm sorry, my dear." He smiled at Karalee. "It's late. Your father will be worried that something has happened to you."

"I do not . . ." Karalee stammered as he led her into the waiting carriage.

"What about my money?" the man with Michael Nolan bellowed, staring after them.

"Move along," the policeman told him, "or it will be you spending the night in jail."

"I would guess the name of Nolan is not altogether uncommon in a city like Philadelphia with such an incoming population of Irish," the man said, after Karalee had explained her predicament. "And matched with the given name of Micheal? There are probably a dozen or more."

"It was only that I hoped . . ."

"I suggest you venture out only during daylight hours,

my dear. Now if you will tell me where you live, I will direct my driver."

The girl who sat next to him was narrow-shouldered. She had a long narrow nose set on a long narrow face. There was little color in her cheeks, but her blue eyes were large and lustrous and their expression of innocence and compassion made her seem beautiful, although she was not.

"Cyril," she said, tugging at the man's sleeve. She put her mouth close to his ear and whispered something Karalee could not hear.

The man nodded gravely and cleared his throat. "Would you be offended if I offered you a few coins? You might buy space in one of the newspapers asking if anyone knows the whereabouts of your family."

The girl smiled and squeezed his arm. Her eyes were wet as if Karalee's story had touched her deeply. But she said nothing.

"No, thank you. I wouldn't feel right in accepting it. But you have been very kind." She hesitated as she stepped out of the carriage. "Cyril Philbrick. Why is it I feel I should know you? It is as if I have heard your name before."

"You might have seen it on one of my buildings down near the water. I am in imports-exports. Shipping."

Karalee shook her head. "I do not think . . ."

Then she remembered. It did not matter. Cyril Philbrick had been the man Jeremy had spoken of aboard ship. The man who had begun with him as a peddler and had become wealthy.

As the carriage moved away, the girl reached out the window to squeeze Karalee's hand. As she did so, she pressed a ten-dollar gold piece into it.

Karalee quickly examined it, then tried to enter the house as quietly as possible.

"Home, are you?"

Anna stood at the top of the back stairs, her gray hair pulled into a waist-long braid, a white nightgown like a flour-sack hanging from her shoulders. As Karalee reached for her door handle, the gold coin slipped from her fingers, rolled along the carpet and landed close to Anna's feet. The woman stooped to retrieve it, held it an inch from her eyes, then plunked it into Karalee's hand.

"I do not have to ask how you earned it." She made a sound like a steaming teakettle and stalked away.

Twenty-eight

When Karalee heard the news, she wept.

Wolfe Tone, the bright hope of the Irish Revolution, had been captured on a ship off Tory Island. He would have escaped unnoticed, except for a man he trusted—a supposed friend, Sir George Hill—who offered him a handshake and called his name. The handshake held the same treachery, it was said, as the kiss of Judas when he betrayed Jesus Christ.

Tone had been sentenced to hang as a common criminal, but in order to save his pride, he had slit his throat with a pen-knife. He succeeded only in severing part of his windpipe and was a week dying—in agony all the while. When Hill heard that Tone's execution would be delayed until the man recovered enough to be moved, Hill remarked only that it was a pity they would not sew up his friend's throat and proceed to finish him.

Karalee had never seen Wolfe Tone, nor had she listened closely enough as the men discussed politics to realize the hope so many felt, that through him their Revolution would succeed. But she knew that he was young and handsome and that he had brought his wife and children to the colonies first, where they would be safe from British retribution.

Karalee wept for this young wife, who would hear the news of her husband's death long after it happened—and through strangers. She would have to know that he died without her kiss and without her touch to reassure him that her love for him would be eternal. Karalee had, at least, been at Patrick's side when the life had left him and so her sorrow would not contain the hollow regret of things unsaid. If indeed there was any comfort in that.

When the spells of dizziness came upon her and she began to lose her usually healthy appetite, Karalee was certain she had contracted yellow fever. She worried only about Daniel, and who would tend to him when she was gone—who would love him. For herself, she regretted only that she would likely not live to see him grown into a man. That she would not watch the rosy babe-face mature into the sun-burned face of a lad—and then into the face of Patrick Roe, as it surely would one day.

She visited St. Joseph's with the intention of dropping her ten-dollar gold piece into the poorbox. Had not Father O'Glanny told them often enough that to gain everything, one had to be willing to give everything? But somehow, each time Karalee came close to the box, her fingers curled about the coin more tightly and at last she came away in shame, still holding it.

You are wicked indeed, Karalee Nolan, she scolded herself. You have been tested and found wanting.

She did not realize until she fainted dead away while serving Eliza and Jacob Whittaker their afternoon tea in the front parlor, that the symptoms she was experiencing—the giddiness and the loss of appetite—were also symptoms of pregnancy. She was carrying Tonaoge's child.

There was no way to keep the truth from her employers now. She awoke from her deep swoon to find the two of them gaping, still fastened in their armchairs, the tea things still upon the floor where she had dropped them. Neither of the Whittakers wanted to touch her. It was obvious that they, too, believed she had contracted yellow fever. Had she not confessed to her condition, she would have been sent into the street without a thought.

It was unfortunate. A dramatic change had taken place in their behavior toward her of late. They seemed almost fond of her. It had begun when Jacob received a letter which agitated him. He called Eliza into the parlor, where they closed the folding doors and whispered together for a long time. When they came out again, they were different. Eliza actually hugged Karalee and called her "dear girl." The following day they hired a girl, Marianne, to help with the dusting, bed-making, and scrubbing. On Saturday when Karalee bundled up and took her brush and pail in order to scrub the front porch, the steps and the sidewalk, a ritual performed each Saturday by those who inhabited every civilized house in Philadelphia, no matter the weather, Eliza had squealed and flown to take them away.

"No, no, dear girl! Your hands are too rough from scrubbing already. Marianne is stronger and more used to heavy work."

The same afternoon Jacob called her into the parlor, asked her to sit down, hemmed and cleared his throat, looked out the window, stammered something about the snow and then dismissed her—a look of helplessness upon his face.

But Karalee could not rely on their changed attitudes to help her now. The Whittakers would be appalled by her condition. Whatever affection they had begun to feel for her would turn to loathing. There would be nowhere for her to go, but to the poorhouse. She was not even certain there would be help for her there.

She braced herself for their indignant raging, but to her surprise Eliza and Jacob sat unflinching as she told them her story. When she had finished, Eliza merely held up one hand and began to count off fingers.

"Let me see—it should be two months before any one notices you are with child. Thin as you are, it could be longer."

Jacob nodded, obviously pleased. "That should be ample time."

Karalee was so taken aback that she merely listened, without asking what they meant by "ample time." Finally Eliza explained.

"As I believe I told you the day we met, I gave birth to two dear little girls, a year apart. Each died in their first months of life, and though I found joy in my sons, I sorely felt the lack of a daughter. Someone to dress in ribboned bonnets and frills, to teach womanly skills, to cuddle upon my knee as one cannot rightly cuddle a boy without taking the manliness from him. And so when my sister died in childbirth and her husband did not want the baby girl as a reminder of his loss, I offered to take her and raise her as my own."

She drew in her breath and when she released it, emitted a single sob, though her facial expression did not change. Jacob rushed to her side and slid a strengthening arm about her shoulders. Karalee was touched, but a little embarrassed by the tenderness she had never before seen them display toward each other.

"She was christened Julianne, my own grandmother's name, and she was lovely. She had gently curling dark hair. She had creamy skin and wide green eyes, which seemed to change to blue whenever she wore blue. Oh, she had a talent for anything she tried. She painted, played at the piano—and my, could she dance. It was as if her feet did not touch the floor."

Eliza was silent for a long time, dabbing at her eyes with a corner of handkerchief, and Karalee began to think that was all there was to the tale. If so, she knew she was expected to make some comment; but she could think of none that was fitting. Fortunately, the woman went on.

"She would have made the perfect wife for a duke, a king. But we made the mistake of sailing to this country. Julianne changed. By the very wildness of the land, she took on a wildness too. Wouldn't you say it was the land, Jacob?"

Her husband nodded. "There is too much freedom here. The guidance of loving parents cannot overcome the influence of outsiders."

"It shames me to tell you this, my dear," Eliza said, "but perhaps, having seen so much of the sordid side of life, you will understand, in spite of your tender years. Last spring—in the middle of April—Julianne fell in love with a common seaman."

"Love? You call it love?" Jacob snorted. "The child was infatuated by his handsome face and by the romantic notions young girls who are allowed to read acquire about life on the high seas."

"Naturally we did not welcome the man into our home, and so she began slipping out in the middle of the night to meet him, though we were not aware of it until later. One day—she was gone. Leaving Jacob and me only a note in return for the years we gave her."

"I am sorry," Karalee whispered, still not sure why they felt it necessary to tell her a tale which seemed to bring them so much shame.

"She will return," Jacob said firmly. "I am confident that in time—perhaps she has already realized her mistake."

"And we will welcome her with open arms. Never a word will be said of her indiscretion. Never. Our family has

216

always commanded respect. Never has there been a whisper of scandal."

"There are those in England who would look down on us because we run this lodging house. We do so by necessity. It was not always so. Ill fortune robbed us of what wealth we had. We were forced to take in lodgers. But we have kept the most respected boardinghouse in the city. We have allowed none but the refined to stay here."

"Now Julianne's father is dying." Eliza twisted her handkerchief as she spoke, avoiding Karalee's eyes. "He did not care enough for her all through these years to write her a single letter or to inquire of her health. But now he is sending someone to see her. His second marriage produced no daughters and there is some family jewelry he wishes Julianne to have. A necklace or two—a brooch—perhaps a ring and a locket. Things that belonged to my sister. This person is on the ocean now and could arrive at any time—tomorrow or a month from now—depending upon weather conditions in crossing the Atlantic. He intends to visit with us, give Julianne the things that are rightfully hers, see that she is well and report back to her father with his findings. The man wishes to die with his conscience clear. To assure himself he did the right thing in giving her up. He claims now to have been thinking only of her welfare when he sent her away."

"I do not understand . . ."

Eliza lifted one eyebrow. "My dear girl, I have tried to paint a clear picture for you." Karalee had suffered through enough of Eliza's fits of impatience to realize the woman was straining for control. She pursed her lips and squeezed her eyes shut before continuing, a false gentility in her voice.

"I cannot inform this person when he arrives that Julianne has run off, we know not where, with a coarse, low-living sailor. I cannot have him return to my sister's widower with the judgment that there was a wildness in my sister's blood which showed itself in the child. That he was correct in ridding himself of Julianne before she could grow into womanhood and disgrace him in his homeland. Or worse—that Jacob and I brought the girl up improperly. I cannot. I would die first."

It was clear enough now what they wanted from Karalee and why they had behaved so differently toward her in recent days. The thought frightened her.

"You cannot wish me to pretend I am Julianne."

Eliza nodded and with a deep sigh settled into her chair. "We do."

"I cannot."

"In return," Jacob said, ignoring her refusal, "we will care for your needs until after your child's birth. We will help you see to its adoption, and then, find you a suitable position. How does that sound?"

"I intend to keep the babe when she is born."

Eliza and Jacob exchanged glances. "Two children for you to raise? Well—there will be plenty of time to decide upon the disposition of the child later," Jacob told her.

"There will be no disposition of my child. I will keep her."

"As you wish. In the meantime, Eliza and I must instruct you in small things, so that there will be no errors. Such as the names of your parents, your birthplace, your age. Julianne is somewhat older. Her birthday . . ."

"I am truly sorry, but I cannot do as you ask. It would be too deceitful. Besides, I would not be believed. Anyone can read a lie in my face."

"We are willing to set aside a small sum—a sum which would be at your disposal, so that you might contact an agency adept at making searches for people lost from each other."

"There are such places?"

"There are," Jacob answered. "Such an agency is conducting a search for Julianne at this very moment. She has been traced as far as Norfolk, Virginia. It is only a matter of time before she is returned to us."

"What of my speech?"

"We lived in Dublin for a time—that much is true. We brought back an Irish nursemaid for you—which is not true. But the excuse will serve. Especially if you speak little. The man will not stay long. Avoid him as much as possible. We will tell him you are shy. Shyness is an attribute greatly to be admired in ladies of quality."

"What of my appearance?"

"None of the family has seen Julianne since she left England, a child in arms. Your coloring is the same as hers. Is it settled?"

"Your lodgers. They have seen me at work."

"With your hair tucked into a cap so that they cannot even tell its color? With clothing that is so ill-fitting you could weigh ninety or one hundred and ninety pounds and no one could guess? No, my dear girl, with a suitable dress and with your hair done properly, no one of them would recognize you. Is it settled?"

They battered her from both sides with their answers and, in truth, they made it sound simple enough. Still she did not like it.

"There must be someone else. Another way. Why not Marianne?"

"The girl is fifteen and appears to be twelve. She is big and clumsy and her hair is fair, at that. Besides, she is not to be trusted. I have already heard her gossiping about her last employers. There is no other way."

"Forgive me, I cannot." Karalee felt as if she were about to faint again. She reached for the back of a chair to steady herself.

"Very well." Eliza stood and began to brush the creases from her skirts. "I will expect you to leave this house before nightfall."

Upstairs Daniel let out a yelp as if he were offering another argument on their behalf. Karalee turned toward the stairs to see to him, but hesitated. "Please. For Daniel's sake. Let me stay a few days longer. I have nowhere to take him."

Eliza smiled thinly. "Since you refuse the request we have made of you, I see no reason whatsoever to grant your request. Perhaps you can go back to your savage lover."

"Eliza!" Jacob's voice sounded angry. "There is no call to speak to the child in such a manner. She is merely overwhelmed by the responsibility we are facing her with. I have little doubt she will reconsider her decision when she has had time."

"It would be wrong," Karalee protested.

"Would it?" Jacob lifted her chin. His hand was icy and smelled of tobacco. "A dying man wishes to know his only daughter is well. Perhaps he feels guilt—as well he should. But who are we to judge?"

"I will not be believed."

"No one will have a reason to disbelieve you. We will be at your side at all times to reassure you."

"It would be such a wicked lie," Karalee whispered. But she had already decided to do as they asked.

Twenty-nine

Not a few young ladies in Philadelphia still wore their hair powdered, but Karalee was relieved when Eliza decided against such a touch for her, though it would have made her appear older. The powdering would have meant having to sit for a long time, wrapped in a wide robe, while her hair was smeared with grease; having her face covered with a paper cone so that she would not be suffocated, as the powder was dusted on by the pound. Her hair would be stiff and sickeningly sweet-scented and the powder would flake off a little at a time onto her shoulders, always to be watched for and brushed away discreetly.

Instead she was allowed her natural hair, but it was crimped with a hot curling iron until it formed a mass of tiny ringlets across her forehead and over her ears. The back was left to follow its own design.

The dress she wore, the other two being held in reserve for the arrival of her visitor, was of soft green muslin, high-waisted, with a gentle gathering at the bosom. A large rosette of darker green was attached to her satin sash at the front of her waist and her full skirt swept the ground. Her wide-brimmed hat of straw was golden tan, with light green and pink plumes at the back of her head.

Eliza was maddeningly attentive, insisting that Karalee nap and that she be in bed by nine each night. She was allowed to do no work, except for needlework, and her supper plate was shamefully heaped, so she would regain her strength and the color of her cheeks. Most of the food she only made a pretense of eating, so that she could slip downstairs and share it with Orson, who was never given enough to fill a growing boy.

She was taken for an outing each day, as if she were a family pet being exercised, always accompanied by Eliza or Jacob, and never more than a few feet from their sight. She was told she needed the fresh air to restore her health, and that it would also be well for neighbors to become used to seeing Julianne in the company of her aunt and uncle.

Her name was Julianne Constance Morrow and she would have a birthday on the fifteenth of February. Her mother's name had been Constance Louise and her father was William Howard Morrow. She had been given so many details to remember that she often woke herself in the middle of the night to find she had been repeating names, dates, and places in her dreams.

She was just as satisfied not to venture out alone these days. There had arisen a new bitterness against the Irish in Philadelphia. William Cobbett, an ex-British soldier, felt a special hatred for the Irish. He wrote and distributed pamphlets warning that there was a conspiracy between France and the "wild Irish." He claimed they were forcing themselves into every branch of the government and when the French invaded American shores, the Irish would begin their campaign of murder and rape. He said they were in the South even now, speaking with Negro slaves, inciting them to rise up and riot when the time was right.

On this day, the weather had warmed unseasonably, though the ice was still thick enough for skating. Jacob left Karalee to watch them as he attended to some business in the market square. Karalee, thinking it was cold when she left the house, had worn a short, but double-tiered cape. Now that the sun was out, she felt uncomfortably warm. She was so busy undoing the intricate loops which fastened her garment at the throat, she did not notice the shadow which fell across her face.

"Karalee."

"Jeremy."

He clasped her hands between his and brought them to his lips.

She might have passed without recognizing him, he looked so different from the Jeremy she had known in the forest and aboard the *Gallant Lady*. He wore a hat, flat-crowned and wide-brimmed, which gave a look of maturity to his face, a deerskin coat which hung nearly to his knees, and a white shirt, open at the collar. His hair was longer, or perhaps it only seemed so since it was not tied at the nape of his neck.

"So you don't hate me?"

"Hate you? Oh Jeremy, I have never been so glad to see anyone. I cannot tell you what it means to meet you like this."

"It was not a chance meeting, Karalee, I'll confess. I've known where you were for some time. I've watched you from far off, walked past the house where you lived and almost went up to knock on the door. But I've been afraid to approach you."

"Afraid of me? Why?"

"It was a devilish thing I did in leaving you in that Indian camp. You had been through such an ordeal, you did not realize what you were doing. I should have fought my way out, dragged you along with me by force, if necessary. Can you forgive me?"

"It does not matter now, Jeremy. It is past."

"You're right. And you have my word to never speak of it again. It never happened."

"But it did happen."

"Karalee." For a moment his face was as bright as it had been the day he introduced himself to them aboard the ship. The day he had made up funny names for the two of them and had made Karalee laugh. If only it could stay this way. If only people did not change toward each other, she thought.

"Karalee, I want to kiss you—now. Come with me. Somewhere."

"I cannot."

"You can."

"My employer will be here soon. I must wait."

"We'll be married. Right away. Hang your employer. Then when spring comes, we'll take the raft . . ."

"If we are truly to be married, Jeremy," she interrupted him, "we must accept what happened in the Indian village and we must speak of it."

"No!" His eyes darkened. The bright moment had flown. "We must not! I am a man of pride. If I can forget what happened—if I have been able to block it from my mind, then so must you. Our lives begin today. There has been nothing up to now. And no one."

Karalee sighed and reached out to smooth his cheek.

How could she tell him she carried Tonaoge's child? Jeremy had not overcome his jealous rage, he had merely buried it, to be dug out again when the memory of it became too much to bear.

"How did you discover where I am living?"

"An old friend. Cyril Philbrick. Remember him? I went to him for a loan and he told me of the beautiful Irish girl he had rescued from a jail cell." Jeremy laughed, his old laugh—his dear laugh—his black anger forgotten for the moment. "I knew before he told me her name that it was you. No one else has such a knack for getting into difficulties."

"I suppose you are right in that."

"I had him show where he had taken you. Then I watched for you. Day after day. Karalee, I want to kiss you."

"Did you get your loan?"

"I did. I am back in business come spring thaw. Karalee . . ."

"Mr. Philbrick is a kind man."

"The devil he is! He's a shrewd man. He knows he'll double his investment, with me doing his work for him."

"Has your leg healed?"

"Damn near lost it, tearing through the bogs with it open, the way I did. But it is well enough now." He took a step backward and studied her. "That's a beautiful dress you are wearing."

"Thank you."

Jeremy waited, as if he expected her to say something more. When she did not, he turned away, pretending to find interest in the skaters.

"Your employer must be fond of you." His voice was guarded. "To dress you in such a fashion. I had the understanding you were a housemaid."

"I am. That is, I am not exactly . . ."

"You are or you are not. Which is it?"

"I am."

"You have found a boardinghouse keeper who can afford to dress his housemaids as well as he dresses his wife?" Jeremy's tongue moved across his lower lip. "Do you want to tell me about it, Karalee?"

"Yes. Oh, yes, I do and I will. I must." She stepped in front of him and clasped his hands again, just as she caught sight of Jacob Whittaker turning the corner at the end of the next street. He must not see them together. He had warned her to speak to no one. To do no more than to nod pleasantly, and then only if it were someone who was known to the Whittakers.

"Tell me."

"Not now. Where are you staying?"

"Where I always stay. The Alden House on Chestnut Street. But why can't you tell me now? I don't like riddles."

"I cannot. He is coming."

"He?" Jeremy followed Karalee's gaze. Fortunately, Jacob Whittaker's eyesight was poor and he had not spotted them yet.

"I demand that you tell me now, Karalee. You do not have to take orders from that man anymore. I'm going to take care of you and Daniel. It's none of the old fool's business what is said between us." He brushed Karalee's hand away and glared at her. "Or is it?"

"Please go," she begged. "I will explain later."

"Explain? It won't be necessary." He touched his fingers to his hatbrim and stalked away.

Karalee watched as Jeremy walked out of her life once again.

Thirty

The young man who rose when Karalee entered and pressed his lips fervently to her hand, was not merely a messenger sent by Julianne's father, as Karalee had been told to expect. He was her half-brother, Peter.

"My dearest, dearest sister. I would have known you anywhere. You look very much like our father."

If it were true, she thought, then Peter must have looked like his mother, as he was her exact opposite. He was overweight enough to strain the buttons of his vest, though not to the point of being considered fat, or even unattractive. He was not tall, but he carried himself with dignity. His hair was golden, not powdered, and worn in a roll over each ear, the back tied with a ribbon. He wore a simple brown homespun suit, with a frill at his shirt opening and snug breeches which reached into his turned-down boots.

He answered all Jacob's questions politely and agreed to Eliza's observations about the weather, but he would not take his eyes from Karalee. All his own questions were directed toward her.

"What a charming Irish lilt you have, Julianne. However did you acquire it?"

And Eliza told him the rehearsed story of the Irish nursemaid, Bridget.

"I understand you play the piano beautifully. I would enjoy hearing it."

"She is too shy to play for company."

"Company? I am not company, am I, Julianne?"

"I'm sure she would rather not."

As time went on and Eliza persisted in monopolizing the conversation, Peter seemed to become increasingly annoyed and he did little to conceal it. At last he stood and cleared his throat. "Mr. and Mrs. Whittaker, I have enjoyed visiting with you, and now I would like to take my sister for a carriage ride. I am sure you will understand. It is my first visit to Philadelphia, and I would like to see something of it."

"Julianne will not be much of a guide, I fear," Jacob said, rising too. "She has been very sheltered. I will . . ."

"I am certain she has been sheltered," Peter broke in, "but I enjoy her company. We have much to talk about and little time."

Eliza reddened. "I do not think it wise, Mr. Morrow. Julianne takes a chill easily and it is unusually cold today."

"We will wrap her up well then, won't we? And if we keep the carriage curtains drawn, I am sure she will be fine. Come, dear."

He cut off each of their arguments and when he had helped Karalee on with her wrap and opened the door for her, he called back, "Do not wait supper for us, Mrs. Whittaker. I am taking Julianne out to dine."

Karalee enjoyed seeing the helpless way the Whittakers, usually so much in command, looked at each other, Jacob sputtering, his cheeks puffed out, drops of perspiration on his forehead, and Eliza's eyes bulging. Perhaps it would do them some good.

She felt very much at ease with Peter, who showed her every consideration. She had never before been assisted in and out of carriages, up and down curbs, across streets and through doorways. He made her feel as if she actually were a fine lady.

"Julianne," he told her over supper, "My main reason in coming all the way to Philadelphia was to ask you to return to England with me."

Karalee nearly choked over her wine.

"Father does not have long to live and he wants very much to see you. He would be proud to know how lovely you have grown to be."

"I could not leave here."

"I understand how you feel. Father sent you away. He has always regretted it. But he loved your mother very much. You were a constant reminder of his loss."

"I bear him no grudges."

"Then you will come?"

"I cannot leave Aunt Eliza and Uncle Jacob."

"I understand. They have been the only parents you have ever known. But . . ." He took her hand across the table. "Couldn't you come back, only for a visit? It would be good for you. Much as your aunt and uncle love you, I believe, and I hope you do not feel me too forward in saying it, they smother you. It is no wonder you have not yet married."

"Peter . . ."

"I did not mean to embarrass you."

"You did not."

"We will have a delightful crossing together, getting to know each other as brother and sister. When we arrive, I will show you the English countryside. It is breathtaking. Perhaps you will not wish to leave. And father—you would give him a few happy hours in his last days."

"I am truly sorry about your father, Peter."

"Our father."

For a moment, he looked as if he might cry; then he gathered himself and took a sip of wine. "Do not give me your answer now, dear. Only think about it. As I wrote you, I am being married in the spring. You could attend the wedding. You would adore Nan—my bride-to-be. She is very young and sometimes silly. She giggles a lot and pokes fun at my weakness for rich foods." He patted his vest front. "But she loves me, and I, her."

"Peter . . ."

"I do not want your answer now. Tomorrow will do well enough and it will give my charm a chance to do its work with you."

"I must explain . . ."

"And I must insist!" He smiled. "Though you are the older of us by three years, I am the visitor, and so have special privileges."

As Peter wished to see the sights, Karalee showed him those she knew: the market square, the State House, Washington's home, the New Theatre on Chestnut Street, and the Anglican Cemetery, where Benjamin Franklin and his wife, Deborah, were buried.

He was such good company, she almost took him to St. Joseph's to show him her painting—until she remembered. Everything she was to him was a lie. She could not be Irish—or a Catholic. She was not even his sister.

"You are entirely different from your letters, Julianne," he told her later in their carriage.

"My letters?" The Whittakers had not told her there were letters.

"I had decided you were—I don't know—more aggressive, perhaps."

"People usually write somewhat differently from the way they speak."

"But not so differently. And I? Am I the way you pictured me from my written words?"

"Why—yes, I suppose."

"I am not sure I like that." He pulled a long face. "I am a poor writer. Nan tells me I compose a letter that is like a page from a school primer. Stilted and impersonal."

"You are charming."

"I believe I am." He smiled. "To think I nearly did not come. It was difficult to leave with Father so ill. He had planned to send someone else with the papers for you to sign."

"Papers?"

"Yes, dear, the papers allowing you to have your money at once—in a lump sum now. Rather than receiving it as you have been, a bit each month."

"Oh."

"One would imagine the change to be very simple—a few words of spoken agreement. But our governments seem to enjoy bogging the smallest transaction down with details. There will be a dozen papers to sign, and of course, copies of each of those papers for you and for father, and for their vaults. Then there must be witnesses to the signing—and then, the witnesses must sign."

Karalee cringed at the thought of it. Something was amiss. She had been told only half-truths. That meant the Whittakers were hiding something.

"I do not think I wish to do all that, Peter. Let us forget about it. I do not want the money."

"Nonsense. You are entitled to it. Father considered your request carefully and agreed with you that the money would help you to make a more suitable marriage. Though from what I see of you, no man would care if you had a shilling."

"You said—my request?"

"Yes. In your last two letters. Julianne, is something wrong?"

230

"No, no, of course not."

"I can tell that there is. You are fearful of the signing. Of the people you will meet in the legal offices."

"Legal offices?"

"You are! My dearest sister, how is it possible to be so beautiful and so unaware of it? If your eyes were each of a different color, if your skin were dough-colored, if your belly were as round as mine, and your nose as bulbous as that of your uncle . . ."

"Oh Peter . . ." Karalee could not resist laughing at the description and at the distorted manner in which he twisted his face.

"There is no reason for you to be shy or fearful. I will accompany you to the signing. I must sign papers too, remember, and I do not tremble at the thought of it."

"I am not afraid."

"There's my girl. And I want you think very hard tonight about returning with me to England. Will you?"

"Yes—I will. I promise."

Thirty-one

"Do you remember Miss Julianne?" Karalee asked Orson, as she handed him the candy cane she had bought for him that day.

The boy squeezed his eyes shut and scratched the tip of his nose. "They said your name was Julianne now."

"Yes. But did you once know someone else with that same name?"

"Is this peppermint?" the boy asked. "I don't like peppermint. I ate some once and the smell of it went up into my nose and burned it."

"No, it is anise."

"What's that?"

"Taste it and see. Did you know another girl named Julianne?"

"There was her before. A long time ago."

"Her?"

Orson stuck his tongue out of one corner of his mouth and began to unwrap his candy cane. He peeled back the paper from one end, licked his fingers so that they stuck to the candy, then licked them again to set them free. "It's ever so sweet."

"Yes, it is. Where is Julianne now, Orson?"

"She lived in this house a long time ago. A long, long time ago. But I remember. I tasted this kind of candy before once."

"Yes, Julianne lived in this house. But it was not so long ago. She went away only last spring."

"She didn't either." He held the flat of his hand level

with his chin. "I was only this tall when she was here. When my uncle first brought me here. He said he didn't want me any more because I was stupid and he brought me here to work. I remember Miss Julianne because she brought me sweets like you do."

"Do you know where she is now?"

The boy rolled back on his cot so that he faced the wall, sucking noisily on his candy cane. "Go away now. I won't talk about it anymore."

"Did she tell you goodbye?"

He rolled over again, to face her, and there were tears in his eyes. "I think you must be stupid too. How could she tell me goodbye? She got sick. Her face got a funny color and she sounded loud when she tried to breathe. I sneaked into her room and saw her lying on her bed. But she couldn't talk to me. 'Cause she didn't breathe at all anymore. They told me she went away. But I could tell she was dead. Like all those other dead people. All lying in the streets. Their faces got a funny color too. I stayed in the house after that so I wouldn't have to look at them."

"Julianne died of yellow fever."

"That's what they called it when they whispered about it."

"But the yellow fever came this summer."

"No. It wasn't last time. It came before that too. It comes ever so often." He sat and held his hand level with his chin. "I was this tall and my uncle brought me here to work because I was stupid and because he didn't want me anymore."

Karalee smoothed his hair back and gave him a light kiss on the forehead. "Thank you for telling me, Orson."

"They made me burn all her clothes in the stove," she heard him murmur as she went upstairs. "They said she went away. But how could she go away without her clothes?"

Thirty-two

Eliza and Jacob Whittaker were in the sitting room waiting for their tea when Karalee confronted them with what she had learned. Neither of them seemed flustered or even faintly embarrassed that she now knew their shocking secret.

"Yes, all right," Eliza said. "So now you know. Julianne Morrow is dead."

"How could you have made up such wicked lies about her then?"

"Very easily." Eliza opened the little glass door of the mantel clock and adjusted the hands. "This clock is one of the few nice things I have left. It has been in our family for generations. I dread parting with it, but it does not keep proper time anymore."

"Mrs. Whittaker, it was a shameful thing you did."

Eliza snapped the glass door shut. "Let you not speak to me of shameful doings. Not with your sinfully conceived child growing within you. I will not have it!"

"Julianne was of your own blood. You told lies about her to get her money for yourself."

"The money is mine by rights. My sister would have wanted me to have it, had she known her only child would not live. She would not have wanted it to go to that flabbellied, pompous little worm who gushes over his 'dearest, dearest sister.' "

"I must tell him the truth. So it is over."

"You realize that Jacob and I have been receiving money for Julianne's care all these years? That we contin-

235

ued to accept it even though she had died? If you tell Peter Morrow that, Jacob and I will be thrown into prison. What will that serve?"

"It is not as though we did not take proper care of the girl," Jacob said. "We were not at fault. Julianne was healthy and strong. The fever struck suddenly. Our lodgers left and there was not enough money to pay our creditors. Who was harmed by our keeping her death to ourselves—certainly not William Morrow, who would only have been grieved to know of her passing?"

"I will beg Peter's pardon for what you have done. He is kind-hearted. I do not believe he will make charges against you."

"Oh, you do not believe he will make charges?" Eliza laughed mirthlessly. "What do you suppose he will think of you when he discovers you are an imposter? That you have been posing as Julianne so that you could share in the money?"

"That is an evil lie."

"As far as your fat little worm will know, it is true."

"I will swear to him . . ."

"You? Swear to him? And he will believe you after all the other lies you have told him? And if for the sake of argument, he were to believe and to forgive, what of his father? If you believe that man capable of human forgiveness, it is only because you do not know William Morrow."

"Have you thought of Orson and what will become of him if we are imprisoned?" Jacob asked. "The boy would likely be thrown into a madhouse with no one to care for him."

"If not Orson, think of yourself. You have allowed us to introduce you to friends and neighbors as our niece, have you not?"

"Yes, but . . ."

"You did not deny it when introduced to Peter Morrow as his sister, did you?"

"No. But I have taken no money from him, nor from you. Only the two dollars a week you promised in return for my work—and not all of that."

"I will swear that I did pay you," Eliza told her. "Anna will swear that she was witness to it. Anna would do anything for me. I will say you planned it all with us and were to get a portion of the entire amount when we received it.

But you became frightened when you discovered you would have to go to the legal offices to sign the papers."

Peter would believe that, Karalee thought. He would remember how terrified she had seemed when he told her she would have to sign so many papers. Perhaps she actually would be thrown into prison.

"Now be a good girl." Jacob lifted her chin with an icy hand. "Play your part for a few more days and it will all be over. No one will be hurt."

"Why don't you run along and rest now, dear." Eliza feigned an expression of concern. "I want you to look beautiful tomorrow. When you fret you get dark circles beneath your eyes."

"I do feel tired."

"You have done quite well. The young man is totally charmed by you. Did you notice, Jacob, how taken he was with her?"

Jacob nodded. "I certainly did. It is a pity you cannot go back to England with him, as he has asked you to do."

"Yes, a pity." Eliza began to laugh. "I would like to see his face—and the face of his father—in a few months, when you give birth to your little papoose."

Thirty-three

Karalee eased her door open and listened for a moment before she went back to get Daniel and ventured into the corridor. The house was deathly silent as it always was at this hour. Jacob would be reading his business reports, hoping to find that one of his fellows was financially ruined so that he might remark on it sympathetically. Eliza would be sitting with her nose in her Bible, searching for a passage to put to memory so that she might flay an underling with it at the first opportunity.

Karalee slid past the partially opened sitting room door, praying that Daniel would not wake and cry out, alerting the Whittakers of her escape. She had played boisterously with him all that afternoon, hoping to tire him into a deep sleep when night came. She could only inch along. The floor-boards could not be counted on to carry her weight without creaking.

It would have been wise, perhaps, to wait until later when all were asleep. As it was, the two of them would be calling for their tea promptly at ten. That was less than an hour away. When Karalee did not come to their call, Eliza would grumble and rant, and come to find out what had happened. It would not give her a chance to get far before they realized she was gone. She did not know what they could do to her, or how they could force her to return, but they were slyly resourceful and such accomplished liars she had no doubt but that they could do it.

She dared not choose the "wicked" hours of the night, as Eliza called them. The footsteps of one sounded like the footsteps of an army on the pebbled streets when the hour was late. A lone woman would be noticed at any time, but after ten the watchman would surely become suspicious of her and she might find herself under arrest.

She paused before the door that led down to the cellar where the boy, Orson, would be sitting, staring into the darkness. She would have wished to tell him goodbye and to tell him that she would always consider him her friend, but she daren't.

The front door whined as she opened it and she froze, waiting to see if someone had heard. Evidently no one had. She pulled it closed behind her, and tucked the blanket over Daniel's face to protect it from the chilled night air. Though she was not certain she would find a welcome where she was going, or even a roof for the night, she was overcome with a sense of relief that she would never have to see the Whittaker house again.

Luck was with her. Tonight there was a dancing assembly at Washington Hall. She would not attract as much attention as she might have at another time. Though it was frowned upon, it was understood that many of the young men mixed the punch with cognac and became quite rowdy. For a young woman to be forced to take her leave from her escort in the middle of the evening was not unknown.

It was fortunate too that Karalee had done so much walking through the city streets, making her fruitless searches. She knew the way well and might have drawn an accurate city map if called upon to do so. She would find the Alden House on Chestnut Street easily.

But would she find Jeremy there? Would he open the door to her? What would she do if his landlord sighted her first and refused her entrance to the building? She had best not think of those things. Daniel was too heavy now for her to carry. Her arms ached before she had even reached the corner.

Jeremy registered no surprise when he opened the door to her. He bustled her in, sat her down with a cup of tea, and probably for the first time in his life did little talking.

He was so tall his head seemed to reach the top of the window frame as he leaned upon the sill, looking out. Karalee could not see his face as she told him her story, and so, thankfully, could not tell what he was thinking—though she could imagine. When she had finished, he was silent for a long time.

"I cannot keep the two of you here," he said, at last. "Or should I say, the three of you? I am not allowed even a female visitor. Certainly not one who stays the night."

"I am sorry. It was only that I had nowhere else to go."

"Damn it, Karalee." His face was pale with anger when he turned to look at her. "Stop being sorry. I am sickened to death of your being sorry. I would want you to come to me. You should have done it from the start. It is only that I am deciding what to do with you."

"It is not your problem."

"Not my problem?" Jeremy began to laugh, quietly at first, then louder and louder until he dropped into a chair, still laughing. "You have never been more wrong. It has been my problem since you turned your bedevilling green eyes upon me. Since your smile first lit up that black hole where we lay. Since you spoke my name and made it sound like a love song. Do you know what I planned to do tomorrow? I saw you, by the way, this afternoon, laughing with that mincing fop. Actually laughing! When I was spending most of my hours in agony over you. I planned to break in the door of your boardinghouse and smash your employer's face with my fist. Then I intended to drag you away by the hair. Not my problem, you say?"

Karalee swallowed the ache in her throat and ran to him, where she knelt at his feet. "Jeremy, you are so good."

He tangled his fingers in her hair, then began to smooth it back into place.

"You would not think me good if you could read my thoughts. Tell me, have you eaten?"

"Yes. I slipped away when they had gone to bed. I decided they could make no trouble for me, without making trouble for themselves."

"And when your 'brother' returns and he does not find you?"

"They are adept at making up tales. Let them tell him I ran off with a sailor—the same tale they told me at the beginning. Though I hate for him to think badly of me."

"Of Julianne."

"Yes—of Julianne. He will not know that they lied, and so will have no reason to send them to prison, though I suppose they deserve it. But since I am no longer with them, they will be sent no more money. It seemed the only way."

"Except that you must not be seen on the streets of Philadelphia." He shook his head. "What to do with you? Wait . . ."

"Yes?"

He snapped his fingers. "I will take you to Cyril. He has a mansion well away from the city, large enough to hold twenty like you and still not be able to find you if you took the notion to hide. I did him many a favor in the old days. He'll feel beholden, if he has a memory."

"How long will I stay there?"

"Until—" he hesitated. "Until afterwards."

"Afterwards?"

"After the child is born," he snapped, suddenly angry.

He rose, and as if noticing for the first time that his room was cluttered, he began to pick up articles of dropped clothing, and to straighten books and old newspapers which lay about under the table and next to his chair. He smoothed over his bed and plumped the pillow. It would have seemed comical to watch him going about such wifely chores, had not the mood been so tense.

"Then we will be married and I will take you with me. By then, surely the danger will have passed."

"I will be alone in Mr. Philbrick's house—with strangers?"

Karalee had always enjoyed knowing that she could stand alone. She had never simpered and giggled, as many of her girlfriends had done, pretending to fear mice or worms, or anything which would make them seem in need of their sweethearts' protection. When she had taken part in games, she had never allowed a man to win, unless it was a true win and she had tried her best to beat him—and never the mind how disheveled or awkward she appeared in doing it. Now the thought of being without Jeremy again overwhelmed her. Was it only Daniel and the baby within her that made her feel so dependent—so vulnerable—she wondered? Or had she truly changed so much?

The round towers and the castles, the bridges and brooks, the green hedges and fields of flowers, the fiddling and the dancing, were only part of a lost girlhood. The streets of Galway, teeming with filthy, starving beggars, the grunting yeoman who had raped her, the raging sea, Theo's poor thin face, and Patrick's blood on her hands and her dress were the only real things. And love was not poetry, or passion which sent you into the clouds, it was only tenderness and gratitude, such as she felt for Jeremy now.

"You will not be with strangers. And you will not be alone," Jeremy said. "I will visit so often you will tire of seeing me. But I cannot expect Cyril to take me under his roof too, can I? Besides, I have much work to do before the season begins. Peddling is not all poling upriver and selling merchandise to willing customers, as I, perhaps, led you to believe. It is searching for the right merchandise. Deciding what items will be in greatest demand by those I visit. Comparing prices and working out figures."

"But I hardly know your Cyril Philbrick."

"Althea will be there, and she has taken a liking to you."

"How can that be, when I do not know her?"

"Althea is Cyril's younger sister. She was with Cyril the night you met him."

"She gave me a ten-dollar gold piece," Karalee said, remembering. "I still have it."

"Althea will be happy for your company. She has always complained that she has a brother, rather than a sister."

"What will she think of me when she finds I am with child?"

"She is tender-hearted. She will pity you."

"I do not like to be pitied."

Jeremy looked at her hard. "Nor do I."

He took a heavy blanket from the closet and folded it onto the floor. Then he placed Daniel, who had already fallen asleep, upon it, covered him with another blanket and tucked it tightly around him. "We had better stop our talking now or Mrs. Alden will hear you and we will lose our roof tonight."

Karalee moved up behind him as he worked over the babe, and when he stood and turned to face her, she threw her arms around his neck and kissed him on the mouth.

"I do love you, Jeremy," she whispered. "I do."

"Karalee . . ."

He kissed her then, drawing her lips within his as if he would swallow her up if he could. He kissed her ears, her cheeks, her neck and then her lips again, until she became so weak she would have fallen to the floor had he released her suddenly.

"To have you in my arms at last, moving against me,"

he murmured against her ear, "and to feel only coat and dress."

He kissed her once more and then removed her cape, throwing it onto a chair. He worked at her dress front, his fingers trembling so that it was a long time until she stood naked before him. She reached for him, aching to feel the heat of his body against hers, the protection and strength of his arms through the night. He was about to lift her, when he looked down at her belly—slightly rounded with child. A look of revulsion crossed his face. He shuddered and turned away.

"You may have the bed. I will sleep on the chair."

"But Jeremy . . ." She reached to touch him, but he pulled away.

"Jeremy, don't do this."

"Go to sleep," he told her, and blew out the light.

Thirty-four

The home of Cyril Philbrick stood high upon the west bank of the Schuylkill, sheltered on three sides by lush green gardens, thick with every kind of tree and shrub capable of withstanding the extreme cold of a Philadelphia winter. As with most splendid mansions of the day, there was no back entrance, but rather two fronts, each approached by its own circular stone stepway.

The riverfront, which fell steeply to the water, was banked with rough stones, tangled with ivy and wild roses, giving it a pleasant, rustic appearance in spite of its elegance. The road-front was stately, with a wide, carved-panel door, a broad porch, Ionic columns and cornices, and a deep, fan-shaped terrace, paved until it touched the green of the tiny glen which screened the house from the eyes of the casual passerby.

Cyril was kindly, but usually preoccupied and often away, seeing to interests in New York and Baltimore. He would return, his arms laden with gifts for Althea, and his perpetual expression of worry would fade for a time as she tore off the bright wrapping papers and colored ribbons and squealed as a child would over his purchases. She would sit upon his knee and cover his face with kisses, planting a special one on the deep frown-crease between his eyebrows.

"Certainly, I spoil her," he answered, when Jeremy commented on it over dinner. "And I will continue to spoil her. As she spoils me. Life was not always fine wines and candlelight dinners for Althea and me. Eight years ago, if you remember, I was a peddler, poling up the river, breaking my back, much as you do now. I took no delight in dodging Indian arrows and counting myself lucky if I returned with my scalp intact. Our parents were alive then to look after Althea and my other sister, Sylvia, who is now married. But it was a struggle in those days for my father to keep bread upon the table, and the little I could contribute did not help much. Althea had one dress and one pair of shoes. Now she has three or four pairs of shoes in each color and the dresses to match them."

As Cyril recounted the trials of his youth and young manhood, Karalee began to realize why he had come to her rescue that night in front of the Quiet Woman, and why he opened his doors to her now, when she was a virtual stranger. It was unfortunate that all men of power and wealth who had also had humble beginnings could not retain the memory of those beginnings and open their arms to others in need.

"There are only the two of us now. And it may well remain the two of us. Althea may marry one day, of course, but she will never have to marry, as my poor sister Sylvia, did, only so that she will not have to go to bed hungry."

"And you?" Jeremy asked. The wine had slurred his speech somewhat and had loosened his manner, not only with Cyril and his sister, but with Karalee. He had remarked on how beautiful she looked in her borrowed dress of pale yellow, and now, as he spoke, he moved his hand gently up and down her arm, in a kind of caress. "Will there never be a wife for you?"

"Me? I doubt it. My early days spoiled me for women of wealth, who do nothing but stare at their own reflections and float about in a cloud of wig powder. Or comb their own hair so high that it stands two feet taller than they do. Take one of them into your arms, and you are never quite sure what might leap out of the tangle and nip you."

"What of simple women then? I remember Meg, at the Three Crowns, eh?"

"Meg." Cyril nodded and took a sip of wine. "Hair like a sunset."

"And Winnie, at the Half Moon. She could never get enough of you. There was a beauty."

"After eight years? They each probably have seven children."

246

"Your memory has faded from too much sitting, my friend," Jeremy told him. "You remember the Indian arrows, and the poling—but you do not remember all the beautiful women waiting on the banks along the way."

"I remember. But could I wed one of them—providing she suited me—and ever be certain it was not the clink in my pockets she really loved?"

Jeremy laughed. "That is a problem which comes from too much gold. And so—one I will never have to face."

Althea was alight with enthusiasm, as Jeremy had said she would be, at having Karalee as a houseguest. She had never been out of Philadelphia, and so was full of questions about life elsewhere. She wanted to know every detail of the uprising in Ireland, of the sea voyage, and of Karalee's capture by Indians.

As Jeremy and Cyril sat in the study talking business or reliving old times, Althea and Karalee would sit in the music room, Althea's eyes wide and often full of tears as the story unfolded. She would repeat names and places as if she were trying to put them to memory.

"Robert Kerrigan," she would say. "I like him. What did he look like?" Or: "Your brother, Theo, sounds fascinating. So brave and handsome. You say he is unmarried? And here—in this country? I should very much like to meet him."

When she spoke of Karalee's family, it was never "if" we find them. It was always "when" we find them. Her confidence renewed in Karalee the hopes which had almost died, that she and her loved ones would be reunited.

Althea played with Daniel as if he were a living toy. She spent many hours brushing his dark curls around her fingers and fitting him in lace dresses with shirred cuffs and tiny ruffles which she bought whenever she went into town. Once she brought back a tiny blue velvet suit with a plumed hat, pantaloons, and a double-breasted jacket. She and Karalee giggled until their sides ached at the sight of Daniel's baby form in such grown-up attire. Althea thrilled over his coos and his attempts at speech as if she were certain he was blessed with an extraordinary mind.

"He will be a physician," she would say, "or a man of science, or a professor. And no woman will be good enough for him to marry."

Karalee would have been content and almost happy had Jeremy not behaved so strangely. He would be tender and loving with her the way he used to be. He would hold her in his arms and kiss her, speak of what they would do when they were married and where they would go. Then suddenly, he would turn away as if he were thinking of something too ugly to bear.

The dresses Karalee wore now were high-waisted, gathered in such a way that her swelling belly was not so noticeable, if she was careful how she stood—and she was extremely careful during Jeremy's visits. Some nights she lay in bed weeping, worrying how he would take to the babe when it arrived. Other nights, she allowed Althea to convince her that once he held it in his arms, he would love it as he had grown to love Daniel.

Then one evening, as they were bringing Daniel into the study as they always did, to say goodnight to the men, all freshly bathed and powdered, Althea paused to tie a ribbon into the baby's curls.

"Speaking of weddings, my boy," they heard Cyril say, "when exactly will we be asked to attend yours?"

"Not for a time yet." Jeremy's voice was terse.

"Do you love Karalee?"

"More than my own life."

"Then there could be no better time than now to be married, if you are set on it. Karalee is good for you. I have never seen you so settled."

Though Cyril was not unkind enough to mention that by standards of decency, the wedding should take place before the birth of the babe, the unspoken thought hung heavy in the air.

"Not settled enough to want a savage to bear my name."

"Karalee," Althea whispered, tugging at her arm. "Come away."

"No. I must hear."

"You will have to get used to the idea of the child, Jeremy. It will not be long before it is here," Cyril told him.

"The child will be taken back to its people where it belongs. We will forget it ever existed and begin to live ourselves."

"Karalee will be satisfied with giving it up?"

Karalee did not hear Jeremy's answer. She could hear only the beating of her heart and the pounding inside her head. She touched her hands to her belly as she felt a jolt of movement within her. Then she turned quietly and went upstairs to her room.

Thirty-five

St. Patrick's day was much the same as another day in the home of Cyril Philbrick. It came and went unnoticed—except by Karalee. In Ireland, it was the day when the first potatoes of the year were planted and the day set aside for prayers to the beloved saint, prayers for his help in uniting Irish people everywhere.

What despair there must have been for that unity in Ireland now, Karalee thought. The Rebellion had failed, its leaders had been brutally murdered, and although she was certain thousands still belonged to it in secret, the Society of United Irishmen had been broken.

Now it was May Day. In Ireland, cattle were being driven to pasture. Farmers and their families circled the fields of new crops carrying torches and singing. Beltane fires were kindled upon the hills to celebrate the coming of summer. Then all hearth fires were smothered, and hastily relit by the holy fire.

Had it not been for Althea's gushing enthusiasm for the warm breezes and the sun and the budding in their garden, Karalee would have been entirely unaware of the change of seasons. A weakness had come over her of late. She had taken to her bed and remained there.

Cyril had just returned from Baltimore after seeing to the purchase of some new land—or had it been a warehouse? There had been dinner guests, one of whom had damned Jefferson in a penetrating voice which had found its way all the way upstairs to Karalee's room.

"The man lies. He lied in his dealings with Washington

249

and now he is doing the same with Adams. I will not vote for a president I cannot trust."

Then Althea was singing for them, her voice thin and high, but sweet—and true. Karalee closed her eyes. She did not notice that Jeremy had entered until she felt her bed sink under his weight when he sat upon it.

"I go on the river tomorrow," he said.

"Will you be gone long?"

"No, not long." He touched his hand to her forehead, as if he suspected she had a fever. "Will you be all right?"

"I will be fine."

"I wanted to tell you I have found a home for the babe when it arrives. With a bakery man and his wife in Germantown."

Karalee dug her fingernails into the palms of her hands, but kept her voice even. "What is their name?"

"I do not think it is wise to tell you. You might decide to visit the child later and that would not be good for you. It is enough that you know they are good people, loving people, and that they have three other children. All girls. They have wanted as many boys, but the wife has been unable to conceive."

"And if I bear a girl?"

"They will accept her. They do not even mind that the mother is Irish and the father Indian. The baker's own brother is a fur trapper, married to an Indian woman in York. I thought it best to tell them, in case . . ."

"In case the babe is born with pigtails and beads around its neck," Karalee said. "Thank you, Jeremy. Would you mind saying goodnight now? I would like to rest."

"Rest! All you have done is rest. What ails you? I expected you would be pleased. You have lain in your bed like a corpse for weeks, sulking because you did not want the child raised among Indians, I suppose, though you did not come out and say it. Now I have made other arrangements for it. I have stayed here with you, when I should have gone up river a month ago. What more do you want of me?"

"I have not felt well."

"It is your mind that is not well."

"Perhaps." Karalee sighed and turned her face from him. With the light from the hall against his back, he was only a black shadow with no features. Not Jeremy at all. "I have heard you say it often enough. Is this why you have kept Althea from visiting me?"

"What would you expect? Cyril has always done everything he could to shield Althea from hurt. Have you thought what your moping is doing to her? She is being packed off to stay with relatives in the morning in the hope they can raise her spirits. She and Cyril quarrelled about it. Something they have not done since they were children. I feel responsible. Is this the way you repay them for their hospitality?"

"I have not wished to harm anyone. I am grateful to them both. And to you, Jeremy."

"Grateful? I do not want your gratitude, Karalee." He gathered her into his arms suddenly with a groan of anguish and crushed her against his chest. "This waiting is more than I can bear. You cannot know what it is."

"I have not held back from you, Jeremy. It is your own doing."

"Have you no idea how much I love you? Don't you realize that everything I do now is because of that love? I know it is difficult for you to understand. Perhaps you even think I am cruel. But later—when you are yourself again—you will be glad."

He held her away from him and lifted her chin so that he could look into her eyes. "I was saving the best news for later when I return. But I can contain myself no longer. I have decided to abandon the wandering life I have led. I cannot realistically take you on the raft with me. That was the foolish dream of a boy."

"The dream of a dear, sweet boy," Karalee whispered, trying to remember how carefree Jeremy had seemed when she first met him—how full of fun and laughter.

"And I cannot realistically part with you long enough to leave you behind me all those months. So, I have borrowed enough from Cyril to buy land. I know the exact spot. It wants clearing, but I have thought each time I passed it, that it would make the ideal spot for a general store. It is remote—but not too remote."

"It sounds dull for you."

"Not dull. Never dull with you by my side helping me. We will work together, you see." He kissed her, then hugged her to him again. "The past will be as if it never was. There will be only you and me. Things will be as they were before."

Had the child been a girl, and Karalee was certain somehow that it would be, she had planned to call her Theresa. Now the babe would not be hers to name. When it was born, she would force herself not to look on it. She would close her ears to its first wails. She could not bear to see it—or to hear it—and then have it lost to her forever.

"Everything changes," she whispered, more to herself than to Jeremy. "Nothing can ever be the same."

He stiffened, and pushed away from her. "We will see about that. In the morning, I will expect to see you at breakfast before I leave, or I will carry you down. I will make no more excuses to Cyril for your lack of manners."

"I could not eat."

"No. Of course, you could not eat." His gaze fell upon the dishes which sat upon her bedside table. He swept them savagely to the floor with his hand. "You could not eat because Althea has had the housemaid bring food up to you. The trays will stop."

The house had been silent for hours. The night had passed and the morning had begun, and still Karalee could not sleep. At first, she thought she actually had drifted off and was dreaming, when she saw the figure in white floating toward her.

"Karalee, are you awake?" It was Althea. She wore a flowing white nightgown and her feet were bare.

"You should not be here. You will take a chill and it will be my fault."

"No, it will be Jeremy's fault. I never knew he could be cruel. His attitude toward you and the baby you carry is monstrous."

"I do not wish to speak of it, Althea." Karalee bit her lower lip, not wishing to weep again. She had tired of weeping. But sympathetic words had their way of wringing out tears, where bitter ones could not. "I cannot blame Jeremy for feeling as he does. Most men would feel the same."

"Jeremy is a jealous fool. He pretends to despise your child-to-be, because its father is an Indian. That is nonsense. He would not be able to abide the thought of any man touching you—no matter the race. He has made Cyril believe you are not responsible for your actions. That you are incapable of making your own decisions."

"He could be right. I am so confused."

Althea smiled. "It is not difficult to make Cyril believe such a thing. Cyril is a darling, but as many men do, he believes that women were born with tiny minds which will shatter if they are overused. He does not like me to read because he feels it weakens me. He pampers me as if I were no older than little Daniel. But I do not mind. It pleases him. Your circumstances are different. We must act. The sun is rising and there is not much time before I am to leave. Answer me quickly. But be certain of your answer."

"What is it?"

"Are you giving up your child because you believe it is best for you and for the child? Or are you giving it up only because Jeremy gives you no other choice?"

Karalee turned her face toward her pillow and squeezed her eyes shut. "Please go away now, Althea. It causes me pain to speak of it."

"Would your mother and father reject you if they knew of the child? Would they despise it, or would they accept it because it is yours?"

"What difference can it possibly make?"

Althea shook Karalee's shoulder impatiently. "This is not the time for weakness. Answer me now. I must know."

"My mother and I have never been close. I am not certain how she would feel. My father would likely be shamed. Oh, not because of what I have done. But because he allowed it to happen. But I cannot imagine him despising my babe in any case. He is a man who is filled with love." Karalee touched her hands to her middle and the tears started down her cheeks, unrestrained. "But I would not care if the world despised me. I do not want to give up my babe. Oh Althea, I do not want to."

"Then you will not have to." Althea leaned closer, her voice a whisper. "First promise that you will not despise Jeremy for what he has done."

"Jeremy? How could I despise him? I owe him my life."

"I heard about it only three days ago, though the two of them have known longer. It was to have been a secret, but I was looking through Cyril's desk for some note-paper and I found the letters."

"What letters?"

"I was aching to run to you with them, but they would not allow me to."

"Althea, what letters?"

"I coaxed Cyril at the beginning—when you first arrived—to make inquiries. An agency wrote to your Robert Kerrigan in Galway. Remember how I questioned you about him? I thought perhaps he might be a key, but I did not want to build up your hopes. They have located your family."

Karalee blinked and fastened her eyes upon the sweep of landscaped wallpaper across the room. The morning light had just struck it. Ladies in wide skirts swept through a grove of poplar trees, carrying dainty parasols and little boys rolled hoops with sticks, along the edge of a glistening blue lake. She could not, for a moment, be certain that she was not dreaming.

"Jeremy has known of this?" she murmured. "And he has not told me?"

"He convinced Cyril that it would be better to wait until you are married. Then you would feel no shame in returning to them."

"Shame? But . . ." Karalee paused, unable to fit any truth into the words Jeremy had spoken to her only a few hours before. "But by then it would be too late. I would have given up . . ."

So that was it. Jeremy realized that if she knew the whereabouts of her family first, she would never willingly give up her child. It would always be there to stand between them.

"Where is my family now?" she asked. "Surely they will come for me soon."

"I know nothing else," Althea told her. "Only what I read in the letters. They will not speak of it to me. It is why they are sending me away tomorrow. Why I had to slip in to see you without their knowing it."

Karalee took a deep breath and threw back her comforter. "Well, they will speak of it to me!" she said.

Thirty-six

Cyril wore a blue brocade dressing gown and a velvet morning cap of orange, set forward so that it covered the place where his hair was thinning. His eyes were dull and squinting, as if he had not yet recovered from the effects of last night's wine.

"If you would set aside your girlish notions of the sanctity of motherhood, Althea, you would agree with Jeremy, as I do. While Karalee has brought me a great number of problems, I am fond of her. She is a fine, decent young woman who has been so misused by fortune that she is no longer clear-headed enough to make decisions for herself."

"Nonsense." Althea held her chin high. "She is as clear-headed as any of us. She knows how she feels."

"Perhaps. But we are not speaking of her emotions now, dear, only her future. Consider this. Would you have, by your own consent, gone to the tent of a savage, subjected yourself to his whims, only to save the life of a worthless stranger?"

Althea touched one finger to her lips and thought for a moment. "I would like to imagine that I would have. Though I doubt I would have found the courage."

"Bah!" Cyril sank deeply into his chair, and extended his arms in a gesture of helplessness. "It is too early in the morning for such serious discussion. In a few hours, after we have eaten breakfast . . ."

"Mr. Philbrick." Karalee held her morning cape tightly around her chemise, so that nothing showed of her night-clothes but the bottom ruffle of her petticoat. "Before long it will be a year since I saw my mother, my father, my little brother and sister. My older brother had only just escaped from a jail cell, where he had been beaten and starved until he was only half the size he had been before, when I last saw him. If you know the whereabouts of my family, you must realize it would only be cruel of you to keep it your secret, even for a few more hours. I cannot believe it of you."

Althea knelt beside him, and clasped his hand to her cheek. "If you believe someone should make Karalee's decisions for her, should not those decisions belong to her mother and father?"

"Jeremy." Cyril rolled his eyes toward the ceiling. "There is too much logic here for me to battle. I shall leave it in your hands."

"Your family is not in Philadelphia. They have not even been informed as yet that you are alive." Jeremy sat in an oversized armchair in front of the window. His back was turned, so that they could not see his face. They could only hear his voice.

"Where are they?" Karalee asked.

"You must not think I planned to keep you from your family only to deprive you of your child, Karalee."

"What else is there for me to think?"

Althea tugged at her brother's arm and lifted her eyebrows meaningfully. "I do not know about the rest of you," she said, "but I have not had enough sleep to last me through the day. I will see you at breakfast."

Cyril rose and allowed himself to be led to the door. "Strange. I make decisions each day which involve thousands of dollars—decisions which decide the economic fate of dozens of other men besides myself. Yet I cannot offer you a sensible solution to this."

"If they are not in Philadelphia, Jeremy, then where are they?" Karalee persisted, when Cyril and Althea had left the room.

"I was afraid I would lose you."

"Because I had found my family? Didn't you think I have enough love inside me for all of you?"

"The man who arrived on a later ship, the man who took them away from the house of the Whittakers, was not your brother, as you supposed he was."

"There is no one else it could have been."

"No?" Jeremy rose deliberately and walked to the desk.

256

He opened a drawer and brought out a stack of letters which he sorted through. He drew one from the bottom and handed it to Karalee. "This one is addressed to you. But I fear I have read it."

Karalee stared at the envelope and the name upon its corner blurred before her eyes. "It is from my brother, Theo. But how . . ."

"Read it."

Karalee handed it back to him. "You must read it for me, Jeremy. My own reading is so halting, I fear, I would miss the proper sense of it. Please."

Jeremy cleared his throat. "Sister of my heart: I was told you were dead, drowned along with Theresa Roe and the twin babes. My heart is full of joy with knowing you are safe. I hope by now you have forgiven me for allowing you to believe that Patrick Roe had died when he sank into unconsciousness. You would not have left his side while there was a breath still in him and you would, no doubt, have been taken. In truth, I did not believe he would last an hour. I must say, he is not the dandy I have always taken him to be.

"Loretta Fallon and I are to be wed come June and I have prayed you and our dear father and mother will be able to return for the grand day. But I know you cannot. It is Loretta's father who holds this pen and writes my thoughts for me, or you would not be able to read them. Besides my scrawling hand, my tears would soil the page.

"By the time you receive this, my darling sister, I hope to Heaven you have all found each other. But if you have not, keep your hopes burning bright. Our dear Lord will not turn his back upon you. In the letter Patrick Roe sent to Robert Kerrigan, he said he had been aboard ship with a man named Otis Wheat, who had bought a farm in a place called Maryland. Wheat promised him a job, and Patrick, in turn, vowed to take care of Mother and Father and the children for as long as they have need of him.

"Please write to me, my angel sister, through Robert Kerrigan, who has been a blessing to all of us. I cannot yet tell you where I make my home next. My love sails with this letter to hold you safe from harm. Theo."

"It was wrong of me, Karalee," Jeremy said, after a long time. "But I wanted you to be safely married to me before you laid your eyes on Patrick Roe again."

"I cannot think . . ." Karalee stammered, overwhelmed

at the thought of seeing Patrick again. "Oh Jeremy, my heart is too full to speak. I . . ."

He opened his arms and she ran into them.

"It is as well," he said, still holding her against him. "Can you imagine me—a clerk? I would become so bored that I would eat until I grew fat. My father was a man of gigantic proportions and I am much like him. I would worry over all those accounting figures I would be forced to keep, until my hair fell out and I became quite bald."

Karalee smiled through her tears as the thought of Jeremy, thin as he was, and with so much hair, ever turning fat and bald. But when she tried to draw away, to look into his face, he would not allow her to move. She could tell from the way his chest rose and fell against her, that he was weeping too.

"I do love you, Jeremy," she said, hugging him fast, wondering how she could ever let him go. "I will always love you."

"As you love your brothers and your father and your Robert Kerrigan? It is not enough for me."

"No. It is a special love that I feel only for you. We have shared so much. Oh, Jeremy, nothing can change that."

"If everything is not exactly as you want it to be—if your Patrick is not as you remember him—if he has changed toward you, remember, I am here."

"I know, Jeremy," she whispered. "I know."

Thirty-seven

May was nearly over before Cyril could spare a man he trusted to accompany Karalee the one hundred and thirty-odd miles to New Della, Maryland, the farming community close to Baltimore, where the Nolan family and Patrick Roe had last been reported as living. He would not hear of her going unescorted, though she begged him and she had decided against writing to announce her arrival. There was no way of being certain a letter would ever reach them and besides, there was too much to be explained.

The man's name was Lance Stoddard and he made the trip several times a year to check company accounts and ledgers. He wore his reddish brown hair quite short and slicked forward as many young men were doing, causing the more conservative ones to jeer that they looked as if they were fighting a high wind backwards. He wore loose pantaloons rather than knee breeches, which gave him a floppy rag-doll appearance.

The job of escorting a woman in Karalee's advanced stage of pregnancy obviously did not set well with him, as he wore a perpetual scowl and a red-faced look of concentration, as if to avoid a glance at her protruding middle. His only words to her were warnings, such as, "Step up easy now . . . no, no, hold fast to my arm . . . slow your pace." Once, when she stumbled over a curbstone and almost fell, he had to clutch his chest and rest himself against a lamp post before he could go on.

She did not know if his displeasure sprang from a fear that she would give birth while under his protection, or embarrassment that those around might assume she was his lady. Whatever the cause of his reticence, she welcomed it. She was too full of her own thoughts to make attempts at light conversation.

What if, as Jeremy had suggested, Patrick Roe had changed? She certainly was no longer the frisky young girl who had cracked his head with hers that day in the glen. It would not be unlikely to assume the misfortunes in his life had altered him as much.

The packet from Philadelphia took only five hours and the fare was a dollar for each of them. They lunched on roast beef, new potatoes, and green peas at a sidewalk table in a fine hotel in Newcastle. Lance informed her, as if he were reading from a guidebook, that Newcastle was one of the oldest cities in Delaware—as if it could be as old as the cities she had known—the cities of ancient kings.

From there, they took a stage drawn by four horses, whose driver wanted another dollar from each of them. There were nine other passengers, tossing and rolling against each other, breathing into each other's faces. A woman who took the seat-room of two with her bulk and smelled as if she had been smoking cigars, chattered incessantly, complaining about the condition of the road, the lack of skill in their driver, and the necessary stops every ten miles or so to water and refresh the horses.

Karalee stared out the window in an attempt to thwart her nausea from the roughness of the ride. The countryside was pleasant away from the dinginess of the city. It changed gradually from the long lines of white-flowered thorn hedges inhabited by blackbirds, to the groves of walnut trees, to the fields where families were hoeing and plows were turning up the rich, brown dirt.

By the time they had boarded the schooner *Lark* in Frenchtown, and Lance had paid another dollar each for their fare, Karalee could have dropped from exhaustion. Her feet were swelling and her back ached unbearably. Still she was determined not to let her escort know.

Their meal, whose price was included in their passage, was a heavy dish with chunks of fatty ham, quartered potatoes and overcooked cabbage, whose odor made her stomach lurch and she had to refuse it. The same woman—the complainer—was seated next to Karalee, and miraculously had no complaint about her filled plate except that it was not piled high enough.

Lance paid another dollar to the stage driver in Baltimore. But only for Karalee's fare. He would not accompany her to New Della. He kissed her hand as he told her goodbye, and gave her the first genuine smile she had seen since their meeting. It was a smile of relief that she was no longer his concern.

Mrs. Wheat, a child-sized woman of forty or more years with colorless brows and lashes, fell on Karalee when she learned who the girl was. She brought out a frayed Bible and prayed with her, then with one hand on her hip, pointed out the log cabin in a wide clearing which she said was the cabin of the Nolan family.

"But do go upon them carefully, young woman," she warned. "Your father will faint away at the sight of you."

The cabin looked newly sodded and sat high upon blocks. A sagging porch ran the width of its front and a half-sawed log served as a step up to it. New trees had been planted on either side, the dirt dark and freshly heaped around their roots.

Her father did not move from his rocking chair as she approached, except to throw up a hand to shade his eyes. Her mother, in a plain dress of gray much like the one Karalee had seen her wearing last, appeared in the doorway, wiping her hands upon her apron, her mouth agape. No one spoke, until Brian, who had been under the house, seeming a foot taller than he had been, ran to her, holding a newborn pup.

"See what I have, Karalee. There are four others and one is speckled," he called, as if she had been away no more than an hour or two.

"This cannot be. It cannot be." Mrs. Nolan crossed herself, and then again. "It cannot be."

"It is." Her father stood and moved toward Karalee as if he feared a quick movement would awaken him from his dream. "It is the answer to a million spoken prayers, and ten times as many which were unspoken."

"Karalee is not drowned, Mama," Shauna cried, moving from behind her mother's skirts. "Those men lied to us. I knew they lied."

"Let me take the babe," Mrs. Nolan said when they had embraced. She swayed under Daniel's weight. "What a fine big lad he is."

"He walks a little when he has a mind to, and he says words."

"The other babe," her mother asked numbly. "Was it . . ."

Karalee nodded. "This is Daniel. Deirdre—it was ship fever. And Theresa also. They . . ."

"Do not speak of it, my heart's darling," her father interrupted, blowing his nose. "We will hear the story later when you have rested yourself. Inside with you now, a gilla, out of the sun. And here, you. Let me take your cloak. It must bear you down with its . . ."

Karalee opened her mouth to protest, but too late. The cloak had already slipped from her shoulders. All eyes were fastened on her middle.

"All the saints in heaven." Micheal Nolan sniffed and his lower lip began to tremble. "My little girl has been wedded since we last saw her. Was he someone you met aboard the ship, or was it . . ."

"Where is your husband then? He was not drowned with . . ." Her mother's eyes widened. "He is a Catholic?"

"What a question to be asking, Sheila. Of course he . . ."

Her parents looked closely at Karalee and then at each other. As if they could read their answer in her eyes they moved together and embraced, her mother's face buried against her father's chest.

Thirty-eight

The kitchen was by far the largest room in the Nolan house, with the fireplace itself measuring at least ten feet across. A heavy pole was set across it, from which hung pots, kettles, dippers, and long-handled forks for cooking. To one side sat the oven, and in front, the settle, which opened up to store extra bedding and closed down for sitting. Every foot of floor space was taken up—with the long table, the benches, the cupboard of dishes, the butter churn, the spinning wheel, and the dye vat.

The room where Mr. and Mrs. Nolan slept was barely large enough to turn around in, with the bed and chest inside it. The children slept in a garret room which was reached by ladder, and Patrick had a jack-bed which folded from the wall. Karalee slept in it now, and would until Patrick returned from his trip, when they would have to arrange something better. They planned to dig a cellar come summer for cold storage, her mother told her, and another lean-to room to back onto the fireplace wall, so that it could share the chimney.

Mrs. Wheat did not give them long to visit before stopping in with a fresh-baked cake to share in return for an ear full of Karalee's adventures during the months they had been separated. Karalee would have resorted to lies in order to save her mother's pride. There could well have been a husband who would join them later—or perhaps had been lost at sea. But to her astonishment, her mother repeated the story accurately and dry-eyed, as it had been told to her.

"It is better to speak the truth aloud and without shame," she said later, "than to have it whispered behind your back."

"I think it a most sorry thing, Mother," Shauna said.

She had just taken the embers from the oven with a long-handled ash peel, and was now sweeping its inside with a birch broom, readying it for the loaves Mrs. Nolan had set. In Shauna, Karalee could catch glimpses of herself at the same age—in the high arched line of her brow, the thick, straight lashes, the too-thin upper lip and the too-full lower one. But Shauna was adept at cooking and needlework, while Karalee had preferred working in the fields with the sun on her face and the feel of dirt between her toes.

"There are many sorry things, a gilla," Micheal Nolan said, fixing his pipe. "Which is it grieves you?"

"There is a grave at the crossroads, on the way to Byrnes. Where Patrick left us off when we rode part-way with him. Nora Wheat showed me. It is grown over with briars so you would not notice unless you were looking. Nora says they buried a young girl there with a stake driven through her. It was because she had taken her own life and it was an unforgiven sin."

"Ay, and it is a sin of the worst sort. If we all left this world when the pain began to heap upon us, there would be none left to people it."

"But could they not take it punishment enough that she would never go to heaven—that she would never look on our Blessed Mother and Jesus?"

" 'Tis not the question a child should be asking." Sheila Nolan gave one of Shauna's braids a sharp yank. "I have told you Nora Wheat is too old a girl for you to trail after. She is a child one moment, when it suits her, and a devilish woman the next. It is she, herself, grieves me."

Micheal Nolan paused, holding his pipe in midair, a look of astonishment upon his face. "And what could the little Wheat girl have done to offend you, my life?"

"The little Wheat girl, is it?" Sheila mimicked. "Nora is sixteen years old and though she is short, she has the full body of a woman. Many in this land have borne two children and laid a husband in the ground by her age. She plans to take the roof from over our heads and the bread from out of our mouths."

"She plans all that, does she?" Micheal made a clicking

264

sound with his tongue and frowned, but he winked at Kara-lee. "The little girl smiles and says good morning to us. She skips rope with Shauna and all the while she is plotting against us."

"Laugh, will you then, when she weds Patrick Roe and we are left to fend for ourselves?"

Karalee felt the strength drain from her at the mention of Patrick's name. She had been here three days and as yet had not laid eyes upon him. The waiting had been almost more than she could bear. The dread—of how he would look at her when he learned of the child that was to be. She had not dared to question her parents too closely, lest they suspect her true feelings toward him, and find further shame in it. She knew only that he had gone with Mr. Wheat to the May Fair in Byrnes to sell some goods and to buy others.

" 'Tis your imagination, my light. The lad does no more think of the girl as a woman than I do."

"You are blind to the way he watches her? I will say it is a disgrace to us all how he carries on with his poor wife not dead a year," she said.

"Carries on, you say? I have not seen it."

"You do not see beyond your jug. She pretends it is all in play. Whirling her skirts high, letting them catch the winds so that her limbs are displayed; pretending to fall in running, so that Patrick will catch her."

" 'Tis not the lad's fault then, if it were true. I say you should be properly grateful for what Patrick Roe has done for us. He has worked as two men since he landed, and it would have been so easy for him were he alone."

"It would have taken the devil himself to abandon us in Philadelphia. I did not say that of him."

"The lad has signed his name to work five years with no payment for Otis Wheat. In return he will receive fifty acres of land, a cow, a pig and a goose or two. He would not have had to take on so cheaply had it not been for us."

"It might be well at that if Patrick and his child-bride did turn us out," Sheila Nolan said. "Then you might take your rightful place as head of the family and walk behind a plow. You might own fifty acres yourself."

The twinkle left Micheal Nolan's eyes. "I am not twenty years of age, my light. A man cannot do as much of any-thing when he passes forty-five."

"Then how is it you are able to do twice the drinking, I am asking?"

Karalee could not bear to hear her parents quarrel, though they had been doing it for so long that she was certain it did not lessen their love for one another. It was only that her father always got the worst of it, and ended seeming less the man. She stretched herself, waited until the babe inside her had settled, then went out onto the porch and down the steps, away from the sound of their voices.

She spotted Brian across the road in the maple grove, watching the sap-gathering. The older Wheat boys and a hired man moved about, fitted with sap-buckets fastened with shoulder yokes, and two of the Wheat girls stood over kettles, stirring endlessly with long wooden spoons, watching so that the sap did not burn and the fires did not go out.

Nora Wheat was bent over a washtub set upon a log-bench in the Wheat's dooryard, stirring half-heartedly with a clothes dolly. The sleeves of her dress were rolled above her elbows and her long golden hair was pinned onto the top of her head, with only a few strands wisping onto her forehead. She lifted one hand to wave Karalee closer.

"Do you feel any pains today, Mrs. Nolan?" she asked, with a stress on the word "Mrs." which made Karalee feel suddenly old.

"A twinge or two. But I have had them each day, so they are likely false."

"You are already big enough to give birth to two at once. It must be difficult to move about."

"Not really, though I have a time getting my breath now and again."

Karalee was more conscious of her bulk than ever, with Nora standing before her, tiny-waisted and narrow, except for her breasts, which were high and startlingly full. Micheal Nolan was not at all observant, she decided, if he could see anything remaining of a child in Nora Wheat.

"I despise the springtime washing most of anything," the girl said, her lips pushed into a pout. "To stand all day over a steaming lye-soap tub loosens the wave in my hair. The air is perfumed with flowers and the birds are chirping to one another and the sun is warm on my arms. But I must stay on mangling clothes which are grimed from a full winter's wearing."

"It is difficult. You are right in that."

"And now Father has even taken Patrick away with him, so that we cannot picnic or romp together through the meadows. He could just as well have taken my brother, Adam or Bow."

Was there actually a calculated look of defiance in Nora's eyes when she mentioned Patrick's name? Karalee wondered. Or was her nature turning to be as suspicious as that of her mother?

"I do believe Father keeps us apart deliberately." Nora smiled and brushed her hair back with a sweep of her arm. "But Patrick and I find our own ways to be together."

Karalee did not want to hear anymore. She turned away, but Nora followed her, wiping her slippery wet hands upon her apron. "Would you like me to help you back to the house, Mrs. Nolan?"

"No. Thank you."

Nora walked alongside her anyway. "I have often wondered how a man must feel about a woman once he sees her—swollen with child. It seems that afterwards, even if he still feels some affection toward her, as he might for the family dog, he would no longer feel desire or longing."

"I do not know."

"I should hate it. When I am with child, I shall send Patrick away once I become ugly and clumsy. I shall not let him return to me until I am lying abed with a pink ribbon in my hair and his babe in my arms."

"You and Patrick are to be married?" Karalee asked, keeping her voice as level as she was able.

"Shh." Nora caught at Karalee's sleeve and stopped walking. "It cannot be for a time. We cannot even speak of it. Patrick's wife being dead only these few months. But you see, they did not love one another."

Karalee's heart sank. "Patrick told you that?"

"He did not have to tell me. Had he loved her, would he behave with me the way he does?"

There was no mistaking the animosity in the girl's eyes now.

"Not knowing how he behaves with you, I cannot answer."

"Patrick is a man. He attempts to behave with me as he once behaved with you, I dare say. But I will not allow him liberties until we are husband and wife."

Karalee began walking again, bracing her teeth against

the intense pain which had started within her. But it grew until she had to stand still and wait for it to pass.

"Are you giving birth now, Mrs. Nolan?"

"My mother is Mrs. Nolan. I am not," Karalee snapped when she could get her breath.

"I only wished to be polite. Though Mother says I need not be. She says you are fortunate you live now instead of a few generations ago. They would have whipped you and sewed the cutting of an Indian's face upon your sleeve. They would have forced you to wear it always, for all to see."

Karalee moved with effort toward the cabin. She had only the length of the yard to go, yet it seemed she would never be able to reach it.

Thirty-nine

They kept the bedroom darkened, and so Karalee could not discern night from day. But it did not matter. She had never known such pain. It would lessen just long enough to allow her to drift into sleep. Then it would wrench her back to consciousness again.

"Why is it taking so long?" she heard her father ask.

"There is something wrong," her mother answered. "But it would be as well for her and for all of us, if she lost the child."

"If she lost the child—if she lost the child." Her mother's words sounded again and again, fading in and out. Then Jeremy was in the room and he had brought with him a man in the garb of a baker. The two of them reached for the child, who had already been born and had grown to the size of Daniel. The child, a little girl, screamed and struggled against them and then Karalee heard herself screaming too.

"Dear Merciful Father," her father cried.

"Drinking will not help, Micheal Nolan."

"It will help me."

Poor little babe, Karalee thought, still only half awakened. You have not yet been born, and already you are despised. Not by me. No, never by me. She threw her hands over her face and began to weep.

"None of that now." Her mother wiped Karalee's forehead with a cool, dampened cloth. "Use the time between your pains to rest yourself."

Karalee thought of the village of the Iroquois and of

269

Tonaoge and Osinoh and the others. There, all children were beloved—wanted. They were raised entirely without punishment. Striking a child was unknown. Osinoh had told her that children often threatened to kill themselves or to scar their own faces if they did not get their way—and so they were indulged.

She was jarred from her half-dream by the sound of Shauna crying somewhere far off. Then Brian joined in.

"Mother, is Karalee going to die?"

"Take the children to Mrs. Wheat until this is over."

"Take them yourself. I will not leave." Karalee wanted to cheer him for standing up to her mother.

"Where is the midwife who was to have come?"

"She will be here when she gets here. She could do no more than we are doing."

"Damn her eyes. I will strangle her with my bare hands if she does not arrive soon." Her father's voice.

No—it was not her father's voice.

"Stay out of that room, Patrick Roe."

"I have stayed out of it long enough, I'm saying."

"It is not the place for you."

"It is the only place for me."

The lamplight from the kitchen swept across Karalee's face and she caught a glimpse of the figure framed in the doorway before turning her head.

"Go away," she whispered.

"I will never go away. Here—take my hand, mavourneen. I want to feel you squeeze hard when it begins to hurt you. Squeeze."

"I am so shamed . . ."

"Hush now." He moved one finger across her lips. "You have made me a father still—with your courage. What a fine lad our Daniel has grown to be."

"He—he is that."

"He remembers me."

Karalee had to smile at his foolishness. He turned her chin gently, so that she faced him and his own smile. "That is better."

"Do not look upon me. I am ugly."

"As all the angels in heaven are ugly. Wait." He released his grip and straightened, wriggling his arms out of his coat sleeves. "Only raise yourself a little. There—now. We put it around you—so—now I can feel what you feel."

"It is not seemly," her mother protested, tugging at him.

"I care not for what is seemly."

The pain rushed upon Karalee again. But when she tensed for it, Patrick held her, stroking her hair, whispering to her that it would pass in a moment—and it did.

"The midwife is here," Sheila Nolan announced, indignant. "Or do you intend to take her place too, Patrick Roe?"

"Not if she knows what she is about." He turned to Karalee. "Do you want me to stay by your side, a lhaie?"

"Mrs. Nolan!" the midwife gasped. "I will not have this."

"Do you, mavourneen?"

"No. I will be all right now," Karalee told him.

He touched a finger to her lips. "And I shall be outside your door."

Forty

Karalee studied the wee face of the babe who wriggled in her arms. She had already wrapped and unwrapped its soft blanket a dozen times to marvel at the perfection of its tiny form. There was no way to say from the rosiness of its complexion, its squinted eyes, and its mouth puckered as if to cry, who it would favor—if it would be dark or fair. It had a wild thatch of black hair, but Mrs. Nolan said that Karalee's own had been the same at birth.

"I have not yet thought what to name her," she said.

"Karalee." Sheila Nolan eased herself onto the bed next to her daughter. "I cannot long keep Patrick from your side. But I must speak."

"What is it, Mother?"

"Gratitude is what Patrick feels for you. You must understand that. Gratitude for saving Daniel's life and for bringing his son back safely to him."

"What are you trying to tell me?"

"I do not wish you hurt, child. Many things have happened to all of us during these past months. They have been as if as many years. Patrick has changed. Oh, I saw how smitten he was with you in Ireland—and him, the shame of it, married to your own dear friend. But now, he has eyes for someone else."

"Nora Wheat."

"Ay. A man such as Patrick wishes his bride to be a virgin. It matters not if he himself is not one."

"Please, Mother."

"I know what I say. You must not have your hopes burning too high. When he looks at you and at your child—the child of a savage—and then he sees Nora, young, pretty—pure . . ." She sighed, and then as if it took great effort on her part, she reached for Karalee's hand. "I love you, my daughter."

"And I love you, Mother."

"Let us speak no more of it." Sheila cleared her throat and swallowed as if she had been embarrassed by the words of affection which had passed between them. She eased the infant from Karalee's arms and cradled it in her own. "I will take her out for the children to see. They have been most patient."

There was a single knock and the door flew open. Sheila hurried from the room, her head bowed, as Patrick entered it. His hair was freshly slick-combed, and his face was sunburned. His shirt was red—coarse-woven and patched. Open at the collar. It fit him too snugly, as if it had been sewed for someone smaller-muscled, and his pantaloons were high-waisted and too loose. He wore scuffed, round-toed boots with canvas-lined tops turned over them.

Poor Patrick, she thought. The dandy, as Theo had chided him, with his saffron-colored ruffled shirts with wide sleeves, his cutaway tailcoat and his shining black slippers. Always so careful of how he dressed—the styling and fit of his clothing. Now he wore what he would have used for shoe rags not long ago.

But—A chquid, she thought too, as he came toward her. He is beautiful. So very beautiful.

For a moment, she thought of him as he had looked that day in the wicker-work dwelling by the sea—his face bloodless, his eyes rolling, his shirt front scarlet.

"I am not a wicked man, Karalee," he had whispered.

She had lost him then, and she would lose him just as surely now.

"I have walked over the hill." He knelt beside her bed, his eyes bright as those of a young boy who has discovered a secret place.

"Your lovely hair has been chopped off."

"It tangled in the fields and came untied. But, as I was saying, there is a spot exactly right for us to raise our house."

Karalee could not resist touching a hand to his cheek. He caught it up and pressed his lips to it. Then he kissed

274

her. His kiss was warm, and sweet as Karalee knew it would be.

"Do not plan a life for us two together," she told him. "You have your life and I have mine."

"What is this talk?"

"You are free, Patrick Roe."

"But you are not free and I will not have you forgetting it."

"Mother has told me of Nora Wheat."

"Told you of—Nora Wheat, is it?" He nodded, a one-sided grin upon his face. "I can vision what you were told."

"She told me how you look at the girl. How you take pleasure in it."

"Nora is a darling little beauty, right enough." Patrick lifted Karalee's chin with one finger. "Let us put the matter straight while it is before us, maneen. I have told you that I love you. But I have not told you I would not look at what is there for me to see."

"Mother said . . ."

"And I have not promised you I would not smile if what I see pleases me."

"Have you been told the babe's father is . . ."

"An Indian. And its mother is a hot-tempered Irish Catholic. Heaven protect us, what a brawler she will be, if we do not watch."

"Whenever you look at me, you will remember that there were others before you."

"Every man dreams one day to marry a girl who has been touched by no other man before him. I will not deny it or defend what is truth. But I would not swap you for another girl because of it. No more than I would swap Daniel for another babe who cries less."

Karalee reached for him, pulled his face down to hers and nearly smothered him with her kisses. When she released him, he sat back on his heels and whistled.

"We will have to do much less of that, mavourneen, if I am to last until we are able to be married. Have you thought of what I have thought of?"

"And what is that?" she whispered.

"That we have two babes—a boy-child and a girl—and I have never so much as touched you."

"I have thought of it," she said.

"Once. Almost." He came closer. "In the glen. Do you remember?"

"I remember."

"It was a wicked thing I did."

"It was."

He came closer still. "But I would do it again."

When their lips had almost touched, he drew back. "Karalee, it will be many weeks before . . . that is, I cannot."

"Tell me about the spot you found for our house," she said.

"Karalee." His lips were nearly upon hers. "How long will it be?"

"Tell me about the house."

"One month? Two?"

"Tell me about the house," she repeated.

Patrick stood and wiped the back of his hand across his mouth. "Yes. It will be over the hill."

He crossed to the window, where he looked out, pointing. "It will be there, though you cannot see it from your bed. It is already our own land, did you know? We will have a fine house-raising, with a feast and plenty of rum. It is bare, hard ground now. But that is as I would wish it to be. We will plant trees and hedges of our own choosing, eh? Then we can watch the land turn green around us. Oh, it will be a grand life, Karalee Nolan."

Karalee listened happily, as Patrick spoke of the home that would be theirs. But he was wrong when he told her she could not see it from her bed. She could see it with her eyes closed tight. And it was not bare. No. There were meadows, and fields, and grassy glens. It was a glorious green. As green as the green of her own beloved land. And there were roses, wild roses.

SPECIAL PREVIEW

LOVE'S SWEET AGONY
by Patricia Matthews

This will be the ninth novel in the phenomenal best-selling series of historical romances by Patricia Matthews. Once again, she weaves a compelling, magical tale of love, intrigue, and suspense. Millions of readers have acclaimed her as their favorite storyteller. In fact, she is the very first woman writer in history to publish three national bestsellers in one year . . . two years in a row!

Patricia Matthews's first novel, *Love's Avenging Heart,* was published in early 1977, followed by *Love's Wildest Dream; Love, Forever More; Love's Daring Dream; Love's Pagan Heart; Love's Magic Moment;* and *Love's Golden Destiny.*

Now that you've finished reading *Love's Raging Tide,* we're sure you'll want to watch for *Love's Sweet Agony,* which will be published in May 1980. Set in Kentucky, it is the story of Rebecca Hawkins, a lovely but fiercely independent young girl more used to training thoroughbred horses and winning equestrian contests than to dealing with the complexities of men. But as the opposite sex begins to enter her life, she finds the sudden flurry of romance, love, and danger to be almost more than her young heart can bear. Three men are after her, but which one represents true love, which one a threat to her life?

As in all novels by Patricia Matthews, the storytelling is exciting, the characters memorable, and the ending a satisfying experience.

Watch for *Love's Sweet Agony* in May, wherever paperbacks are sold.

*LOVE'S SWEET AGONY**

by Patricia Matthews

Right across the street from the racetrack stood a hotel that had gained national prominence during the Civil War, when it was used as General Grant's headquarters. Now that Grant was president of the United States, his one-time occupancy of the hotel made it a popular place with visitors to Cairo, and it was always the scene of bustling activity. But it was even busier during the three days of the Alexander County Fair, since it was here that most of the jockeys, drivers, trainers, and owners stayed.

It was eleven in the morning, and the crowd was very large. Men and women were packed into the lobby, and the noise level was so high that normal conversation was next to impossible. Everyone yelled at everyone else in order to be heard, which only intensified the bedlam. Men waved drinks and cigars and even hands full of money as they tried to place last-minute wagers on the races that would begin soon. Women, too, were caught up in all the excitement, and were no less vociferous than the men, so that occasionally a high-pitched shrill of laughter would ring out above everything else.

Only the drivers and jockeys were quiet. They were already dressed in their brightly colored silks, and they stood out in the crowd like gay flowers among cabbages. Like all athletes since the time of the Roman

Games, they were introspective before competing; alone with their thoughts, they prepared themselves mentally and emotionally for the contests that lay before them.

But not all the drivers were in the lobby. Some were still getting dressed, including the driver for the Hawkins entry, Paddy Boy. The cherry-red blouse which was the Hawkins color lay across the bed, and the driver, in trousers, sat on the edge of the bed pulling on a pair of highly polished boots. Then, with the boots on, the driver walked to the dresser and stood in front of the mirror.

Rebecca Hawkins smiled at her reflection. "I wonder what would happen if I showed up at the race like this?" she mused aloud. She giggled at the idea. "I bet I would create such a furor that I'd win handily. Perhaps we'd better save this idea for the Kentucky Derby." She laughed, making her breasts jiggle, and she laughed even harder.

On the dresser in front of Rebecca was the winding cloth which she used to bind her breasts for the races. She had to conceal her true identity when she drove, because the rules and by-laws of all the races specifically stated that the drivers and jockeys must be men. If her true sex were discovered, she would be disqualified. Of course, she and her grandfather could hire a driver, but the expense of that would erode their winnings, and the winnings were very necessary if they were ever to buy their own thoroughbred farm.

When they first began racing, Rebecca had talked Hawk into the subterfuge, and he agreed reluctantly, but only until they could afford a driver. From time to time he still threatened to hire a driver, but Rebecca knew that he never would—unless she was found out. For Rebecca was better than any driver they could find; even her grandfather admitted that.

Still, it was not right that she should be forced to masquerade as a man.

Though the reasons were clear enough to her, the whole thing seemed terribly unfair to Rebecca. For while other drivers were able to reap the rewards of public acclaim for their victories, she had to be content with the secret knowledge of her successes. It was also unfair, she decided now, that she should have to hide her true sex from Gladney Halloran and Steven Lightfoot during the times she drove.

Rebecca frowned, puzzled. Now why had *that* thought popped into her head? She had been thinking of the race and the eventual farm that she and Hawk hoped to buy, and logically there was no reason to think of Gladney or Steven. And yet, suddenly and inexplicably, she had thought of them.

Her face flushed red. She was angry at herself for allowing such unwelcome thoughts to surface. And yet she didn't know what to do about it.

She also didn't know what she could do about the way she was reacting to such disquieting conjectures. For she felt a lightness in the pit of her stomach and a strange, warming sensation lower down. She thought of Gladney's kiss the night before, and her reaction to it, and the feeling of giddiness intensified.

Rebecca studied her image more closely, paying particular attention to her breasts. She felt a heightened sensitivity in them. The two mounds of flesh, which had been little more than an annoyance to her in the past, suddenly took on a new perspective. She studied them now not as something which had to be covered to enable her to drive the sulky but as evidence of her womanhood.

She knew that men liked to look at women's breasts for she had seen them do so. Did they like to touch them, to caress them? And if so, what did it feel like to them? And what would it feel like to her, if a man did touch them?

Rebecca touched one breast lightly, hesitantly, embarrassed by the act. There was a strange, flaming heat flowing from her flesh, and she could feel it in her fingers. That was odd, very odd indeed! She had touched her breasts many times in her life, but never before had she noticed such a phenomenon, although, she realized, never before had she touched them in such a deliberate fashion.

She moved her finger along the pale, rising mound, stopping just outside the aureole. There was a tingling sensation there, and she noticed that her nipple had drawn into a tight rosebud. Daringly, she stroked the nipple, and was amazed and a little frightened by its sensitivity. She wished that Gladney had touched her there last night, when he kissed her. It would have been interesting to see what happened. She wondered if Steven would touch her there, if he ever kissed her. Did he want to kiss her?

Abruptly, Rebecca squeezed her eyes shut and put both hands down on the dresser, gripping the edges tightly. What had come over her? What was happening to her, that she could allow these thoughts to hold sway over her mind? She reminded herself angrily that she had a race to drive, and there was no time for such distracting fancies.

When she opened her eyes again, Rebecca began to bind her breasts slowly and deliberately, wrapping the band around her tightly until her torso was a smooth, unbroken line from her shoulders to her waist. Her breasts were no longer visible even in profile and her disguise would be effective. But this time she was aware, as never before, of the heat and mass of the flesh she had bound, as her breasts strained to be free.

Only two rooms down the hall from Rebecca, a woman was experiencing what Rebecca was thinking about. Her name was Stella—the only name she had given Steven Lightfoot. She was small, with long black hair and an elfin figure. From a distance she looked astonishingly like Rebecca Hawkins, and it was for this reason that Steven had been drawn to her. Stella was a business lady, she had told him, plying her trade among the prosperous men drawn to the fair. She had quoted a price, and Steven hadn't quibbled. Now they were in his hotel room, nude together upon the bed, and Steven was tracing his fingers lightly across her skin, across her breasts, and stroking down across the taut satin skin of her stomach.

"Ummm, that feels good," Stella murmured, looking up into his eyes.

"Close them."

"Close what?"

"Your eyes."

"Why?"

"Because you have beautiful eyelashes, and I like to look at them."

Stella did have beautiful eyelashes, but that wasn't the real reason Steven wanted her to keep her eyes closed. They were blue, while Rebecca Hawkin's eyes were gold. And when Stella's eyes were open, he couldn't hold the image of Rebecca in his mind's eye.

Stella pulled his mouth down to hers and they kissed, long and deep. One of his hands nestled in the small of her back, just above the sweet rise of her buttocks. The other moved up to cover her breast and closed gently around it, skillfully kneading the nipple.

Stella arched under his hand. "Ohh!" she said, when finally the kiss had ended. "Oh, my! I'm glad everyone doesn't make love like you do."

"Why?" he asked, puzzled by the rather strange remark.

She smiled shyly and winked. "Because if they did, I'd do this for free, and then I'd probably starve to death."

Steven had to laugh. Then he kissed her again, as he moved over her. He continued to touch her with skilled, tender strokings, feeling his own blood run hot now, as the woman boldly, hungrily returned his caresses with her own, just as eager.

Either she was eager for him or she was a damned good actress, he thought. He was not a frequenter of whores, so he had no yardstick by which to judge. Yet he was sure that this woman was not acting—her passions were aroused. This pleased him enormously.

"Ah, yes, yes!" she cried out. "Now! I'm ready for you! Hurry, lover!"

Steven entered her with gentleness, but Stella would not have it that way. With a moaning sound of pleasure, she surged to meet him, and urged him to greater effort with hands and mouth. He buried his face in her hair and felt her responding to his quickening strokes with obvious delight. All his senses were engaged in the ecstasy of the moment, and when he felt her quivering beneath him in a shuddering release, he could hold back no longer.

Still, even in that moment of supreme pleasure, his thoughts were of Rebecca Hawkins.

* * *

Patricia Matthews

**...an unmatched sensuality, tenderness and passion.
No wonder there are over 14,000,000 copies in print!**